Black and White and Dead All Over

A Midlife Crisis Mystery

by

Marlo Hollinger

This book is fiction. All characters, events, and organizations portrayed in this novel are the product of the author's imagination or are used fictitiously. Any resemblance to actual persons—living or dead—is entirely coincidental.

For information, email **Cozy Cat Press**, cozycatpress@aol.com or visit our website at: www.cozycatpress.com

ISBN: 978-1-939816-95-5

Printed in the United States of America

Cover design by Paula Ellenberger
www.paulaellenberger.com

1 2 3 4 5 6 7 8 9 10

To my real life "Steve." Thank you for always being there.

Chapter One

"So, here it is. What do you think?" My new boss, Jeff Henderson, looked around the newsroom as proudly as the father of quadruplets achieved without the help of any kind of fertility drug. "Pretty nice, huh? Can't you just smell all the history that these walls have seen?"

Looking around, I felt my eyes widen in dismay and my nostrils crinkle in disgust. All I could smell was years and years of brown bagged lunches combined with endless cups of coffee and stale cigarette smoke.

What a dump! I thought, and although I didn't actually say what I was thinking out loud as I stood in the general reporters' room at the *Kemper Times*, I was positive that my face reflected what I was thinking. My husband, Steve, always says that whatever I'm thinking or feeling is right there on my face for the whole world to see, making me a particularly bad poker player, liar and person to ask if you want to know if your new jeans with the blingy pockets make your butt look big. With a major effort, I rearranged my face into more neutral lines and smiled brightly at Jeff. "Well," I stalled, "it certainly is..."

I was stuck for the right word to describe the room that we were standing in other than "disgusting." With dingy walls that I assumed had once been white but had cured to a shade probably best described as greige—sort of grey and sort of beige—and ratty looking cubicles that gave the entire room the feeling of a fly-by-night call center, the hub of the local newspaper was not at all what I'd expected. Granted, Kemper is a mid-sized town and I didn't expect the reporters' room of the *Kemper Times* to be on par with the *New York Times* or even the *Milwaukee Journal,* but this was pathetic. Where were the hustling reporters, pencils stuck behind their ears as they scrambled to write the next big scoop? Where was the gruff but lovable city editor, waiting to dispense words of wisdom and bucking up his employees with well-earned pats on the back and praise for their latest efforts? Where was the ink-scented, rolled up shirtsleeves ambiance that screamed truth, justice and the First Amendment?

Then again, if I was painfully honest with myself, the *Kemper Times* had just hired me as a part-time general reporter and Girl Friday, so it was pretty obvious that their journalistic standards weren't on par with those of the *New York Times,* the *Milwaukee Journal's* or even the *National Enquirer's*. I have a degree in psychology that I earned over thirty years ago and my only experience writing has been of the volunteer variety for the schools my kids attended while they were growing up—reports on bake sales and plugs for local renditions of *Our Town* or *Les Miz.* Oh, and the Christmas newsletter I reluctantly enclose every year with our cards to friends and relatives ("*Tyler is still looking for a job, our daughter Jane's boyfriend turned out to be married, and we're keeping our fingers crossed that we won't have to replace the hot water heater this year since the air conditioner died in August.*").

If the *Kemper Times* had decided that I was general reporter material, well, let's just say that it wasn't exactly a ringing endorsement for them. Truth be told, I'm not so sure that *I'd* hire me to write for a daily paper, but I wasn't about to put up an argument. The powers-that-be at the local paper had offered me a job, I'd grabbed it, and now I was in the middle of getting the grand tour. I learned a long time ago not to look a gift horse—or anything with a steady paycheck—in the mouth.

"It certainly is what?" my new employer Jeff asked as we surveyed the empty newsroom side by side. He was a few years older than me, had a receding hairline and wore a brown cardigan sweater that reminded me a great deal of the one that Mr. Rogers used to wear on *Mister Rogers' Neighborhood.* He seemed pleasant but a little on the slow side to be a newspaper publisher. I couldn't picture him making a snap decision on whether to cover a fire at a daycare or a hostage situation in city hall. He struck me as far too ponderous to make any kind of snap decision other than if he wanted mustard or mayo on his sandwich.

Well," I replied as I continued to search my mind for a tactful response, "it's bigger than I expected."

"Actually, the newsroom is a lot smaller than it used to be," he informed me in an I'm-surprised-you-didn't-know-that kind of voice. "We used to be down in the basement where there's a lot more elbow room but over the years we've consolidated operations."

"Consolidated operations?" I repeated.

Jeff shrugged. "You know—downsized. When someone quits or retires, we don't necessarily replace them. It makes for more work for almost everybody but it keeps our overhead lower."

I gave a little chuckle. "I'm glad you hired *me* if you aren't doing much hiring."

"Yeah, well, we'll see how that works out. You're part time so if you can't cut the mustard it will be no big deal to can you. Plus, we're counting on you to fill the gaps of some of the people we've let go so it's not like we'd go out of business if you don't work out."

Great. Ten minutes into my new career and my boss was already talking about firing me. I was not about to let that happen. No siree. This job was meant for me and I was going to make it work out. "I'll make sure I do the best I can," I promised, feeling like a Girl Scout who was trying to earn all of her badges at once.

"I'm sure you will. You came highly recommended."

"I did?" That was news to me. "Who recommended me?"

"Well, no one actually *recommended* you but Kate Weston—the editor—read the writing samples you submitted and said they didn't suck out loud. That was good enough for me." He looked around the newsroom again thoughtfully. "I think it's smart to have all the reporters together in the same room. It's easier to keep an eye on everyone that way. You know—no goofing off. We can't afford too many cameras or listening devices to keep tabs on employees everywhere but this way we can see what's going on the old fashioned way, with our own eyes and ears. Oh, and, of course, we read everyone's emails."

Listening devices? Cameras? Reading emails? Was that even legal? Apparently so. "Do you work in here too?" I asked.

Jeff threw back his head and laughed heartily at my obviously ridiculous question. "Are you kidding me? This place would depress the hell out of me after about five minutes. My office is at the other end of the hall, right next to Kate's. We're management," he added in the same you-should-know-that tone. "Management never bunks with anyone else. After all, rank has its privileges."

At least he was honest. An elitist, perhaps, but honest. I looked around the room again and silently counted up the cubicles. There were twenty-four. "How many reporters are on the staff at the paper?"

"It fluctuates," Jeff replied. "Journalism isn't a high-paying career so we do lose a lot of our reporters when they find they can't live on what we pay them." His voice took on a self-righteous tone. "It takes good, hardworking, dedicated professionals to run a daily newspaper who are more concerned with putting out a quality product than making a million dollars. Journalism has never been about making money. It's about performing a much needed community service. That's why I'm so glad you've joined us, Debbie. I can tell that you have down-to-earth values and don't worry about things like raises or benefits."

Wondering how he thought he knew that I didn't worry about raises or benefits since this was only our second meeting and also wondering if management was included in the low pay part of his speech, I gently corrected him. "My name is DeeDee."

"Oh, right. DeeDee. Sorry. I'm lousy with names."

"That's okay. It happens a lot. Where are the rest of the reporters?"

Jeff shrugged. "Who knows? There really isn't all that much of a reporting staff left, anyway. Just Bob, our prize-winning journalist, Frank, Ren, and Sam—our award-winning photographer. You'll meet all of them in due time and I'm sure you'll get along just fine. There might be a few bumps in the road to becoming a true team—there always are—but you'll make it, DeeDee. I'm sure you will."

I swallowed nervously. The people he'd just mentioned were names I recognized from reading the *Kemper Times* and they were all true journalists with actual degrees in journalism. How were they going to feel when they discovered that the newest reporter was completely inexperienced when it came to writing news stories as well as unpublished? "I certainly hope I will."

"So, any other questions before you get started?"

"Um, what about Caroline Osborn?" I asked, naming the sole female reporter on the paper and the best writer of the bunch, in my opinion. "I love her articles. I always read her stories first when I see her byline."

"Oh. Caroline." His voice became flat. "I'm sure she's around here somewhere."

"She's amazing. She really knows how to connect with the readers."

Jeff raised a skeptical eyebrow. "If you say so but I'd have to argue that she only connects with middle-aged, female readers."

It was my turn to raise an eyebrow since Jeff had just described me. "Oh?"

"Not that there's anything wrong with that," he hastily added, obviously realizing his *faux pas*. "Many of our readers are middle-aged and female. It's just that Caroline has been told—repeatedly—that there are other people who read our newspaper and that if she ever wants to win an award like Sam or Bob has, she needs to get with it. Caroline is something of a rabble rouser, as I'm sure you'll quickly discover, and I have no doubt that she'll glom onto you since you're also a woman. Just don't pay any attention to her and never believe anything she says without checking with me or Kate first, all right?"

So much for team spirit. Not wanting to make a promise that I wasn't at all sure I'd be able to keep, I said, "I'll do my best."

"That's all I want to hear. Now let's find a cubby for you and then you can get started."

I followed Jeff to the back of the newsroom, still almost unable to believe that I was actually starting my first day as a professional reporter on a real newspaper. It was exciting and a little intimidating too. The *Kemper Times* office might look like a dump but I was sure that working there was going to be a highlight of my professional career. Being a reporter sounded so much better than being a self-employed caterer, my last job. Being a reporter sounded exciting and glamorous and successful, three things my previous job hadn't been in the least. Actually, exciting, glamorous and successful were three adjectives that I'd never been able to apply to any portion of my life.

Jeff stopped before a cubicle at the back of the room and paused. "You can have this one," he said in a voice that sounded like he was giving me a set of keys to a high-rise condominium overlooking Lake Michigan complete with wool carpeting, stainless steel appliances and a built-in maid. Eyeing the cubicle and the half inch of dust covering every flat surface, cobwebs filling up the corners and large jagged holes in the blue-grey burlap-esque fabric on the walls, I answered, "Great! I love it!"

Truly, it wasn't all that hard to sound enthusiastic because I felt enthusiastic. My secret hope was that Jeff Henderson would be so impressed with the articles that I churned out that he'd offer me a column in the paper that would immediately become syndicated and that not only would I become famous, I'd also have some serious money to plop into Steve's and my retirement account, something I've never been able to do as a stay-at-home mom. I was pretty sure that I had read that that was how Erma Bombeck had gotten started. She worked for a weekly newspaper and her boss arranged *everything* that needed to be done to get her syndicated.

I read once that Erma Bombeck hadn't even known what her boss was up to until it was a done deal. Maybe Jeff Henderson would do the same for me. I sure hoped so. Steve and I weren't looking at a barren retirement but it would be so wonderful to be able to plump it up a bit and feel like I was finally pulling my weight, financially speaking.

Jeff seemed pleased as well as a little surprised by my enthusiasm. "I like your attitude, DeeDee."

"I'm happy to be here," I assured him.

"All right, then. You get settled and once you get your bearings, how about if you make a fresh pot of coffee? I've got a killer hangover so make it strong. And make sure you scrub out the pot first. No one's cleaned it in ages."

Making coffee and scrubbing out coffee pots obviously fell under the Girl Friday portion of my job description. But I wasn't complaining. Making coffee was one skill that I truly excelled at. "Um, where is the coffee pot?" I asked.

"In the break room." Jeff gestured vaguely toward the doorway. "You can't miss it. It's right down the hall." Giving me one last encouraging smile, Jeff began to walk away.

I stopped him in his tracks with another question. "Jeff, do you know when I'll get my first assignment?"

"Your first what?" A quizzical expression covered his features.

"Writing assignment. Story. Article. For the paper?" My heart sank a little bit beneath the blue cotton sweater I was wearing. Oh, dear. I hoped I hadn't heard wrong when Jeff had offered me the job. He had hired me as a general reporter as well as a Girl Friday, hadn't he? Or had I, in my shock on hearing a job offer, heard him say reporter when he meant something else altogether? Like cleaning lady or customer service rep? But he wouldn't be giving me a cubicle if I wasn't on the reporting team, would he? "You do want me to write for you, don't you?"

Still looking puzzled, Jeff stared at me for a long moment before answering me. A little unwillingly, I tried to imagine how I looked to him: early fifties, light brown hair, blue eyes, a few extra pounds around my hips, an all-too-eager expression on my face. Something about the blank look in his eyes told me that he wasn't seeing Diane Sawyer or Barbara Walters while he stared at me. A light bulb finally seemed to snap over his head. "Oh, right! Sure. Of course, I want you to write for us, DeeDee, and I'll have an assignment for you in a day or so but right now I want you to get used to being here and take care of a few other things—housekeeping things—and then we'll see where we stand, okay?"

Patting me on the arm, Jeff started to leave the newsroom once again. He paused before he was all the way out the door. "When the coffee's done, bring me a cup, would you? Black with two sugars. Thanks, hon."

Feeling a little deflated, I waited until he was gone before turning back to my new home away from home. Before making the coffee I wanted to clean up my cubicle. In a nearby supply closet I found some paper towels and Windex and set to work. The whole cubicle really was pretty disgusting. The dust was so thick that it was hairy and there were mysterious and very sticky stains on my new office chair. As soon as I got my first paycheck I'd have to go to Office Max and pick out a new chair for myself. After ten minutes of fairly intensive spraying and wiping, my cubicle sparkled. It didn't look new—it hadn't looked new since 1975—but it looked a lot better. It would look even better once I pinned some pictures of Steve and the kids on the walls and maybe brought in a plant or two. A geranium, perhaps, or a jade plant. Satisfied, I threw out the paper towels, filling the trash basket to the brim. Now on to tackle the coffee pot.

No one had come into the newsroom since Jeff had left but in the break room I finally found another human being. Sitting at an old Formica table was a man reading a dog-eared copy of *Cosmopolitan* and talking to himself. He seemed to be rating the merits of the models in the magazine, but I couldn't tell for sure as he was talking very quietly, mumbling more than anything else. Not wanting to surprise him, I shuffled my feet a little, cleared my throat and bumped into the door on my way into the room. "Hi," I said brightly once I made it all the way into the break room.

The man stopped his mumbling monologue and eyed me suspiciously. He was in his early fifties and had graying hair, heavy jowls and an annoyed expression on his face that looked permanent. "I thought you were supposed to clean on Sundays," he barked, his voice a gravelly mess from what had to be years and years of tobacco and alcohol abuse.

"I'm DeeDee Pearson," I said. "I just started working here today."

"The cleaning people always work on Sundays when nobody is around so that you don't interrupt our creative flow."

"I'm not with the cleaning crew," I replied. "I'm a reporter." My, how good that felt to say!

The annoyed expression morphed into something far more menacing. "Since when are we hiring reporters? Every single time I've asked for a raise for the past three years I've been told that there are no raises because the paper is too broke. So how could anyone have hired the likes of you? What are they paying you with, Monopoly money?"

"I don't know..." I began before he interrupted me.

"Who hired you?"

"Jeff Henderson." Jeff had said it would take a few days for me to feel like a part of the team but if the rest of the staff was like this guy, it was going to take more than a few days. A few decades would be more like it.

Mr. Gravel Voice looked me up and down, taking in my blue cotton sweater, khakis and Avon jewelry in one long, condemning gaze. Even a blind person would have been able to read his thoughts at that moment: *Soccer mom. Cupcake baker. Housewife.* "Where'd you go to J school?" he questioned.

"Excuse me?"

Long sigh. "Journalism school. I'm assuming that at some point in the last century you attended journalism school and that's why Jeff hired you."

"Just who are you?" I asked with a little laugh. "Do you work for the paper too?"

I'd hit a nerve. The man drew himself up and gave me a glacial stare. "I'm Bob Meredith."

Ah, I should have recognized him from the grainy photo in the newspaper that accompanied his column that ran every Saturday: *The Weekly BM.* That photo had obviously been taken around the same time the newsroom had been furnished since Bob had aged considerably since he'd posed for it. "Oh, of course. My son reads you all the time."

He looked slightly less annoyed with me. "Everyone reads me all the time," he said grandly. "I'm a three-time winner for Best Column in a Newspaper with a Circulation of Less than 50,000 in our state."

"First place?" I politely asked even though I have never personally been a fan of his column. Bob

Meredith tended to write about things that my son Tyler found hilarious when he was in junior high, things like boobies and bathrooms and people embarrassing themselves in all kinds of different ways. His column was sort of an *America's Funniest Home Videos* in newspaper form.

"No," he snapped. Bob Meredith stood up and slapped his copy of *Cosmo* shut. "Damn contests are rigged. Everybody knows that. You have to be married to someone or sleep with someone on the judging committee to win first prize. I got three honorable mentions."

"That's too bad," I sympathized although I privately thought that he'd been lucky to get those.

"I'll live. So let's get back to you. How much are they paying you?"

Small wonder this man became a reporter since it obviously didn't bother him in the least to ask all kinds of personal questions. I was going to have to learn how to do that which might be an issue since I've never been too good at asking personal questions. "Not that much," I assured him, "and I'm only part time."

Bob seemed to like hearing that. "All right then. I guess you won't be able to be too much of a drain on the newspaper's finances if you're part time."

"I don't plan on being any kind of a drain," I said somewhat stuffily.

Bob didn't appear to notice that I was offended. "So what are you doing in here?"

"I'm going to make some coffee. I'm also a Girl Friday in addition to being a reporter."

The smirk on Bob's face grew bigger. "Well, then when you're done with the coffee, would you vacuum my cube? I spilled popcorn a few weeks ago and it's still crunching under my feet."

"If I have the time," I said deftly. Something about Bob Meredith told me that doing one thing for him would lead to another and another and another. I didn't want to become more Girl Friday than Girl Reporter if I could help it.

"You do that," he said. He glanced at the watch on his hairy wrist. "Time for this wordsmith to go. I'm interviewing the mayor this afternoon."

The mayor! I could hardly wait until I got an assignment like that. "That sounds exciting."

Bob Meredith rolled bloodshot eyes. "Nothing is exciting anymore, young lady. Give yourself a few months and those pretty stars will be out of your eyes too."

"It was nice meeting you," I told him, forgiving him a little for his interrogation since he'd called me 'young' lady. I haven't been a young lady for quite some time.

"You too—what's your name again?"

"DeeDee Pearson."

"Welcome to the jungle, DeeDee Pearson. Since you seem like a nice person I'll give you a heads up and warn you to make sure your first check is good before you cash it. The paper's been known to have cash flow problems over the years."

That was *not* what I wanted to hear. "Oh, I hope that doesn't happen!" I already had plans for my first paycheck. After I bought a new office chair the rest was going directly into a new savings account I had opened and was calling RETIREMENT.

"We all do, my dear, but it has in the past and will again in the future I'm sure. Welcome aboard and I wish you all the luck in the world."

He didn't say it like he meant it. Bob Meredith said it like I was a sucker and we both knew it. Snapping his rolled up magazine against one heavy thigh, he marched out of the break room.

Once Bob left, taking his black cloud with him, I walked over to the coffee pot and sniffed its contents. I instantly recoiled. *Whew!* The coffee in it smelled like motor oil and had about the same consistency. Not wanting to, but knowing that I had to, I lifted the lid of the coffee maker and peeked at the insides. Big mistake. Small clumps of fuzzy mold dotted the underside of the lid, and the coffee filter had obviously been used and reused several times.

Oh, my gosh! They drink this swill?

I carried the coffee pot—at arm's length—to the sink located on the opposite wall. Hot water, detergent followed by a healthy splash of bleach would have to improve things. Then I'd scrub out the coffee maker. Honestly, how could anyone make coffee in something that was so downright disgusting?

I turned on the hot water tap and waited for the water to get warm. And waited. And waited but it never seemed to get past tepid. Sticking an impatient finger under the stream of water, I wondered if the entire building was in such crummy shape. The working conditions at the *Kemper Times* were probably breaking at least a thousand OSHA rules and were probably worthy of a news story on its own. Finally, after about five minutes, the water got a little warmer. I filled the pot to the brim, added a squirt of detergent and began to scrub away at the thick coffee build up on the sides of the pot. One thing was for sure: I was *never* going to drink coffee at work. I'd bring my own Thermos from home along with my own cup. If the coffee pot was so disgusting, what were the bathrooms like at the newspaper? A voice behind me interrupted my grim thoughts.

"And just what in the hell do you think you're doing?"

Turning, I saw a tall blonde woman standing in the doorway of the break room, hands on slim hips and eyes narrowed. She looked extremely annoyed. With me.

Startled, I told her, "I'm cleaning the coffee pot," holding it up so she could see it. "It was filthy."

The blonde looked disgusted. "Any moron could see that you're cleaning the coffee pot and I know from bitter experience that it was filthy. What I want to know is why you're doing that?"

"Because I was told to?"

"Are you asking me or telling me?"

She reminded me of my junior high gym teacher, a sadist in a jogging suit who used to mock us over our weak upper body strength when no one in the class could climb the rope past the halfway mark. This gal looked to be around thirty, however. An age that was far too young for the Nazi stance she was taking with me over cleaning the coffee pot. Drawing myself up to my total five feet five inches, I reminded myself that I was old enough to be Miss Snip's mother and answered her in a far more forceful tone than I had used before, a tone that was reminiscent of the one I used with my kids when I wanted them to change the kitty litter, I said, "I'm telling you. Do you have a problem with that?"

She narrowed her eyes and looked me up and down for several long moments much in the same way that Bob had a few minutes earlier. "I don't know yet. Who are you?"

"DeeDee Pearson." *Professional journalist* I silently told myself as a reminder that I didn't need to quake or quiver in front of anyone.

"Do you work here, DeeDee Pearson?"

"Yes, I do. I just started today."

"And what, pray tell, is your job title?"

Even though I knew that I didn't have to answer her, my innate good manners forced me to. Well, either my innate good manners or my innate doormat self, I wasn't sure. "I'm the newspaper's new general reporter."

The blonde started to laugh. "You?" she asked between giggles.

This little lady was starting to annoy me. "Yes, me," I said somewhat huffily. "Is that funny?"

The blonde got a slight grip on herself. "No, not really but you look like you should be sitting at a PTA meeting or off protesting for some boring green cause outside the state capital building," she said in a tone that implied that the people who did those things had some seriously loose screws. "Are you really a reporter?"

"Would I have been hired if I wasn't a reporter?" When in doubt, always answer a question with a question.

"Are you kidding me? This dump would hire a monkey if it could tap out a decent sentence on a keyboard and if they could get away with paying it in bananas instead of real cash." The hurt I was feeling must have showed on my face because she stopped herself. "I'm sorry. I'm being unspeakably rude."

I had to agree with her on that one but since she'd stopped giggling, I forgave her. I tend to forgive people immediately if they apologize and if they seem sincere. "That's all right."

"No, it isn't. There's no excuse for rudeness but there's something about this place that seems to bring it out in all of us. If you don't lose half of your manners coming in the door, believe me, you will in a month or so. It's a matter of self defense. I'm Caroline Osborn, by the way. Also a general reporter."

So this was Caroline Osborn. She was much prettier and a lot younger than I expected. "It's nice to meet you. I think you're the best writer on the entire paper."

Caroline looked pleased. "Well, that's very kind of you to say. Of course, at the *Kemper Times* I don't exactly have a lot of competition for that title. There's Frankie Two-Face, the sports writer; Bob Meredith, the resident pervert; our photographer, Sam Weaver—don't get me started on him—Ren Peterson and of course our dear boss Jeff." Caroline looked more than a little disgusted as she listed her coworkers. "Oh, and Kate, the editor and resident shrew. Did I leave anyone out?"

"I don't know," I replied. "Frankie Two-Face?" I questioned. "I never read the sports section but surely that isn't his real name."

"No, of course not. It's Frankie Austin but I call him Frankie Two-Face because he's the most hypocritical person on the planet." She eyed the dripping coffee pot I was still holding. "Why are you cleaning the coffee pot? That isn't a job for a general reporter."

"It isn't?"

"Of course not! I used to wash it because it made me sick to look at it but after a month or so I realized that I was the only person who ever performed that little housewifely duty so I stopped immediately. I buy my coffee at the gas station on my way into work. You will learn, DeeDee, that the 1970s never happened at this newspaper and that all of the men who work here would be more than happy to return to the days when women were second class citizens and stockings were still held up by garters."

Oh, boy. I'd clearly caught Caroline on a bad day. "Well, since I already started cleaning it I'll just go ahead and finish," I told her. "I hate to leave a job half done." I didn't add that I also had an order for a cup of coffee from our boss waiting to be filled since I had no doubt that Caroline would welcome that news flash about as much as she'd embrace a rabid grizzly bear. Although I had known Caroline for under five minutes, I couldn't imagine her getting a cup of coffee for anyone, including her own mother.

Caroline shrugged. "Suit yourself. It's your first day and all, so I'm sure you're still a little bit dazzled by the glitz and glamour of thc wonderful world of journalism." She laughed again. "Believe me, it will be game over by the time you go home tonight."

Caroline walked over to an ancient avocado green refrigerator, opened it and pulled out a Diet Pepsi that had been marked with the initials *C.O* in fluorescent pink that covered the entire label. Seeing me look at it, she explained, "I always mark whatever I put in there or else that rat fink Bob will steal it. I suggest you do the same. He's stolen enough Diet Pepsis from me to start his own bottling company. He's a great admirer of Joan Crawford and always adds vodka to his Pepsi just like she supposedly did. See you later," Caroline said as she sailed for the door. "I have an interview with the high school principal. I can't wait to hear him lie about how advanced his students are and how there are no sex, drugs or rock and roll happening at Kemper High. It's so refreshing to have a job where you can expect to hear nothing but the gospel truth all day long."

"Maybe he'll surprise you," I suggested.

Caroline shook her head and smiled somewhat cynically. "I used to be surprised but not anymore. You won't be either after very long, DeeDee. It doesn't take long for the fairy dust to settle and reality to give you a nice, sharp poke in the rear end. Not around here, anyway."

A small shiver ran down my spine since that was almost the exact same thing Bob Meredith had said to me. "I think I'm going to like working here," I said in my most positive and Pollyanna-ish voice that even revolted me just a little.

Caroline half laughed and half snorted. "Keep on thinking that, DeeDee. Maybe it will keep you from self-medicating like the rest of us."

Caroline left the break room. Job satisfaction appeared to be something that needed working on at the newspaper. No, job satisfaction seemed to be something that was totally missing at the *Kemper Times.*

I turned back to the coffee pot resolutely. That was their attitude, not mine. I was personally thrilled to be working for a newspaper, something I had wanted to do ever since I was in high school and used to watch *Lou Grant* on television and dreamed about working for someone who was gruff but loveable like Ed Asner. Although I never told my husband Steve, I always found Ed Asner to be sexy in the extreme. And while Jeff Henderson looked nothing like Ed, working at the *Kemper Times* might turn out to be like working at Lou Grant's newspaper, the *Los Angeles Tribune*. Besides, I was getting paid. Who could ask for anything more?

After seventeen minutes of extensive scouring, the coffee pot finally lost the dark brown film it had and almost sparkled and my mood had returned to its normal, optimistic level. I filled the pot with more tepid water and a little bleach and left it to soak while I cleaned out the coffee maker. Another few minutes and Jeff Henderson would have a great cup of coffee sitting in front of him. In spite of Bob and Caroline's dire predictions, I knew that I was going to love working at the newspaper.

Chapter Two

"So, how was it?" Steve asked the moment he got home from work. My husband, Steve, is a college professor and although for the most part he enjoys his job, he also has one of those ten-year calendars where he has the day he's slated to retire circled in red. While he likes teaching, Steve's had it up to his eyebrows with academia and all of the accompanying boot licking, back stabbing and general Roman forum-like atmosphere. I suspect that he's been vicariously enjoying my venture back into the working world so that he can hear about what other options are out there once he's done with the classroom.

"It was…interesting," I replied. I was cutting up veggies for crudités. Our daughter Jane was coming over for dinner to celebrate my new job and would be arriving in a few minutes. Jane had been dropping in for dinner a lot ever since her latest boyfriend had turned out to be not only an incurable romantic but also to have a wife and three kids stashed in a town twenty miles away. I considered it my motherly duty to cheer her up as much as possible. I also considered it my duty to remind her on a regular basis that there were many, many, *many* other fish in the ocean and that one of these days she would find a winner.

I finished with the celery and started on the carrots. As I worked at the familiar task, the stress of my first day at the newspaper slowly drained off of me. As a rule, I don't like first days of anything. They're always tough and it's always a good feeling when they're over. Second days are almost always better.

Steve perched on a kitchen stool and helped himself to a celery stalk. "Interesting good or interesting horrible?"

"Not really either. Just interesting," I repeated. "Nothing like what I expected but I think it's going to be all right."

"What did you expect, DeeDee?" Steve asked with a grin. "People rushing around and shouting, 'Stop the presses!' like in some old movie from the 1930s? Or did you expect to see Lou Grant sitting at the city desk and barking out orders?"

I laughed too. "I suppose I did," I somewhat sheepishly admitted. "Actually, the newsroom was pretty empty the entire time I was there. I met two other reporters but that was it."

Steve picked up another piece of celery. "I suppose they were all out on stories."

"That's what Jeff said."

"Jeff?"

"Jeff Henderson. The publisher, editor-in-chief and my new boss who is nothing at all like Lou Grant. He's tall and quiet and very laid back. I guess my biggest surprise was the building itself."

"How so?"

"Well," I explained, "I expected a newspaper to be a little spiffier than the *Kemper Times*. It looks nice on the outside but the inside is pretty run down and everything looks like it was bought at a fire sale."

"There isn't much money in journalism," Steve replied.

"I know but even the computers are old and slow. I thought everyone would have the newest technology out there."

"Look at it this way," Steve suggested, "neither of us are exactly technologically savvy. Now you won't feel out of place."

Steve has a way of always making me feel better. "Good point. If I had to be technologically savvy, I'm sure I would never have landed this job although to tell you the truth, I'm still not sure why they hired me. I didn't do much today other than make coffee."

"You have to get your feet wet," Steve pointed out.

"I know but I didn't feel like a reporter. I didn't really feel like anything. Like I was a visitor instead of an actual employee. One nice thing happened, though. Jeff said that Kate—the editor—liked the writing samples I submitted. I guess that's how I got the job."

"You're a terrific writer," Steve said encouragingly, "but I want you to remember one thing: if you don't like it, you can quit. No job is worth being miserable over and I want you to be happy. It's not like we'll starve to death without your paycheck. We'll manage. We always have."

I stopped cutting up the carrots to walk over to where he was sitting and gave Steve a long, warm, heartfelt kiss. Steve had always been wonderful—maybe too wonderful—about my lack of any kind of career that had perks, benefits or a pension plan. During the years when our kids were growing up, I never gave much thought to the future but ever since Jane and Tyler officially became adults, I've found myself thinking more and more about what it was going to be like when Steve and I retired. That lack of kicking in for savings for our golden years from my end was getting to me. Although I knew Steve didn't see it the same way and that he'd wanted me to stay home when the kids were young, I still felt a little like a parasite. A middle-aged, slightly plump parasite. "Thank you," I told him sincerely once I was done kissing him, "but I'm sure it's going to be fine. You know how I've always wanted to be a writer and now I am. Well, sort of."

"You've always wanted to be a romance writer," Steve pointed out. "There's a world of difference between writing hot, sweaty bedroom scenes and churning out a story on the latest town council meeting. Fiction and journalism are worlds apart."

"I certainly hope so!" I replied.

"All I'm saying is that if you don't like it, quit. There are plenty of other jobs out there, ones that aren't as stressful as reporting."

"How do you know reporting is stressful?"

"I saw a report online about the most stressful jobs and being a reporter was one of the worst. In addition to being stressful, it also has lousy pay, bad hours and a high turnover."

"Even lousy pay is better than no pay," I said a touch stubbornly. "Which is what I've had for way too long."

"I just don't want to see you get into something that is too much for you."

"Too much for me? Because I'm too old?" I demanded.

"Whoa," Steve said quickly. "Of course not. You aren't old at all. All I'm saying is that if you don't like it, quit. I want you to be happy more than anything else."

"I'll be happy. I'm going to love it. I think being a journalist is just about the most glamorous job in the world. Remember Robert Redford and Dustin Hoffman in *All the President's Men*? It was journalists who changed the course of American history."

"You just like Robert Redford movies," Steve replied.

"Only the ones from the 1970s," I said, "when his hair was so blond and sexy and before he got his eyes fixed. Men should never have their eyes fixed. Promise me you'll never get your eyes fixed."

"I promise," Steve said, "although it isn't something I've given a whole lot of thought to. But back to the subject, I don't think that writing stories for the *Kemper Times* is going to be anything like discovering corruption at the presidential level and writing about it for the *Washington Post.*"

"You never know," I said. "Maybe I'll discover a big story right here in Kemper."

Steve looked doubtful. "I'd prefer it if you'd just stay out of trouble."

"Don't I always?" I asked. Steve opened his mouth again and I had the distinct impression that he was about to remind me of what had happened on my last job, when I was a self-employed caterer and one of my customers had died right after eating the very first meal I'd ever catered—although it had nothing to do with the food I'd prepared. I spoke quickly before he had the chance to bring up that unfortunate incident. "I hope you're hungry because dinner is going to be spectacular." Wiping my hands on a red and white checked dish towel, I glanced at the kitchen clock. "Jane said she'd be here at six. Do you know if Tyler is joining us?"

Steve shook his head. "I haven't seen your son today. Are you sure he's up?"

Not wanting to get into yet another discussion on Tyler's habits, sleeping and otherwise, I changed the subject. "Are you going to change out of your work clothes before dinner?"

"You bet I am. I hate dressing like a professor. I always feel like a fraud. Come upstairs and keep me company," he requested. "I want to hear more about your day. Did you get an assignment?"

I set the vegetable tray on the kitchen table. "No. Jeff said he'd have an assignment for me soon."

Steve and I started toward the staircase. Padding through the familiar house where Steve and I have spent the majority of our married years, it seemed somehow sweeter to me after spending half the day away from it. No doubt about it, I'm truly a homebody, happiest in my very own nest. It was going to take some getting used to, having to leave home every day.

Up in our bedroom, I decided to get out of my work clothes too. I peeled off my khaki slacks and sweater and put on yoga pants and a T-shirt and felt the instant relief of wearing non-restraining clothes that didn't pinch me at the waistline. That was another plus of being a stay-at-home mom for so many years; I never had to wear anything other than sweatpants or jeans along with a comfy top. I had the feeling that I wouldn't even remember how to put on a pair of pantyhose. Well, that was a point in favor of being a journalist. No one ever expected them to be dressed up since everyone knew they didn't make enough money to buy decent wardrobes.

Steve stepped out of his slacks and hung them up in our closet. "Did you get a chance to mention your idea for a weekly column to your new boss?"

"I thought I'd hold off on that one for a little while."

"Good idea," Steve agreed as he put on pair of jeans. "Give it a week or two but be sure to tell him you want to write one. I know you'd be a hit."

Is it really any wonder why I'm so nuts about my husband? It's like living with my own personal cheerleader. "I'll bring it up as soon as I'm feeling more comfortable," I promised.

"Then we could really retire in style."

"Would you stop worrying about retiring already?" Steve came over and wrestled me onto the bed. "I married you for your body, not your money, remember?"

"Hello!" a voice called from the back door. "Mom? Dad? Tyler? Anybody here?"

"That's Jane. She's early." I wriggled out of Steve's embrace somewhat reluctantly. It felt pretty wonderful to be pinned underneath him.

"I'll be down in two minutes," Steve promised. He touched my arm as I walked past him on my way out of the room. "DeeDee, I'm really proud of you. It takes a lot of courage to try something new."

I quickly kissed him. "You mean it takes even more courage to try something new at my age."

"At any age," he said. "You're wonderful."

Kissing him again I said, "So are you."

"I can't believe you're actually working for the *Kemper Times*," Jane said after accepting a glass of chilled white wine from me. "That is so cool, Mom!" Steve, Jane and I were sitting at the kitchen table enjoying veggies and dip and a glass of wine before dinner.

"It is," I agreed as I tried not to notice how quickly Jane drank her wine. I don't think I'll ever get used to serving my kids wine instead of juice boxes. "I kept having to pinch myself to make sure I was really awake and not dreaming. I only applied there because I read an article once that said when you're looking for a new job, apply to all the places where you'd like to work and the newspaper was my first choice."

"Sounds like a good strategy to me," Jane said after finishing her glass of wine and reaching for the bottle to pour herself another. "You've always written stuff so why not get paid for it? You shouldn't volunteer all the time. People take advantage of you that way."

Steve's eyes met mine across the kitchen table. Life is always so logical when you are twenty-eight years old and make more money than your parents combined. "She's getting paid for writing now," Steve said.

"Once I get an assignment I will be," I added. "So far I'm getting paid for cleaning the coffee pot out."

The back door opened and our son Tyler loped into the room. The door slammed behind him making the knickknacks on the kitchen window sill bounce and Steve, Jane and I jump in our seats. Tyler has always entered a room like a hurricane rushing down a cornfield. "Sorry I'm late," he said.

"I wasn't sure if you'd be here at all," I told him, "so you aren't really late."

"I wasn't sure either," Tyler replied. "How was your first day, Mom?"

"Come join us and she'll tell you," Steve suggested.

After grabbing a lite beer from the refrigerator, Tyler took his place at the table. For a moment I was transported back to a sweeter time when the four of us ate together every single night and the only things we had to worry about were report cards and how much money the tooth fairy should leave. Of course, back then, both Jane and Tyler drank milk instead of beer and wine and neither of them had tattoos or piercings or married boyfriends. What can I say? Once a mom, always a mom.

"Did you meet Bob Meredith?" Tyler asked eagerly. "His columns are awesome."

"His columns are disgusting!" Jane informed her brother with all the imperiousness that older sisters have bestowed on younger brothers throughout the ages. "Small wonder you like them. He has the sense of humor of an overgrown adolescent with a challenged pituitary gland."

"He does not! That guy's hilarious, although a person has to have a sense of humor to appreciate that quality in another person so that pretty much rules you out, Janie."

"I happen to have a wonderful sense of humor but since it's a mature sense of humor, you'd never appreciate it."

"You do have a mature sense of humor. Sometimes I think you were born seventy-five years old," Tyler replied. Jane threw a carrot stick at him.

"Let's have some peace while we eat, please," I suggested.

"So did you meet him, Mom?" Tyler asked again.

I nodded as I thought about the grumpy old man I'd met in the break room. "Yes, I did."

"That is so cool! Is he as funny in person as he is in the paper?" Tyler asked.

"Well, no…but I'm afraid I never found his column all that funny in the first place. I guess it's an acquired taste."

"Like liver and onions," Jane suggested. "Or arsenic."

"He's a comic genius," Tyler assured me. "Can I come down to the paper and meet him sometime?"

I couldn't remember Tyler ever being so interested in anything I'd done before and I was flattered. "Sure," I said, "as soon as I get used to working there myself, okay?"

"What we need to concentrate on is a great story idea for Mom to cover," Steve said. "Something that will make her really stand out."

Leave it to Steve to read between the lines and be able to tell that I was a tad hurt that I hadn't gotten an assignment yet. I suppose that I was being a little impatient—after all, it was my first day on the job—but I had kind of expected to have more to do than cleaning out the coffee pot and bringing four cups of coffee to my new boss over the course of the morning. I suppose after thirtysome years of marriage, it doesn't really take ESP to read each other's thoughts. By this point it's pretty hard to hide anything from each other. "Yes," I agreed, "help me come up with a truly knock-your-socks-off story that will make Jeff Henderson stand up and take notice of his new cub reporter and wonder how he ever got along without me."

Tyler wrinkled his smooth forehead as he thought. "There's talk that a new tattoo parlor will be opening up downtown this summer," he offered. "It's going to be pretty unique—a tattoo parlor and a bar. Cool idea, huh? I might try to get a job there."

"That's a terrible idea! You have a few drinks and wake up with a map of Australia tattooed on your butt," Jane said. "Although it would be a cool idea if you tried to get a job anywhere. You aren't getting any younger, baby brother."

"I *am* trying," Tyler told her. "It's a tough job market."

"Especially when you don't really have any talent," Jane replied sweetly.

"That's enough, Jane," I said a little sharply. Jane can go too far when it comes to needling Tyler. "Tyler will find a job he likes soon enough."

"Enrollment is up at Kemper College," Steve told me, ignoring our squabbling offspring, "although I know that's not too exciting."

"That's a thought," I said, wracking my own brain to see if I could come up with something myself but my mind drew a complete blank. The only interesting thing I'd heard lately was that the former president of the PTO was having a fling with one of the town's garbage men and that was only hearsay and not anything that could be printed in the newspaper anyway.

"There's something big happening at Kutrate Kemicals," Jane said slowly. "No, never mind. It's not really a story yet."

"What is it?" I asked, pouncing on her hesitation like a cat on a mouse. It was obvious that my nose for news was quickly developing. "What did you hear?"

Jane finished her second glass of wine. "Rumor has it that Kutrate is coming up with an exciting new weight loss product." Jane had been working as an accountant at Kutrate Kemicals, Kemper's largest employer, since graduating from college.

"Why would a chemical company be getting into something like that? I thought your company just made things that like vitamins and prescription medicines that people don't really need and eventually end up killing them," Tyler said.

Jane looked at her younger brother with the disdainful expression that she had perfected back when they were both still in diapers. "We make all kinds of different products, Tyler, and for your information, the weight loss field is huge. People spend billions on different kinds of weight loss tools."

"Just another way to separate fools from their money," Tyler told her. "If you want to lose weight, eat less. It's pretty simple."

"Simple for you," I told him, looking at his six foot four, one hundred and seventy pound body. "It's not so easy for everyone."

"Exactly," Jane agreed.

"What is the weight lost product?" I inquired. Whatever it was, I hoped it worked. My own jeans were getting a little tight around the waist band and I really didn't want to move up a size. Not when I had a closetful of jeans that were size fourteen.

"It's all very hush hush," Jane responded. "I'm not supposed to even know about it but a friend of mine in R and D—that's research and development—told me a little bit about it." Her face turned red and I wondered just how good of a friend she was talking about. "Actually, he's the person who invented it. He's really a chemical genius."

"Your secret is safe with the four of us," Steve told her. "We're family. You can trust us."

"Well," Jane said, "It's pretty technical. I'm not sure you'd understand it."

Steve and I smiled at each other. "Probably not," I agreed, "but maybe if you dumb it down we might be able to get a little idea of what it is."

"All right but you have to promise me that you won't tell a soul."

"We promise," Steve said solemnly.

"You too, Tyler?" Jane demanded.

"Who would I tell? No one I know cares about weight loss. Speaking of food, when are we going to eat, Mom?"

"As soon as your sister finishes her story," I promised.

"What are we having?"

"Chicken enchilada casserole."

Tyler's face lit up. "All right! Would you hurry up already?" Tyler asked Jane. "I swear I won't tell anyone what your company is up to unless it's totally illegal and needs to be reported to the EPA."

Satisfied with our vows of secrecy, Jane began. “Fritz, he’s the inventor, has come up with a product that kills appetite. A couple of squirts and people aren’t hungry anymore.”

Steve, Tyler and I stared at her. “That sounds pretty unbelievable,” I said.

“It sounds impossible,” Steve agreed.

“So what does it smell like? Food?” Tyler asked.

“No, Tyler,” Jane said. “If it smelled like food that would make people more hungry, lamebrain. I knew this would be too complicated for you.”

“Then what does it smell like?” I asked as I tried to imagine what it would be like to spray something into the air and suddenly lose my desire for chocolate chip cookies to go along with my afternoon cup of coffee. It sounded like a marvelous idea that would make Kutrate Kemicals at least a billion dollars.

Jane’s eyes darted around the kitchen as if she was looking for hidden corporate spies hiding behind the microwave. “The company is working the bugs out on that one,” she said in a hushed tone.

“What does that mean?” Steve asked.

“Right now it doesn’t smell too...pleasant,” Jane explained. “But it will. I have every confidence that Fritz will solve the odor problem and we’ll be on the market within the year. After that, the sky’s the limit. Can you imagine? Fat loss in an aerosol can! It should win the Nobel Prize and really put Kutrate Kemicals on the map.”

“It sounds too good to be true.” It really did. Spraying something in the air that made a person lose weight would beat the heck out of sweating at the gym but having been around the weight loss block at least a thousand times in my own lifetime, I couldn’t help being more than a little skeptical about Kutrate

Kemicals new miracle product. There had to be a downside to it somewhere.

"It's going to change the weight loss industry," Jane said. "Fritz is sure of it. May I have another glass of wine? It will be my last one," Jane said hastily, "so you don't need to lecture me on drinking and driving for the millionth time. I know my limit. Fritz explained all about body chemistry to me and I know I need to quit after three glasses or it will turn to fat. He's really amazing. I could listen to him talk for hours."

Steve and I exchanged another glance. It sounded like our daughter had something of a crush on this Fritz person. Well, an employed chemist would be an improvement over her last choice, a married creep.

"That's very interesting, Jane. Do you think I could contact someone at Kutrate about doing a story on the new product?"

"Mom! I just said that it's a secret. Of course you can't do a story on it. Not yet."

"Will you tell me when I can approach your company about it? It would be great to be able to bring something like that to my boss."

"Of course I will. I'll do some digging and talk to Fritz."

By the way Jane's eyes lit up when she said Fritz's name, my suspicions were confirmed. Jane was definitely interested in this Fritz person. "I'd love to meet him," I said lightly.

"Now can we eat?" Tyler inquired.

"Yes," I told my always starving son, "now we can eat." After finishing my glass of white wine in a long gulp, I got up to get the casserole out of the oven as the conversation at the table turned to another topic.

"A spray that makes you skinny," I said to Steve later that evening after Jane had gone back to her apartment and Tyler had gone out. Steve and I were in our usual spots in the family room in front of the television set, both in our bathrobes and respective recliners. "All you have to do is smell it. Doesn't that sound amazing?"

"It sounds impossible to me," he replied as he reached for the television remote. "Hey, *Bullitt* is on TCM! Let's watch."

"But if it did work," I continued, "wouldn't that be something? People are always looking for a fast, easy way to lose weight."

"How do you know it would be fast and easy?"

"What could be easier then spraying something in the air and then not having an appetite? It sounds great to me."

"It sounds like hogwash to me."

Glancing over at Steve's small paunch and then down at my own Jell-o-esque tummy, I silently disagreed with him. "Well, I hope it works," I said.

"Me too but it doesn't sound like it's going anywhere. Fat loss in a spray? No way can that work." Steve settled back in his recliner and turned his attention to the television screen. Although he's seen *Bullitt* approximately three hundred times, he's always transfixed whenever it plays. I looked at the screen too. It was the scene where Steve McQueen was telling Robert Vaughn to work his side of the street and Steve would work his own. I've always wanted to tell someone that.

Steve and I sat in companionable silence watching the movie. To be honest, I wasn't paying much attention. My mind was on two things: my new job and what Jane had told me. I so wanted to do well at the

Kemper Times and what could ensure success more than coming in to work with a scoop about a painless, easy weight loss product that was going to be manufactured in our very own town?

"I wonder…" I said thoughtfully.

Steve pulled his eyes away from the TV. "What do you wonder, honey?"

"I wonder if Jane would introduce me to that chemist. Maybe he'd tell me a little more about that weight loss product so I could have some background information before the company is ready to go public."

"I kind of doubt that. I'm sure Kutrate Kemicals is going to plan a huge publicity campaign. They aren't going to want any leaks now."

"I suppose you're right," I agreed. "I think I'm going to take a shower and then go to bed," I said.

"You'll miss the chase scene," Steve said.

"I've seen it," I replied, getting up and dropping a kiss on top of his head. "Many times. Don't stay up too late."

On my way out of the room I grabbed my laptop. I had a little homework to do after my shower and I couldn't wait to get started. At the top of my list was the question: just how many fat loss plans were out there?

Chapter Three

In a word: thousands. Maybe hundreds of thousands. Although I was certainly no stranger to diets, I'd always stuck with the boring counting calories plans that took forever to work but did, eventually, make my pants fit more comfortably—until I started eating more calories and wound up back where I started. After surfing the internet for an hour or so I fell asleep with my mind positively clogged with ways to lose ugly fat and become the skinny swan that purportedly lived inside all of us. Liquid diets, pills, fasts, high colonics, low colonics, calorie counting plans, candies, cookies, bars, exercise regimes straight out of Dante's inferno—while I had always known that dieting equaled big business, I hadn't realized quite how big a business losing weight truly was. That night I had a dream that I landed the story on Kutrate Kemicals latest fat loss technique and woke up just as Jeff Henderson was telling me that I was up for the Pulitzer.

Jumping out of bed, I felt more energized than I had in decades. This story had all but been delivered to me with a big red bow tied around it. I had to write it. It was meant to be. Now all I had to do was get the green light from Jane to talk to Fritz and I'd be good to go. I knew that it was too soon to approach the powers that be at Kutrate Kemicals at the moment but I was dying to cut my teeth on another story. Maybe Jeff would have my first assignment ready for me. Humming happily, I got dressed and did my hair and makeup in record time. The early bird catches the worm—or the story, hopefully.

"No, DeeDee, I don't have a thing for you."

I focused on the small blob of scrambled egg clinging to Jeff's tie as I tried to hide my disappointment to Jeff's response to my question about whether or not he had an assignment for me yet. Although a part of me was ready to slink back to my desk without arguing—the weak, scaredy-cat, completely chicken part—another part of me wouldn't let that happen. Weak, scaredy-cat and chicken were not part of a true journalist's persona. "Um...why not?" I questioned in what I hoped was a friendly but professional tone.

Looking up from the story he was editing, Jeff stared at me in much the same way he might have stared at a mouse who'd jumped onto his desk and questioned his judgment over the kind of cheese he'd put in his mousetrap. Pushing his glasses up with his forefinger, he said, "I don't really need to give you an explanation. You work for me, remember? Besides, this is your second day on the newspaper. As I told you yesterday, I want you to get used to working in a journalistic environment before sending you out on a story. Now would you run and get me some more coffee? I don't know what you did to that coffee maker but that coffee you made yesterday tasted like something from Starbucks. Nice job." Jeff held his coffee mug out to me and waved it slightly in the air.

I reluctantly reached for his coffee cup. My hand stopped mid-air as I remembered Caroline's warning from the day before. The one about the men who worked at the *Kemper Times* still being stuck in the Dark Ages when it came to women's liberation and how I shouldn't be doing anything as demeaning as cleaning out the coffee pot. I was pretty sure that Caroline would also see getting coffee for the boss just as—if not more—demeaning. Then again, as Jeff had just pointed out, it was my second day at work. Plus he was not only my boss but also the editor-in-chief of the newspaper and its publisher. I pretty much had to do whatever he wanted me to do. Surely after a few more weeks I'd be able to tell them that playing waitress was not part of my duties, not even as the newspaper's Girl Friday, but until then it wouldn't hurt to go along to get along. "Coming right up," I said, taking the mug out of his hand. "I hope you'll have an assignment for me soon, Jeff. I can't wait to get started. I've been trying to think up some stories I could do and I might have a lead on something quite exciting…" My voice dribbled back down my throat as Jeff shook his head.

"DeeDee, there's one rule at the *Kemper Times* that I'd like to make perfectly clear: you aren't paid to think." Jeff spoke so calmly, so matter-of-factly that for a few seconds I couldn't believe what I'd just heard.

"I beg your pardon?"

"We didn't hire you to think. You're here to do whatever else we tell you to do without questions."

"Well, sure, but don't you want my input?" In every television show that I'd ever seen about newspapers, every movie, every novel, every single article about the world of journalism the reporters *always* tossed their story ideas into the ring and usually the editor barked at them, "Cover it! The truth must prevail!" Or something to that effect. Then, after the reporter trotted off after the hot lead, the editor would shake his head in admiration over the spunk that his reporter was showing.

"Not particularly," Jeff said, scratching his jaw absentmindedly. Apparently Jeff Henderson and I didn't watch the same television shows. "Leave the story ideas to the experts. That's what we're paid to do. Now how about that coffee?"

Knowing a dismissal when I heard one, I left Jeff's office and headed for the coffee machine, hoping that I wouldn't run into Caroline on my way. Since Jeff's coffee mug was neon green with inch high letters that spelled out *JEFF* on the side, it would be pretty obvious to everyone within a hundred yards what my latest assignment was at the *Kemper Times*.

Halfway down the hall, I passed an office that had been empty when Jeff had given me the grand tour the day before. Glancing inside. I saw a petite woman sitting behind a battered metal desk that was a dead ringer for Jeff's desk. The paper must have gotten most of its furniture at some kind of going out of business sale back in the 1960's. The woman had light brown hair that she wore in a flip style giving her a Gidget Goes Journalist look. Smiling at her automatically, I continued down the hallway with Jeff's mug.

"Hey! You! Stop!" She had a squeaky voice that instantly made the hair on the back of my neck stand up.

Backing up a few steps, I peered into her office again. "Are you speaking to me?"

"Damn straight I am! Who are you? What are you doing here?"

My eyes dropped to the brass nameplate on her desk. *KATE WESTON*. This must be the infamous Kate Caroline had mentioned the day before. This was also the woman who'd liked my writing samples enough to recommend me for the job. "I'm DeeDee Pearson." I waited for her to recognize my name.

Apparently, I hadn't made that big of an impression on her because she looked at me blankly. "What are you doing here?" Her eyes narrowed as they dropped to the mug I was holding. "And isn't that Jeff's coffee mug? What are *you* doing with it?" She sounded like I was planning to pour rat poison into Jeff's coffee just like the secretary did in *9 to 5*.

"I work here. Jeff asked me to get him a cup of coffee so I was on my way to do that."

"*You* work here? Since when?"

My feelings were beginning to get a little hurt the way everyone at the paper sounded so surprised upon learning that I was on the staff. "Since yesterday morning."

"As what?"

"Ummm, as a general reporter." Kate Weston was the editor so it seemed to me that she should have been aware of the fact that there was a new hire on board but apparently I was wrong about that. "You're Kate Weston?"

A pleased look passed over her small features. "You've heard of me?"

"No, I read your nameplate," I said, gesturing toward the nameplate on her desk.

Kate looked disappointed. "Oh. Well. I'm the editor and as such, I'll be the first one to read your copy—you do know what *copy* is, don't you?"

"Yes, I do."

"Good. The last fool we had in here didn't have a clue as to what I meant when I asked for his copy. He thought I wanted him to copy what other reporters had written. Can you believe that?"

"What happened to him?" I asked.

"What do you mean?"

"Is he still working here?"

"Of course not! We have *very* high standards. If you aren't good enough, *wham!"* Kate made a whacking movement with her hand against the top of her desk. The metal vibrated loudly when she hit it. "You're out of here."

"You fired him?"

"You bet I did!"

"So where is he now?"

"How should I know? The last I heard he was working at KFC but I don't know how long that gig lasted and I don't care."

My dream of retiring from this job was starting to fade. It was late August and I was starting to think that I'd probably be lucky to last until the holidays were over. "So what does an editor do?" I asked. "Forgive me if that's a silly question but I want to learn everything I can about the newspaper."

She shook her head, making her flip bounce. "Are you kidding me? I do everything around here. Mainly, I write brilliant editorials. I have a column too. I'm sure you've read it."

Here was my chance to mention my idea of writing a column. Taking a deep breath, I plunged in. "I've always wanted to be a columnist. As a matter of fact, Erma Bombeck is one of my heroines—"

Kate interrupted me and continued as if I hadn't responded. "I think my best column was the one when I wrote about my nephew graduating from kindergarten. It took my sister forever to make sure his little robe fit just right and then he blew everything by wetting his pants. Well, I wrote about that day in detail and then had the column framed so he'd remember his big graduation fiasco forever. I try to write with a lot of pathos but also with a great deal of wit. I think I really nailed it with that one."

I somehow doubted that her nephew would agree. "So how does that work having two columnists on the paper?" I asked.

"What do you mean?"

"Well, there's you and Bob Meredith. How does that work out—isn't there a lot of competition?"

Kate raised her eyebrows and a smug smile curled around her lips. "Competition between Bob and me? I suppose there could be—if he was anywhere near as talented a writer as I am. Besides, he writes humor and I write a more slice of life type of column. They're quite different. Plus he appears on Saturdays, and Sundays are all mine. Sunday is the big day in newspapers, FYI. That's why I always get Sunday for my column. Rank has its privileges."

Jeff had said the exact same thing to me the day before and it was obviously a motto that management at the newspaper lived by. I held up Jeff's coffee mug. "I guess I'd better get Jeff's coffee for him. I don't want to get in trouble with the boss on my second day at work."

"Look," Kate assured me. "I'm your boss too and if I want to talk to you, Jeff's going to have to wait for his coffee. Have you gotten an assignment yet?"

"No…"

"Some old broad is retiring from the library and this is her last day. You could cover that one. It would take a real moron to screw up a story like that. Blah blah blah. Knows the Dewey Decimal system by heart. Blah blah blah. Can't wait to spend time with the grandkids. Blah blah blah. I could write it in my sleep."

"I would love to write that story," I told her.

"Well, we'll see. If Jeff hasn't given you anything yet there must be a good reason." Kate picked up a coffee mug off the top of her desk and held it out to me. "As long as you're headed that way, fill me up, would you? Just a splash of creamer. Just a splash. I'm watching my figure."

Since she had a figure like a skinny twelve-year-old that didn't seem necessary but I silently accepted her empty cup. "It was nice meeting you," I said.

"Ya, you too, DeeDee." Kate smirked. "That's a funny name. So old-fashioned. How old are you?"

Was this woman for real? "Ahhh…old enough to know better than to answer that question," I said.

"I'm guessing that you're pushing fifty pretty hard, right? I can always tell by the eyes and the neck and both of yours are starting to look a little baggy." She squinted at me through over-sized eyeglasses. "I use Crisco on my neck," she confided. "Keeps it as smooth as a baby's patootie. Sometimes I cover my whole body with Crisco, climb into a pair of flannel jammies and get into bed, all greased up like a chicken about to go under the broiler. I heard Doris Day used to do that with Vaseline but I prefer Crisco. Goes on easier."

"Isn't that awfully messy?" I tried to picture Steve's face if I got into bed covered in Crisco but couldn't do it.

"Not really. It's mostly absorbed by the morning. Doesn't matter though—I don't do the laundry. That's hubby's job. He does all that stuff—cooking, cleaning, laundry. All the boring stuff." She snickered. "He makes a wonderful wife. That's why I married him—he takes good care of me."

It was beyond the power of my imagination to drum up what kind of man would marry a woman like Kate Weston but apparently there was one masochistic enough out there to have done it.

"How about you? You married? Any kids?"

"Yes, I'm married and I have two grown children, Jane and Tyler."

"They live in town or have they flown the coop?"

"They live in town. Jane works at Kutrate Kemicals and Tyler's between jobs right now." He'd been between jobs for about three months, but I didn't see any reason to share that with this woman. Frankly, I was surprised she'd asked me anything personal at all. Five minutes into our relationship and she didn't strike me as the kind of person who was interested in anyone else, especially not the help.

Kate's eyes widened. "Oh," she said, "you're the one who submitted the Christmas letters as your writing samples. I remember you now. I said you'd probably be okay at this job so in a sense I got you hired." Kate laughed loudly. "You owe me, kid!"

"I'll remember that," I said weakly.

"See that you do. I always call on people I've done favors for."

"I'll get your coffee," I said, wanting to get out of her office in the worst kind of way. "How's that for a favor?"

"Miniscule. Make it snappy," Kate ordered. "I'm like that old commercial with David Niven. I hate to wait. I'm sure you remember that one, DeeDee. It's from the good old days, just like you."

Giving her an extremely small smile, I exited Kate's office. Steve had always told me that I had the gift of being able to get along with anyone. Walking through the newsroom where my new colleagues—all half a dozen of them—were sitting hunched over their computers, heads down and eyes glazed, I had the distinct impression that getting along with the people who worked at the *Kemper Times* was going to be pretty much a challenge along the lines of fitting into my junior prom dress without the assistance of a tub of some of Kate's Crisco and a spatula or some of that miracle weight loss spray that Jane's company was going to put out. Maybe that would change over time. I hoped.

In spite of the fact that I brought Kate her coffee in record time, the assignment on the retiring librarian never materialized. With nothing to do other than fetch coffee for Jeff every half hour or so, I decided to do some more digging on weight loss plans so that I could compare them to what Jane had told us over dinner the night before. It truly sounded too good to be true—losing weight by smelling an air freshener? But inventors had come up with a lot of amazing things over the years. Just look at the Thighmaster and Silly Putty.

"What are you doing?"

Caroline Osborn startled me by appearing over my left shoulder.

"Oh, just some research," I said as I clicked on the red *X* in the corner of the screen. I wasn't fast enough.

Caroline read the screen before it vanished.

"Weight loss? Are you thinking about going on a diet, DeeDee?"

"I'm always thinking about it," I replied. "Thinking about it but not necessarily doing anything about it."

"Yeah, I know how that is. Well, just a word to the wise. Don't let Kate catch you surfing the web for personal things. She'll have your head on a platter. Not on company time and all that crap."

"It wasn't really for personal use," I began but then stopped. I didn't have enough information to suggest a story on the new fat loss spray and even if I did, I didn't want to tell Caroline about it. If there ever really was a story to do and the paper gave it to Caroline instead of me—a likely scenario—that would be way too painful.

"Yeah, right, and my 'research' on vacation packages to the West Indies isn't for personal use either." Caroline smiled at me knowingly. "Just don't get caught," she advised. "Kate's a real stinker about what can and can't be done on company time."

"Thanks for the warning," I said sincerely. It was nice to have someone fill me in a little on how things were done at the newspaper.

"Anytime. If you're not going on a diet, how about having lunch with me today?"

"Sure," I readily agreed.

"Noon," Caroline said. "We'll have a real girl talk and get to know each other." Although her tone was more than a tad sarcastic, I was looking forward to getting to know Caroline. Yes, she had a somewhat brusque personality but she was a journalist and I wanted to find out more about her.

"Sounds good," I said.

"See you then." Caroline sashayed off and I turned back to my computer. After she left, I returned to my research. Maybe I should make a list of the different kinds of diet aids that were currently available to the public. It would take me forever but it would be nice to have the background if I ever landed the story about Kutrate Kemicals' newest product. I pulled a yellow legal pad out of my desk—brand new and purchased by *moi* for my new career—and started to write. Within twenty minutes I had four pages of different products. No doubt about it, losing weight was huge.

All this research was making me hungry. I've never been able to understand how people can stay on diets for weeks at a time. Just reading about other people losing weight made me want to head for the nearest Dairy Queen and buy half a dozen Dilly Bars. I'd have to call Jane and see if there was any progress on getting her company's weight loss product on the market. I'd do that as soon as I got home.

"So how's it going?" Caroline asked me at precisely twelve-oh-seven. We had left the newspaper together and walked the block to the Budapest Café, a small restaurant located in what had once been a funeral home. It was my first visit there since the whole idea of eating in a former funeral parlor creeped me out, but Caroline didn't seem bothered in the least. "Are you enjoying being part of the *Kemper Times* family?"

I laughed and took a sip of ice water. "Well, to tell you the truth the family part has pretty much eluded me so far."

Caroline smiled knowingly. "You mean that you haven't been swept away by the warm welcome you've gotten?"

"Not exactly." I glanced around the room to make sure that no other newspaper employees were eating there. The new owners had decorated the restaurant in a style that was vaguely reminiscent of Persia or maybe somebody had access to props from the community theater's production of *The King and I.* Long curtains were draped along every wall, giant pots of petunias were positioned in all the corners and the waiters and waitresses were forced to wear Harem pants and *I Dream of Jeannie* velvet bikini tops for the females and little velvet vests trimmed in gold brocade for the males. "Actually, you're the only one who's really talked to me so far."

"I'm not surprised. Everyone who works there is so miserable that they probably haven't even noticed that a new face has joined the ranks."

A waiter came to take our order. He was young, around my son Tyler's age, and his velvet vest was black to match his black gauze Harem pants. He looked so humiliated that I decided to leave as big a tip as I could manage. "I'm Virgil and I'm your server today. What will it be, ladies?"

Caroline looked him over, her eyes lingering on his flat, well-muscled torso. "Hello, Virgil."

Looking up from his pad, Virgil's own eyes widened in recognition. "Caroline! My favorite reporter! What are you doing here?" Virgil didn't glance in my direction but that wasn't a surprise. I've noticed that once women are over forty, they become invisible to younger men, even younger men wearing black gauze Harem pants.

"Having lunch, silly. What else would I be doing here?"

Virgil giggled and some of his macho mystery vanished. "Sorry. I'm just not used to seeing you in the daylight."

"Virgil!" A voice called from the back of the restaurant. "Snap it up."

"I'll have a glass of Merlot and your lunch special," Caroline told him. "I wouldn't want to get you in trouble with your boss."

"I'm always in trouble with that broad." Virgil turned to me. "And what will you have, ma'am?"

"What is the lunch special?"

"It's on the board out front." He adjusted the fez hat he was wearing so that it sat more neatly on his dark curls.

I squinted but could barely make out the board placed in the front of the restaurant much less read what was written on it. "That's all right," I assured him. "I'll have the lunch special too but just ice water to drink."

Virgil nodded before leaving us. As he was walking away, I noticed that he was wearing those shoes that curl up at the toes. I wondered how he walked in them.

"He is such a doll," Caroline breathed once Virgil was out of earshot.

"Have you known him for long?" I asked, brushing away at a fly that was apparently determined to dive down my throat.

"Oh, a few months. He has a degree in archeology but he can't find a job that pays better than being a waiter. Those harem pants net him some pretty great tips."

"That has to be a tough job market, especially in the Midwest." I don't know why colleges offer degrees in areas like archeology and philosophy. I mean, really, how many jobs can there possibly be in either field?

Caroline shrugged. "Maybe I should join him and work here. One of these days I'll find a new job and then I'm going to quit so fast that Jeff Henderson's square head is going to spin. I plan on giving absolutely no notice."

"Are you looking for another job?"

"Only all the time but it's like being in a jungle with way too many tigers fighting over the same few pieces of meat."

Caroline was starting to depress me although I knew she was right. "Yes, my son Tyler hasn't had much luck finding a good job." Or finding any job, actually but I didn't see any point in sharing that with Caroline.

"What's his degree in?"

"He hasn't finished college yet. He's taking some time off to find himself." So far Tyler had been searching for himself for over five years.

"Well, good luck to him. Does he live at home with you?"

"Yes, he does."

Caroline sighed deeply. "I bet he's cute too. Why are all the cute guys unemployed or working at crap jobs and still living at home with their mommies?" She shook her head. "Whatever. I swear, I'm going to stop looking for guys in my age bracket and start going for old coots with pensions. At least they'd be able to take me out to dinner once in a while. So, you met the Dragon Lady?"

I knew immediately who she was talking about—not that it was too difficult to figure out. With just three women working at the newspaper, the Dragon Lady was pretty obvious. "I met her. She is a little…challenging."

Caroline snorted. "You don't have to be diplomatic with me. I know what a pain in the butt Kate is. Rude, smug, know-it-all—and that's when she wakes up in a good mood. Watch out when she's in a nasty mood."

"Um…is there any way to tell?"

"Not really. To tell the truth, her good moods and her nasty moods really aren't all that far apart."

Virgil returned with a wine glass the size of a small fish bowl and set it in front of Caroline. Smiling her thanks at him, she took an enormous swallow. "That's better. After working at the *Kemper Times* for seven years, I finally understand the stereotype of the hard-drinking newspaper person with the bottle of bourbon or vodka or whatever stashed in a desk drawer, only I'm strictly a wino. You have to drink or you'll go nuts."

"Because the work is so stressful?" I asked.

"Because we work for such jerks and get paid peanuts for the privilege. Has Kate given you an assignment yet?"

"Not yet."

Leaning back in her chair, Caroline looked perplexed. "I don't get that. Why did they hire you if they aren't going to use you? The rest of us are drowning in work and they have you making coffee and cleaning off tabletops. What are they paying you?"

"I beg your pardon?" Bob Meredith had asked me the same question the day before. I had been brought up to believe that talking about money in general and salaries in particular was extremely uncouth, so uncouth that I never knew how much my father made until Steve began to do his taxes. It was then that I learned that Daddy really could have bought me a pink Sting Ray bike for my seventh birthday if he'd wanted to and that there had been absolutely no need to keep the household thermostat at 65 degrees all winter long throughout my entire childhood.

"How much are they paying you?" Caroline repeated. "You don't have to tell me if you don't want to. I'd like to know for my own edification but if it makes you feel weird or anything, that's okay. I understand how it is with your generation."

All of Dear Abby's instructions about how to respond when someone asked a highly personal question refused to surface in my brain. "I'm starting out at nine."

Caroline blinked. "Nine what?" she asked before taking another sip of Merlot.

"Nine dollars an hour," I reluctantly admitted since I had the distinct impression that my hourly wage was not going to impress the woman sitting across the table from me.

Caroline came perilously close to spewing a mouthful of red wine all over the dirty tablecloth. She managed to swallow it but was still sputtering when she spoke again. "Are you crapping me? They're paying you nine measly dollars an hour and you accepted? You do know that nine bucks an hour isn't that much more than minimum wage, right? You could probably do better for yourself working as a cocktail waitress even at your age and with your legs."

For the first time in a long time I was glad that my son was unemployed since his jobless status was saving him from dating Caroline. "Well, yes, but hopefully I'll get a raise in a few months."

Caroline shook her head. "Don't count on it. The last raise I got was about four years ago and it didn't even come close to being a cost of living raise. I can't believe you accepted that kind of a salary, DeeDee. You're a professional writer. You deserve more than nine dollars an hour!"

"I'm not really a professional writer," I admitted. "Actually, most of my writing has been for the schools my kids attended and our Christmas newsletters. Nothing all that big."

"Doesn't matter," Caroline told me with an emphatic bounce of her wine glass. "The point is that the newspaper hired you as a professional journalist and even though it's as plain as the nose on your face what they're up to, they should be paying you more than nine dollars an hour."

It wasn't plain to me so I asked, "What are they up to?"

"It's pretty obvious that they don't care if you can write or not. They're going to use you as an in-house janitress and maybe toss you a story once in a while so that you can brag to your book club buddies that you're a reporter."

"I don't belong to a book club."

"Yeah and I doubt that you belong to the Society of Professional Journalists either."

"Why would the management at the paper bother to hire me if they didn't plan on using me as a reporter?"

"I just told you why: because they're cheap! If they can get away hiring a—a *mom* instead of someone with an actual degree in journalism, then why not?"

Caroline said the word "mom" the same way some people said "hooker." Stung, I refused to believe what she was telling me. She had to be wrong. I waved for the waiter. When Virgil shuffled over, I ordered a glass of Chablis for myself. Virgil was blessedly fast with my wine and I took a deep sip while wondering if the newspaper business wasn't getting to me already. "I seriously doubt that there was any kind of orchestrated plot to hire me just because I didn't ask for more money."

"Maybe not but you should tell them that you won't work for less than twelve dollars an hour. Have a little pride, DeeDee. Nine dollars an hour? Are you freaking kidding me? You could deliver the newspaper and make more than that."

"I can't ask for more money now. I said I'd take the job at nine."

"But don't you see that by accepting a professional job at such a low salary, you're bringing down the entire journalism field? Pretty soon management will expect you to sweep out the bathroom before you go home at night."

"I leave at noon."

"That's beside the point. You have to ask for more money, DeeDee. That's simply all there is to it."

I toyed with the stem of my wine glass, troubled by the turn our conversation had taken. "So you don't think I'll ever actually get an assignment?"

Caroline looked like she was torn between wanting to knock herself between the eyes and wanting to knock me between the eyes. "Don't be a dope. Of course they'll give you a story. They'll give you every crappy story that comes down the pike because you're new and don't know anything."

Maybe I was a dope but I felt a wave of pure relief rush through me when I heard Caroline's prediction. I'd never tell my lunch companion, but I would have worked for even less just to be able to call myself a journalist and *not* because I wanted to brag to my book club—provided I had a book club—but just because I thought it was such a cool job. "Look, I know it isn't very much money but I think it's exciting to work for a newspaper. I'm not young like you, Caroline. I don't have that many options open to me at this point in my life. I'm thrilled that I have been hired to work in a field filled with people I admire."

Caroline rolled her eyes. "Right. Have you met Ren Peterson yet?"

"No, I don't think so. Who is he?"

"One of those people you admire so much. Ren is the editor of the *Lifestyles* section. He has the cube at the far end of the room. Right next to yours as a matter of fact. Nice looking guy with light brown hair?"

"Oh, sure. He looks a little bit like Tom Cruise."

"Yeah, if Tom Cruise was on the verge of a nervous breakdown. Ren started out as a perfectly normal person last year and then they gave him the *Lifestyles* section on top of all of his other duties around the paper. He's gone from a pleasant human being into someone wound so tight that one wrong look, one offhand comment and he's going to flip out."

"Um, what's your point?" I asked.

"If you allow management to take advantage of you the way they obviously plan to, you're going to hurt each and every one of us. Why should they give us raises when they can get the likes of you to work for nine dollars an hour? Do you really want to be responsible for pushing Ren over the edge?"

"Caroline, I don't even know Ren." Although Caroline seemed to have a sincere interest in how I was being treated, there was no way that I could see myself marching into Jeff's office the next morning and telling him that I wanted a raise after working at the newspaper for all of two days. "Maybe after six months or so, then I might feel more comfortable asking for more money but not until then. I appreciate your concern, Caroline, but I have to do things my way."

"Your way sucks," Caroline argued. "By accepting that crummy salary, you're bringing down journalistic standards everywhere. I don't suppose you're in our union yet either."

Thankfully, Virgil returned with two lunch specials and set them down in front of us with a flourish before I had the chance to tell her that I didn't even know there was a union at the newspaper. "There you are, ladies, curried tuna. Careful, it's hot." He winked at Caroline. "I told the cook to make yours extra spicy. I know how much you like hot things."

Caroline winked back at him. "You got that right, Virgil."

"Another wine?"

"Why not?"

Virgil vanished then returned almost instantaneously with Caroline's second glass of wine. "Enjoy."

Picking up my fork, I sampled the tuna curry and instantly almost tore the roof of my mouth off. "Oh, my!" I panted as I lunged for my water glass.

"It's a little on the spicy side," Caroline conceded, "but for $3.99 a plate, what do you expect? You get what you pay for." There was an almost menacing glint in her eyes as she spoke and it didn't take a genius to figure out what she was telling me, namely that I'd already botched my entrance into the world of journalism by accepting such a low salary.

Slowly I ate my tuna curry, ignoring the burning sensation that accompanied every bite. While I agreed that Caroline had a point, I also wasn't in the position to start anything. All I wanted was a job. Was that so much to ask for? "This is very good," I said after a few minutes.

"It's all right," Caroline replied. Her pretty face grew determined. "Someday I'm going to have a job that gives me an expense account. When that happens, I'll never eat lousy tuna curry again, I can promise you that." She looked a little bit like Vivian Leigh swearing that she'd never be poor again in the scene right before the intermission in *Gone with the Wind.*

I believed her. There was something about Caroline that told me that she was the kind of person who always got what she wanted sooner or later. I continued to eat my tuna curry half wishing I'd gone home for lunch instead.

Chapter Four

"Don't be too hard on yourself," Steve told me later that night. We were both in our recliners with the news on, cocktails in our hands, and the tension of the day was quickly draining away. Dinner (lasagna) was in the crock pot, our son Tyler was out with friends and the house was blissfully serene. Taking a long sip of Chablis, I intended to make it even more serene. Steve continued. "You know what's right for you, not Caroline Osborne. Personally, I think it would be pretty dumb to ask for a raise a few days after being hired."

"Exactly. Besides, if all I'm going to do at the paper right now is make coffee and do some cleaning, then I don't think I can complain about what they're paying me," I said and then I sighed. "Caroline doesn't agree with me. She made me feel like I was a traitor to journalists everywhere because I settled for nine bucks an hour."

"You aren't a trained journalist, honey."

"You've got that right!" I took another sip of wine, my forehead furrowed. "She did kind of make me wonder why the paper bothered to hire me in the first place," I admitted.

"Don't do that to yourself. You gave them your writing samples and they must have spotted potential in them or else they wouldn't have hired you. Isn't that what that Henderson guy said? And he's the publisher so he should know what he's talking about."

"I guess he edits stuff too," I said.

"See? He knows what's good. And that the editor spotted potential in what you'd written, right?"

"Yes, but—"

"But nothing. A newspaper wouldn't bother to hire someone as a reporter if what they really wanted was someone to clean for them. That's way too complicated. The *Kemper Times* isn't exactly known for being run by a group of evil geniuses and if you don't believe me, read their editorials sometime."

"That's what I think too," I said, feeling relieved to hear Steve's take on my new work situation. "Besides, I'm sure I'll get a raise once I'm there for a while."

"I know you will. They'd be nuts not to keep you. Give yourself some time and let them see how terrific you are. In the meantime, don't listen to Caroline Osborn. She sounds a little on the bitter side."

"She's very bitter, which is a shame because she's a lovely girl and obviously quite smart and talented. I think she hates working for the paper but I can't tell if it's the *Kemper Times* in particular or newspapers in general. Maybe she's burnt out. When I get to know her better, I'm going to suggest she get some job counseling. She's too young to be so mad."

"Well, if anyone can help her out, you're the one, DeeDee. You did a great job with Jane. She's always had her head on straight about what it takes to make it in the working world and that job she has at Kutrate Kemicals is fantastic. It's such a relief not to have to worry about our daughter. Now Tyler, on the other hand—"

"Did I tell you that Tyler has another job interview tomorrow?" I said, interrupting Steve before he could get started on how our son apparently lacks having any kind of career goal other than becoming the next Eddie Van Halen or George Harrison or whoever Tyler's latest guitar hero might be. I know Steve loves Tyler but I also know how frustrated he is over Tyler's seeming lack of ambition. Steve is an extremely focused person, just like our daughter, while Tyler is a free spirit, just like yours truly. I'm sure that once Tyler decides what he wants to be when he grows up he's going to do just fine. I'm not worried about him…too much, anyway.

Steve perked up. "He does? Where?"

"I'm not sure."

"I certainly hope he gets something soon. He's getting way too old to sleep until noon every day. Say, you never told me. Did you get an assignment today?"

"No, not yet."

"It sure would be great if you could cover what's happening at Jane's company, that weight loss thing. That sounds like a real scoop."

"I know. That kind of story might even get picked up by the AP. I'd love that."

Steve reached over and squeezed my hand gently. "It will happen, DeeDee. After you've been there awhile I'm sure you'll have more stories than you can handle and as soon as Jane gets the green light she'll tell you and you'll be the first journalist to write about the story."

"I hope so but in the meantime I'll try not to be so impatient. I have the feeling that I'm not going to feel like I really belong at the newspaper until I get that first assignment."

"You'll get it," Steve assured me.

We both turned our attention to the news then but I have to admit that I was only half listening to what was happening in the rest of the world. I was more interested in what was happening in my tiny corner of it, namely my brand new job and what Caroline had implied over lunch that day. I sure hoped that it wasn't what Caroline had said—that the paper wanted me more for my dusting skills than my writing skills and that I was a reporter in name only. If that was true it seemed like a pretty sneaky thing to do to a person. But as Steve had said, it would be stupid to pretend to hire me for one job only to have me do another. What would be the point of that?

Ours is not to reason why... My mother always said that whenever she couldn't figure something out and I supposed she was right. Either Jeff or Kate would give me a story sooner or later or I'd continue to make things sparkle down at the paper and never interview anybody but the guy who came in to clean the bathrooms once a week—provided I happened to be at work on a Sunday. Either way there wasn't much I could do other than try to absorb as much newspaper ambiance as much as I possibly could. That and keep bugging Jane about the weight loss spray story. Jeff said he didn't want input from his reporters but surely he'd bend the rules if one of his reporters came across a really huge story, wouldn't he?

Feeling better, I decided that the next day when I went to work I was going to do my best to get to know some of the other reporters a little better. I wanted to make a niche for myself at the newspaper and to do that I was going to have to like the people I worked with as well as like the work I was doing. After living with me for all these years, I know me pretty well. I have to be comfortable in my surroundings to perform at my optimum.

Tomorrow. Open mind. Positive attitude. This is all going to work out just fine.

Squaring my shoulders firmly, I got up and went into the kitchen.

"Where are you going?" Steve asked.

"To get our dinner. I'm starving. Being a sort of Girl Reporter has really given me an appetite."

"Well, I'm not a Boy Reporter but I'm starving too. I'll take an extra big serving of lasagna."

"You got it," I told my husband. "Want to eat in front of the TV since no one else is home?"

"Sounds like a plan," Steve agreed.

"Are you DeeDee?" A man with sleepy-looking eyes paused next to my cubicle where I was busily using a toothpick to clean out the gunk that had accumulated between the desktop and the fabric covered wall.

"Yes," I told him, happy to hear my name said out loud. Three days on the job and I was starting to feel invisible.

"I heard there was fresh meat in the newsroom. How are you doing?"

Fresh meat? Well, that was one way to look at it. "Fine. Great. I'm very happy to be here."

Looking around the still empty newsroom, the man sighed. "Yeah, well, it beats standing on the corner with a sign announcing to the world that you're homeless, I guess."

"Um, what's your name?" I asked. It felt wonderful to be talking to another human being. Who would have dreamed that journalism would be so lonely?

"Frank Austin. Sportswriter and resident blogger *extraordinaire.*"

This must be the Frankie Two-Face Caroline had mentioned. He didn't look two-faced. He looked like a pretty nice guy. "It's nice to meet you, Frank. You said that you blog? What do you blog about?"

Frank stared at me as he picked at a scab on his left thumb. "You've never read my blog? It has the highest readership on the paper."

"I'm not really into reading blogs," I admitted. "I like books."

Frank stared at me like I'd just admitted that I liked eating sweat socks. "Everyone reads blogs. Or they should." His voice became a touch patronizing. "I suppose it's a generational thing."

Since Frank and I were about the same age I felt comfortable disagreeing with him. "I'd say it's more a technological thing. Blogs seem so cumbersome to me. You have to find them and pull them up—it's a bother."

"Cumbersome? You're out of your mind. It's a lot easier to read a blog than it is to read a book or a newspaper. Better graphics too."

"Well," I said doubtfully. "Maybe you're right. I'll have to check yours out."

Frank laughed. "If you plan on working here for longer than two weeks, you're going to have to do more than that. All of the reporters are required to have their own blog. Didn't anyone tell you that?"

"No…are you serious?" My stomach sank. What on earth would I blog about? I was a wife, a mom—I had nothing to write about on a blog! "You're kidding, right?"

"I'm dead serious. We have to Twitter and do Facebook too. I suppose no one told you about those either?"

I shook my head. Of course I had heard of Twitter and I had a Facebook account but the only things I posted were pictures when Steve and I went on vacations and snapshots of any extra big tomatoes my garden happened to produce. "How often do we have to do those things?"

"At least once a week. More if possible but it usually isn't possible. I mean, there's just so much to blog about in a town the size of Kemper."

"But what are we supposed to write about?"

Frank gave me a small smirk. "If I could tell you what to write about, DeeDee, why would the paper need to keep you around? I could do all of your writing and then management could give me a raise."

He had a point. "I suppose you're right. Well, I guess I'll have to take a crash course in blogging."

"I guess you will," Frank agreed. "Good luck with that. Where'd you go to J school?"

"Where did you go?" I asked, turning the question around.

"The U along with everyone else. I thought maybe you went to someplace a little more impressive like Northwestern or the University of Missouri and that's why they hired you at your age."

"Actually my degree is in psychology." From a city college but there was no way that I would share that tidbit with Frank. I wasn't sure how much lower my reputation at the paper could go but I wasn't in any hurry to help it along.

Frank laughed. "That should come in very handy working around here. Hey, I almost forgot. There's a reason I'm talking to you. I'm supposed to tell you to go see Kate. She has an assignment for you."

"Really?" I leaped up out of my chair, almost knocking it over in the process. "I thought Jeff handed out the assignments."

"Kate…Jeff…there's not much of a difference between the two of them. They're both demanding, arrogant and can't spell worth a darn."

Jeff Henderson appeared behind Frank. "Who can't spell worth a darn, Frank?"

Turning around, Frank instantly morphed into the perfect employee. "My next door neighbor's kid. It just amazes me how he could be in high school and still not know how to spell 'separate.' What are kids learning in the public school system these days anyway?"

Jeff shrugged. "Tell me about it. My own kids can't spell either and their teacher told them that's what spell check is for on their computers. I don't know why we pay teachers those outrageous salaries with our tax dollars." He looked at me. "Kate wants to see you, DeeDee. I told her it was all right to give you your first assignment. I know how much you've been looking forward to it and I really can't be bothered with something so minor."

"No one ever forgets their first assignment," Frank said in a tone of voice so sincere that it was almost nauseating. "I know I'll never forget mine and I also know how much I've appreciated each and every assignment you've ever given me, Jeff."

"Well, support the winners, that's what I always say," Jeff responded, "and with your batting average, you are most definitely one of our stars, Frank."

Leaving Jeff and Frank to enjoy their mutual admiration society in private, I headed for Kate's office, my heart pounding with anticipation. I hoped that my assignment would be something human interest oriented. I had the feeling that hard news and I were not going to like each other very much. I'm pretty much a wimp when it comes to things like blood, gore and violence, and while Kemper is for the most part an uneventful town, I still didn't want to be sent out to cover a car accident or anything else that might end up with blood-stained sheets covering still warm bodies. I'd had enough of that during my last foray into the working world.

At Kate's office, I knocked on the door. "Kate? Jeff said you wanted to see me."

Kate was sitting in front of two large computer screens, the expression on her small face intense as her eyes darted back and forth between them. I glanced at the screens too and was surprised to see that she was watching what appeared to be surveillance cameras. One shot looked like the lobby of the newspaper and the other screen was of the back entrance where trucks picked up the papers that were ready to be delivered. "Where is that woman?" she muttered.

"Who?" I asked.

"Natalie Cooper. She's our customer service rep but she's never at her desk. This is the third time today I've caught her sneaking off."

"Maybe she's in the bathroom," I suggested.

"I certainly hope not." Kate pulled her attention away from the screens. "Bathroom breaks are scheduled for ten o'clock and three for her. She shouldn't be anywhere but at her desk."

"Well, nature calls," I said weakly. Kate scheduled bathroom breaks for her underlings? Talk about micromanaging.

"Not on my watch," Kate replied. She stared at me for a few seconds, apparently unsure of who I was. "Oh. DeeDee."

"Yes. Frank said you wanted to see me," I repeated.

"Right. I have an assignment for you."

"Great!" I responded. "I've been looking forward to getting an assignment."

Kate ignored my bubbling enthusiasm. "Go to this address and talk to Meryl Cunningham." She held out a slip of paper for me.

Stepping into her office, I took the paper out of her hand and saw that it was for an address out in the county. "Ummm…what am I supposed to talk to Ms. Cunningham about?"

"About her lead in the community theater's production of *Ten Little Indians.*" Although she didn't add a 'duh' at the end of her sentence, she did say it like I was supposed to know that vital bit of information through osmosis or extra sensory perception.

"Oh, I didn't know that the community theater was doing *Ten Little Indians.*"

"Well, they are," she said, clearly bored with our conversation. "I want about 800 words and I'd like them ASAP. That means 'as soon as possible.'"

"Yes," I said, "I know that."

"Then what are you waiting for? You want a driver? Perhaps a chauffeured limousine?"

"No, I was just wondering if you wanted me to bring the photographer with me."

Kate sighed loudly, sounding like a tire rapidly losing air. "I suppose so."

"Um, how do I find a photographer?"

"Do I have to do everything around here?" Kate asked. "Maybe you'd like me to take you by the hand and lead you to where you're supposed to go?"

"I'm sorry, it's just that I'm new at all of this and no one has told me too much…" My voice dried up and dribbled down my throat under Kate's laser-like glare.

"We have one photographer," she said slowly and clearly like she was talking to someone who had just landed from Mars. "His name is Sam Weaver and his desk is the first desk in the newsroom. Go and tell him to come with you if he's free. If he isn't, try to take some photos with your phone. But if the photographer is free, drive together so the two of you can't double charge for mileage. Got it?"

"Thank you," I said although I felt like sticking my tongue out at her.

"Amateurs," she muttered under her breath before turning to her computer screens, her attention back to searching for the hapless Natalie Cooper.

"All right. I'll see you later." Needless to say, I wasn't surprised when Kate didn't say good-bye, but I didn't really care. My good mood had returned full blast. I had my first assignment and it wasn't for anything gory. I happen to love theater stories and I knew that talking to Meryl Cunningham was going to be fascinating. I could hardly wait to get started.

"I'm not driving you." Sam Weaver didn't look up from the *Cosmopolitan* he was reading, the same issue Bob Meredith had been looking at the other day. His cubicle was two down from mine but this was the first time I'd ever seen him. He was big with a beard and longish brown hair. I had never seen him before but I'd seen plenty of his photos. He was a good photographer and had worked for the newspaper for as long as I could remember.

"Kate said we should drive together so we both wouldn't need to charge the paper for mileage."

"Yeah?" Sam lifted an eye from the magazine and fixed it on me. "Well, you can go tell Kate that she can shove her cheapskate attitude right up where the sun don't shine. I'm not driving you. What am I supposed to do while you're doing your interview? Twiddle my thumbs and count red convertibles driving down the highway?"

"I don't know," I responded since I really didn't know what he was supposed to do while I interviewed Meryl.

Sam finally tossed his magazine down and gave me his full attention. "What's your name again?"

"DeeDee Pearson."

"Well, DeeDee, since you're new here I won't hold it against you that you wanted me to drive my vehicle, use my gas, oil and tires to drive out to the middle of nowhere. For your future reference, I don't drive anybody but myself."

"Uh, I suppose Kate knows that?"

Sam snorted. "Yeah, Kate knows that. Just like Kate knows not to ask me. Notice how she told you to tell me? That's her m.o. Get someone else to do the dirty work all the time and never get her own hands dirty. That broad is seriously asking to be whacked."

I tried to laugh since he had to be kidding. "We won't get in trouble if we don't drive together?"

"This isn't junior high, honey. We're both over twenty-one and can make our own choices without Kate's approval."

But would we both get paid for mileage? I was too chicken to ask Sam that question. "Well, I guess I'll see you out there then."

"What's the address?"

"I beg your pardon?"

"I need the address so that I can know where I should go with my trusty camera and amazing photographic talent," Sam said in the same super slow, overly patient tone of voice that Kate had used on me, only he sounded like he might be talking to someone who was just coming out of a coma. "Would you please give it to me?"

"Oh, of course." If Sam wanted to make me feel like a dope, he was doing a marvelous job at it. Flustered, I scribbled down the address on another piece of paper and handed it to him. "It's out in the county."

"Yes, I can see that by what you've written down. I've been at this game a long time, little lady, and I know not only our entire town but the whole county as well as I know my wife's backside. There's really no need for you to clarify directions for me."

Oh, boy. Another charmer employed by the *Kemper Times.* Gulping, I nodded and left without saying another word. Then I went to my cubicle and got the reporter's notebook that I'd purchased for this exact moment. Written on the cover was *DeeDee Pearson* along with my cell phone number. Looking down at the notebook, I couldn't help but smile. An assignment at last.

Once outside, it was easy to forget Sam and his rude attitude. It was a gorgeous late summer day, the humidity was low and I was on my way to my very first assignment as a reporter. Pointing my car in the direction of County Road 19, I began to drive toward Meryl Cunningham's house.

On the way, I went over the questions I planned on asking her. About a thousand years ago, I took a journalism class in high school and I could still remember my teacher, Mrs. Silber, pounding *who, what, when, where, why and how* into our adolescent brains. She claimed that asking those questions and having a pushy personality were all anyone needed to succeed as a journalist. *You don't need a fancy schmancy degree,* she told us repeatedly. *All you need are guts! Guts and at least three active brain cells and you could work for the* New York Times*!*

Well, the time had finally come to put Mrs. Silber's theory to a test. I knew the questions but I was a little doubtful over whether or not I could be all that pushy. Pushy really isn't my nature but surely I wouldn't need to be too pushy with Meryl Cunningham, a local actress who would undoubtedly love talking to the press.

Driving past corn fields that were almost ready to be harvested, I wondered if Mrs. Silber was still alive. If she was, it would be nice to get in touch with her and tell her about my new job at the newspaper. She'd probably be happy to hear that one of her journalism students was now in the business. As soon as I got home, I'd have to see if she was on Facebook. Humming happily, I steered my minivan toward Meryl Cunningham's house, more than ready to hear about the community theater's upcoming production of *Ten Little Indians.*

Chapter Five

"You should have called first!" Ms. Cunningham told me sternly though her screened door, heavy arms crossed over an equally heavy bosom. Dressed in a faded bathrobe printed with purple roses the size of large cabbages, her blonde hair sticking up in tufts like cotton candy and her wide face totally devoid of makeup, Meryl was somewhere in her late fifties or early sixties and she looked like I'd just roused her out of bed although it was after ten in the morning. Then again, she was in the theater so maybe she hadn't gone to bed until dawn.

"Oh, I'm sorry. I guess I thought my editor had been in touch with you," I apologized. Great. My first interview and I'd already committed a faux pas. Mentally, I kicked myself. Of course I should have called Meryl to set the interview up. What had I been thinking? That she'd somehow know I was on my way out to her house? *See? You aren't a real journalist! Caroline Osborn would never make a mistake like that!* I tried to ignore the nasty little voice in my head. My self-esteem was suffering enough without me adding to it. "Would you like me to come back at another time?"

Peering past my shoulder, Meryl eyed my mini-van with its Kemper city sticker stuck on the windshield. "You drove in from Kemper?"

I nodded. The drive had been about twenty miles, not exactly a marathon, but still a good distance.

Meryl sighed dramatically, so dramatically that I half-expected her to do a corny moue with the back of one hand pressed against her forehead and the other hand pressed dramatically across the doorframe. "I *suppose* we could do the interview now but I hope to God that you didn't arrange for the photographer to come out today too. An artist needs time to prepare for photographs far more than for a print interview."

As if on cue, Sam Weaver's silver pick-up truck pulled into the driveway and stopped behind my mini-van. Although I'd only had one conversation with Sam, I had the distinct impression that he wasn't the type of person who liked to reschedule appointments. As a matter of fact, I was pretty certain that if I did suggest we reschedule, he'd beat me to death with the long lens on his expensive-looking digital camera. "I'm sorry," I said sincerely, "but that's our photographer now. This is my first interview and I guess I'm a little green. I didn't think things through too well."

Meryl's finely plucked eyebrows rose impressively, reminding me of twin curtains going up on opening night. "A little green? My dear, you are positively emerald." She squinted at Sam. "Is that Sam Weaver?"

"Yes, it is."

Meryl immediately began patting her cotton candy hair and sucking in her stomach. "Well, I guess it's all right. He's a very good photographer and I don't want to pass up the opportunity of having my picture taken by a true genius. Let me change and toss some make up on. Let him in, help yourself to some coffee and I'll be down in five minutes." Meryl left me standing on her front porch to face Sam alone. I watched as Sam got out of his truck, pulled a camera bag from the front seat and then stomped over to join me on Meryl's front porch.

He looked about as thrilled to be there as a vegan at a meat packers convention.

"Hi there!" I said cheerily. "You sure made it here fast!"

"Where's the subject?" he asked, ignoring my friendly welcome. "I've got seven more assignments to do today so I'd like to get this one over quickly."

"She's freshening up," I said while shooting a silent prayer skyward that Meryl freshened up quickly. Genius or not, instinct told me that Sam Weaver was not the kind of person who liked to be kept waiting by anyone. Instinct and the way he was tapping his foot against the wooden porch floor in a staccato rhythm that Ricky Ricardo would have appreciated. "She'll be right down."

"She's not ready?" Shoulders sagging, he sat down on the porch steps. "What is with these people?" he demanded in a whiny voice. "Why can't they be ready when I get there? Don't they realize what a busy man I am? That damn newspaper needs to hire another photographer. I've got too many assignments and not enough hours in the day."

"Why doesn't the paper hire another photographer?"

"Because Jeff is a cheapskate. I mean, come on! How many papers have the publisher also acting as the chief editor? That guy gives new meaning to the word tightwad. He has his lamebrain nephew takes photos on the weekends and then only if there's an emergency, like a train derailment. The rest of the time it's all up to me."

That did sound a little daunting but since Sam was already feeling quite sorry for himself, I didn't want to add to his pity party. "I'm sure Meryl will be right out," I said.

"She'd better be," he said darkly.

"You know how actresses are. They can get ready faster than anyone else on the planet. They have to since they need to change so quickly between scenes, you know—change costumes and put on different makeup…" My voice faded away and dwindled down to a mere squeak under Sam's glare.

"Good Lord, an actress. What's her name again?"

"Meryl Cunningham."

"What do you want to bet her real name is Mary?"

"Why would she change it?"

Sam rolled his eyes toward the cloudless blue sky. "Because perhaps maybe she's heard of another actress who's done pretty well for herself who goes by the name Meryl?" He shook his head. "These small town actors are the worst. Never made it anywhere but they act like their community theater production of *Our Town* is the greatest things since the invention of the push-up bra. Talk about phony baloney."

Sam Weaver's photographs were the high point of the *Kemper Times.* He definitely had talent and most of the pictures he took looked like they could be in a much better newspaper. Looking at him, I wondered why he'd bothered to stay with such a small paper. "Who are your favorite subjects?" I ventured to ask, hoping to take his mind off the ticking of his wristwatch.

Sam shrugged. "Pets are good. They can't talk to you. Hunting shots are always great. I'd have to say anything without people. Especially actors or actresses. Talk about giant egos. Only thing worse are local politicians."

Thankfully, Meryl's screen door opened and she stepped out on the porch. Swathed head to toe in a filmy pale blue dress that was a huge improvement over the ratty bathrobe, she had managed to achieve a miracle over the past five minutes. The frowsy looking woman who had opened her front door for me had vanished and was replaced by a handsome, commanding presence who all but screamed the *thea-tah*. "Good morning," she said to Sam, enunciating perfectly. "I'm so pleased to meet you."

Sam quickly got to his feet. "Sam Weaver, award-winning photographer. It's a pleasure meeting you, Meryl." His transformation was as amazing as Meryl's and his attitude had gone from whiny and complaining to charming and professional in an instant.

"How delightful, Sam," Meryl breathed. "I've always admired your talent. Whenever I see one of your photos in the newspaper, I ask myself what you're doing at a small town paper like the *Kemper Times.*"

I was happy that Meryl had asked that question since I'd just been wondering the same thing. Sam chuckled. "That's a mystery to me too, Meryl, but you know there's a lot to be said for working at a smaller newspaper. I have my freedom and that means a lot to me."

"Freedom is a lovely thing," Meryl replied, placing one perfectly manicured hand on his arm. "I don't know what I'd do if I wasn't free myself. No husband anymore, no boyfriend, my children are all grown and on their own—I'm a totally free person." Her heavily shadowed eyes peered intently at him. "Totally free," she emphasized.

Sam smiled back at her. "How nice for you."

Pleased, Meryl dropped her clutch from his arm and smiled triumphantly at me as if we were in competition for Sam's attention. I smiled back while longing to say, *He's all yours, honey.* "Now how do you want me?" she purred.

Looking around the porch, Sam pursed his lips. "The light's not bad out here. Why don't you sit on your porch swing and we'll see what happens?"

"All right." Meryl daintily walked to the swing and sat down, her skirt flouncing out around her. I was completely impressed with how she'd managed to shave at least twenty years off her looks in under five minutes. Once Sam left, I'd have to try and find out how she did that. She glanced over at me. "Did you get coffee for Sam? Oh, and for you too."

"No, I didn't. Sam, would you like some coffee?"

"Sure," he agreed.

"It's on the stove," Meryl instructed. "Cups are in the cupboard right next to it. You can't miss them."

Obediently, I trotted into Meryl's small house. So far, so good in spite of Meryl's initial bad mood and Sam's grumpiness. I didn't want any more coffee but I poured a cup for Sam, pausing for a moment to study a large collage Meryl had up on the wall of her kitchen. It consisted of pictures of Meryl from what had to be two dozen plays. It was obvious that the woman had been in the acting game for a long time. She had been quite stunning when she was younger with good bone structure and pretty eyes. After studying the collage for a few moments longer, I returned to the porch just in time to hear Sam say, "You're kidding me! She didn't call you first?"

My good spirits plummeted a notch or two. Had Meryl been telling Sam how I'd neglected to call to set up an interview before coming out to see her? It sure sounded that way. I slowed my steps to hear her response. "Well, in her defense she said that this is her first interview—although that does surprise me. She looks pretty old to be just starting out as a reporter, much older than I am."

"I'm sure the paper got her cheap," Sam replied. "Our management isn't exactly known for hiring top drawer talent."

"Except for you," Meryl cooed.

Sam laughed. "Of course."

The two of them were getting along swimmingly. I almost hated to interrupt them but sensed that cowering in Meryl's front hallway while waiting for Sam to leave wouldn't exactly further my reputation as a rising middle-aged reporter. "Anyone for coffee?" I asked, stepping out on the porch.

"Sure. We're all done here." Sam accepted a cup and sat down on a glider.

"You're done? Already?"

"That's how professionals do it, DeeDee. We know our subjects, we get what we need and we call it a day."

"That was the best shoot I've ever had," Meryl assured me, sounding like she'd just wrapped up shooting the cover for an upcoming edition of *Vanity Fair*. "I've never been handled quite so professionally before. Sam, you really know your craft."

I glanced over at Sam to see what there was about him that would cause such a high octane reaction from Meryl but I drew a blank. Kind of tubby, in need of a haircut and wearing a Minnesota Twins T-shirt that had a large mustard stain on it, I was missing whatever allure Meryl was finding but that was okay. I didn't want to find him alluring. I just wanted him to be nice to me. "Well, as soon as you're done with your coffee, Sam, Meryl and I can get started." I really didn't want to interview Meryl in front of Sam. Not just because it was my first interview but also because I had the feeling that he'd hang onto every word, correct me when I made a mistake and then report all of them to everyone else down at the paper.

"I don't mind if you start while I'm still here," Sam said as he put his feet up on a wicker ottoman.

"I thought you were in a hurry. I thought you had seven other shoots for today."

"I do but I also deserve a coffee break. Go ahead. Start your interview."

Since he hadn't offered me too many alternatives and since I'd also look like a wienie extreme-o if I refused, I gave him a tight smile before turning to Meryl. "Is that all right with you, Meryl?"

"Of course it is." Meryl was sitting in one of those wicker chairs with a huge fanning headrest. Very Morticia Adams. "Fire away."

Trying to get my hands to stop shaking, I pulled out my reporter's notebook, flipped back the top and asked my first question. "Um, let's see…where did you grow up?"

Meryl launched into her background with gusto. "I was born in Kansas City, Kansas, although I won't tell you when that blessed event occurred. I grew up in Springfield, Illinois, where I met and married my dear late husband Howard and had our five children. Do you want their names?"

"Sure," I agreed somewhat recklessly. My handwriting was already deteriorating and even I could see that there must be a better way to interview someone that didn't involve writing down every single word they said.

"Michael, Michelle, Melissa, Mortie and Max."

"Cute," I commented as I struggled over spelling out Melissa. Was Melissa spelled with one *s* or two? My brain seemed to be taking a sudden holiday to the Bahamas. "When did you get interested in acting?"

"Oh, my, let's see…I think I've always been dramatic. At least, that's what my grandmother used to say. I can still remember her telling me, 'Meryl, you have talent and it would be a shame not to share it with the rest of the world. That's why I'm such a strong believer in Community Theater. We might not reach huge audiences but I always feel that we're helping improve people culturally one performance at a time. I remember my first grade teacher telling me—"

"DeeDee, would you walk out to my truck with me?" Sam interrupted. I looked up at him in surprise. "I have something I need to give you before I take off." Sam got to his feet and smiled quite charmingly down at Meryl. "Thank you for the coffee and for being such a delightful subject. It was a pleasure meeting you."

"The pleasure was all mine," Meryl told him, still gazing at him like he was a combination of Warren Beatty and Liam Neeson all rolled into one delicious package.

I followed Sam down the porch steps and to his truck which was parked about a hundred feet away. I couldn't imagine what he could possibly have in his truck that he would want to show me. "What is it?" I asked. "What did you want to give me?"

"Listen," he spoke in a quiet voice, "don't let that woman talk your ear off. I've met a million broads like her and she'll be dragging out her baby albums and showing you her first teeth and locks of hair when she was still a natural blonde if you let her. You've got to take hold of the interview, DeeDee. Get what you need and then get out of there."

"I don't want to be rude," I began but Sam cut me off.

"It's not being rude. It's called saving your life. That woman is obviously starved for attention and if you let her, she'll be yakking from now until sunset. Believe me, DeeDee, I'm telling you this for your own good since you obviously have zero newspaper experience. You need to grow a pair."

"Ahhh..." Not knowing quite how to respond, I finally said, "Well. Thank you, Sam. I'd better get back to Meryl."

"I mean it," he said as I walked away, "do what I'm telling you and save yourself." With that, he climbed into his truck, threw it into gear and roared down Meryl's gravel driveway leaving me behind wondering how I'd ever manage to 'grow a pair' on the short walk back to Meryl's front porch.

Three hours later, I wished that I'd listened to Sam. "...and that's when I got my very first role in our local community theater." Meryl had barely paused to take a breath since she'd started her monologue. I didn't even need to ask questions. She had already provided more than enough information for a three-part, hardcover biography with barely any prompting from me. Finally, I broke in. "Well," I said, "I think I have enough information for our article." Kate only wanted 800 words. I was sure I had at least 8000 words written down in my notebook. My hand was killing me.

"But we haven't covered my latest play!" Meryl said. Thankfully, my cell phone rang. Peeking at it, I saw that it was someone calling from the paper.

"Excuse me. I really have to take this."

"Of course," Meryl pouted. "Do what you have to do."

"DeeDee Pearson," I said, feeling relief as my right hand slowly began to uncramp.

"Where the hell are you?" It was Kate and she sounded more than a little peeved.

"At Meryl's house," I said, wishing I had a better answer.

"Still? I told you I wanted a short piece on her upcoming play and you're still there? What are you doing, writing it in longhand and then having her correct it? Get your ass back to the paper now. That story was due an hour ago. You're only paid until noon, DeeDee. It would behoove you to learn how to work more quickly."

"I'm on my way," I said. Hanging up, I turned to Meryl. "That was my editor. I've got to get back to the paper and write this up."

"Of course! I'm sorry if I ran on a bit. You know how it is...I start talking about my love of the theater and time seems to disappear."

Maybe for her it had disappeared. For me it had stood still. "Thank you for agreeing to be interviewed." I got to my feet.

"Anything for the press," Meryl said airily.

"One more question—is Meryl your real name or your stage name?"

Meryl's eyes narrowed. "It's my real name. I was using it far before that Streep woman came along—not," she added as she quickly backpedaled, "that I'm older than she is. I'm a little younger, actually, but I have been going by Meryl forever and in my opinion, she might be a well-known movie star—although some of her pictures from the last few years have been real dogs—I'll always be the First Lady of Community Theater."

I nodded. "Well. All right, then. I should be going. It was a pleasure meeting you, Meryl."

"When is this story running?"

"Tomorrow, I believe."

"Wonderful!" Meryl followed me out to my car. "I wish we'd had more time to chat, dear. Are you sure you have enough material?"

"Positive," I assured her.

She was still talking as I drove away and although I felt more than a little rude, I also felt as if I was escaping from a human volcano that was spewing sentences—all beginning with the word "I"—instead of lava.

"Phew. Thank God that's over," I said out loud as I drove back toward town. The clock on the dashboard told me that it was close to noon. I still had to write up the story so it looked like I'd be staying late at work that day. Well, that was all right. I didn't mind staying late since it was really my fault that the interview had taken so long in the first place. I was sure that as I got more experience I'd be able to time things a little better. It was like cooking. When Steve and I first got married, I could never figure out how to time meals so that the potatoes were done at the same time as the meat and the vegetable. Journalism had to be pretty much the same thing.

Shaking out my right hand as I held the steering wheel with my left, I sure hoped that I was right.

Chapter Six

Kate was standing by my cubicle when I got back to the paper. Arms on her hips, lips a thin bright red line and her right foot impatiently tapping inside a most unattractive taupe-colored sneaker, she wasn't exactly the Welcome Wagon. "Look who's here," she drawled as I tossed my purse on my desk.

"Hi, Kate," I said breathlessly. The reporters' room was located on the third floor of the newspaper building and there wasn't an elevator. Climbing up the steps reminded me daily of how out of shape I was getting but if I lasted at the paper, I was sure to get toned pretty fast.

"'Hi, Kate,'" she mimicked in a high squeaky voice, an action that immediately set my nerves on end and brought back too many memories of mean girls who mocked my athletic skills during junior high gym class. "Do you have any idea of what time it is?"

"Um…" I glanced at the clock on the wall. "Twelve seventeen." Wow! Twelve seventeen? I'd made great time coming in from Meryl's house.

"You should have been back here by nine-thirty, ten at the penultimate latest. What took you so long?"

"My subject was sort of long-winded," I began to explain. "She had a little trouble getting to the point."

"Well, for Pete's sake, you should have cut her off! Sam came back here and told us how she'd cornered you. He said you looked just like a fly trapped in a spider web. You need to learn how to control these situations, DeeDee. I know you're new to this game but come on! You aren't some teenager. You're an adult woman who should know how to say, 'Thank you. I have all I need.' You need to wise up!"

I shot a glance over at Sam Weaver's cubicle and caught him leaning back in his office chair as he eavesdropped on Kate and me. So much for hoping he might keep his mouth shut as a professional courtesy. "I am sorry," I repeated. "Next time I'll know better."

Kate waved my apology away. "Sorry doesn't cut it in journalism. I wanted that story an hour ago."

My blood was beginning to boil so I answered her a little more sharply than I normally would. "If you'll let me get to work instead of wasting more time telling me how I messed up, you'll have it before I leave."

"You're damn straight I'll have it before you leave! That's your job, cupcake, now get to it." She slapped away from me, her skinny thighs swinging underneath the leggings she was wearing like thin twin metronomes as she walked and talked loudly to herself. "Honestly! It's like working in a damn daycare around here. What do I have to do? Babysit each and every single one of you so that you do what you're supposed to do? We aren't paying you to sit around with your fingers up your collective noses, we're paying you to work!"

Thankfully she had reached her office by that point and went inside, slamming the door shut behind her and muffling the rest of her monologue.

For a moment or two I sat at my desk and quaked with anger. I simply wasn't used to being spoken to that way. Kate acted like she was my kindergarten teacher and I had been tardy coming in from recess. It was not a sensation that I enjoyed reliving in the least.

"Don't let her get to you," a soft voice advised.

I looked up from my computer. A young man was leaning around the petition, pity in his large brown eyes. "I'm Ren Peterson. We haven't met yet."

Automatically, I held out my hand for him to shake. "DeeDee Pearson."

"Nice to meet you, although I should have introduced myself sooner."

"You haven't been here while I've been here," I pointed out, my nerves calming down a little. Ren had a soothing voice, like a radio announcer's, that was quite welcome after Kate's high pitched screech.

"True enough. They keep us so busy around this place that I feel like most of us are barely in the newsroom these days."

"I'm sorry we had to meet right after I was scolded. I feel like I was caught stealing a candy bar or something."

"Don't," Ren advised. "That's her goal. Like I said, don't let her get to you."

"Is she always like that?"

Ren nodded. "Always. Kate suffers from a malady called DPD."

"What's that?"

"Defective Personality Disorder. There's a lot of that going around here. I'm hoping it's not contagious. The best thing you can do is try not to take it personally. Believe me, you'll have to learn how not to take it personally if you want to stay here."

I smiled. Ren seemed like a nice enough person although he was too young to have such dark circles under his eyes. I recalled that Caroline had said how overworked he was and I believed it. His cubicle was piled so high with papers that I could see stacks threatening to topple over the wall that separated his side from mine. "Thank you for the advice and I'll try not to let my blood pressure get too high. Now I guess I'd better write this story before she comes back to bite my head off again."

"Don't worry," Ren said before vanishing back into his cubicle, "if she doesn't bite your head off about the story you're working on now, she'll find some reason to bite it off about the next one. Kate is never satisfied."

Wonderful. Turning toward my computer, I began to tap out my very first story for the *Kemper Times.*

Writing up Meryl's interview turned out to be far easier than the interview itself had been and as I wrote the last sentence, my self-confidence was slightly recovered although I realized that in spite of the fact that I'd learned who was Meryl's college roommate back in 1978, I hadn't asked about the dates and times of her upcoming play. A quick telephone call rectified that and I worked the information into the article. Finally satisfied with what I'd written, I rubbed my eyes. It hadn't been easy but I'd written my very first story for the *Kemper Times.*

Now what?

I realized that I didn't know what I was supposed to do next since on the job training seemed to be pretty much non-existent at the *Kemper Times*. "Ren?"

His head appeared around the cubicle again. "You rang?"

"I have a dumb question for you."

"There are no dumb questions." Ren grinned. "Actually, that's not true. There are a million dumb questions but I doubt that yours is one of them. What is it?"

"What do we do when we're done with a story? I mean, who do we send it to?"

"Who else?"

My heart sank. "Jeff?" I asked hopefully.

Ren shook his head sorrowfully. "Kate. When you're ready, just send it to her as an email attachment."

"DEEDEE!" Kate's voice bellowed out from her office. "Are you done YET?"

Hurriedly I scanned the story one more time before sending it on to Kate. "Just finishing up," I called back.

Immediately Kate appeared in her doorway. "There is no need to shout," she snapped. "We work at a newspaper, not on a farm or in a factory. I'll thank you to remember that."

It was becoming more and more apparent that I couldn't win with this woman and I was beginning to wonder why I would want to. "All right," I said in the most pleasant tone I could manage between gritted teeth. "I'll remember."

"You just do that one little thing," Kate said before going back into her office, her door slamming shut behind her.

"Charming, isn't she?" Ren whispered.

"I think I've seen cobras that had more charm," I replied.

With a barely suppressed sigh, I sent Kate my story and then got to my feet and walked over to her office. Time to make nice with the dragon lady. I knocked softly on her door.

"What?" Kate shouted.

I opened her door and stepped inside. "I just wanted to say I'm sorry about calling back to you," I apologized in as friendly a tone as I could muster. Okay, I didn't like the woman but she was my boss. I needed to figure out a way to get along with her. "I didn't mean to shout. I just assumed that since you called to me that it would be okay for me to call back to you."

Kate ignored my apology. "Did you finish your story?"

"Yes. I just sent it to you."

"I'll let you know what corrections need to be made."

"All right." I lingered for another moment or two to see if she had anything more to add. When she didn't say anything, I turned to leave.

"Where do you think you're going?" Kate instantly barked.

I turned back to face her. "Excuse me?"

Kate punched up her email and found the one that I'd sent her without bothering to answer me. I watched as she opened the attachment. A second later she looked at me triumphantly. "The story you just sent me is 778 words. I said it should be 800."

"You wanted exactly 800 words?"

"You'll find that I never say what I don't mean, DeeDee. Now, you can wait while I read 778 words, can't you?"

"I didn't know that you wanted me to wait."

Kate chuckled, showing off tiny white teeth that looked exactly like baby Chicklets. "I'm a pretty fast reader, DeeDee, but even a moron can read 778 words in a few minutes."

"So you want me to stand here while you read my story?"

"How am I supposed to give you fresh feedback if you slink away from me while I'm reading?"

This woman was the limit. No, she was obviously from the outer limits. Job or no job, regular paycheck or not, I didn't have to take that kind of crap from her or anyone else. "Kate, I've never slinked anywhere or away from anyone in my entire life."

She wasn't listening to me. "Your opening line is good but your overall style needs work," she said, looking up from her computer. "Plus it's too passive. Newspapers are all about action, DeeDee, action. Re-write it."

"Now?"

"You'd rather wait until the play is over?" she questioned. "Re-write it in a more active voice and it will do. It's not great but for a first crack, it's not the worst piece of journalism I've ever read."

"Kate?" Bob Meredith came up behind me. Right behind me. I was still standing in the doorway when he joined us, pressing his right hip against my left hip, a completely unnecessary move, I might add, since there was ample room in the doorway for both of us. "Got a sec?"

"Of course," Kate replied, looking past me and beaming at Bob. "Always for our ace reporter. What's up?"

Bob glanced over at me. "Are you done?"

Since he had me pinned against the doorjamb like an unfortunate centipede, I wrenched my hips away in a quick swivel and nodded curtly. "I'll do my re-write right now," I told Kate.

"Well, that's mighty decent of you, DeeDee," Kate responded, "especially since that's your job. And don't put these hours down on your time sheet since you could have had this all wrapped up if you'd managed to conduct your interview in a normal amount of time."

Not being able to come up with any kind of reply that would add to our conversation, I went back to my cubicle. I might even have slunk but I was too mad to be able to tell. As I left I heard Bob Meredith say, "Time sheet? She's hourly?"

"What else?" Kate asked. "All of our new hires are hourly from now on. Saves the paper a ton of money. No bennies either."

Caroline looked up as I blindly moved past her. "I can't stand that woman," I said through gritted teeth. "She's awful."

Caroline nodded her head. "To know Kate is to hate her and the worst part is that she's such an idiot that she doesn't even know how we all feel about her. She thinks she's wonderful and that we all think she's the greatest boss since Henry Ford, can you believe that?"

"Then she's highly delusional."

"You got that right."

I gave myself an all over kind of shake. "All right. I'm okay now. I'd better get back to my story before she starts picking on me again."

"Did she make you re-write it?"

I nodded. "It's too passive."

"Next time, turn in a kind of sloppy first story," Caroline advised. "Kate never lets anyone get away with their first draft. She always has to criticize it, always wants changes. It's a power trip for the old windbag."

"I'll remember that," I said.

Once I was back in my cubicle, I got to work on my re-write. Re-writing the story didn't take as long as writing it the first time had, especially since I was fueled with venom for my boss. My ire also helped me turn my passive writing into something that was a lot more active and, I must admit, more interesting. My finished product made Meryl Cunningham and her community theater group sound like they'd just blown into town from Broadway.

When I was through, I looked up to see if Kate was still in her office. From my vantage point, I could see

Bob Meredith's shoulder in the doorway and I could hear the low rumble of his voice. Every few seconds Kate's grating laugh punctuated their conversation.

At least one member of the newspaper knows how to get along with her.

Frankly, I didn't know how Bob did it. I found Kate to be one of the most loathsome people I'd ever been unfortunate enough to meet. With a resigned sigh, I sent the story to Kate, sat back in my chair and waited for her verdict. It was closing in on three o'clock and I still had no idea of what I was going to fix Steve and Tyler for dinner.

"DeeDee!" Kate's voice filled the office.

Reluctantly, I got to my feet and walked slowly to her door. "Yes?" I asked when I reached her desk.

"Your second draft is better," she told me. "Not perfect but I'll be able to fix it up and polish it. By the way, you went over the word count by thirty-three words. Watch that next time."

"I will," I promised her.

"I've got another assignment for you. There's a new bakery in town and they're introducing a new type of cupcake. That sounds like something you can handle. Go there as soon as they open tomorrow and talk to the owner. And don't take forever. I want that story by eleven o'clock."

My spirits lifted slightly. "All right. I'll see you tomorrow."

Kate looked at the clock on the wall. "Must be nice to work part-time," she commented.

I couldn't help myself. "And it must be nice to work full-time with benefits and a living wage for a salary." Caroline would be proud of me.

Kate looked surprised. "I wouldn't work for anything less," she assured me. "I'm no idiot."

Feeling more than a little idiotic myself, I got my purse and left the building, thrilled to hear the door slam shut behind me as I headed for the parking lot.

"So how'd it go today?" Steve had such a big smile on his face and looked so eager to hear about my day that I almost didn't have the heart to burst his bubble. Almost.

"It was a good news/bad news kind of day," I told him. We were in the kitchen eating leftover spaghetti and stale garlic bread, both of which tasted wonderful. I am a nervous eater and from the moment I'd gotten home from the newspaper, I'd downed approximately 7,000 calories, mainly in junk food.

Steve is an eternal optimist. "What was the good news?"

"I got my first assignment."

"You did? DeeDee, that's great! What was it?"

"I interviewed a woman from the community theater group about her part in the group's next production."

"Well, tell me about it," Steve insisted. "How'd it go?"

I toyed with a strand of spaghetti, my nervous appetite finally leaving me. Now I just felt sort of...blah. Let down. Marginally depressed and wishing with all my might that I could just cut to the chase, win the lottery and retire three days into my new career. "Not too well."

Steve's face fell. "Oh, honey, why not? What happened?"

"It was my first interview and I let it go on for too long. Sam—the photographer—told me to cut it off but I couldn't figure out how to do that. Meryl—she's the actress I interviewed—was talking and talking and talking, and it seemed rude to interrupt her. I had the feeling that she didn't have too many people who would listen to her so I did. That was a mistake."

"I don't think it was a mistake. You were being kind."

"Kate didn't think so."

"She's the editor, right?"

I nodded. "And resident witch. She chewed me out for taking too long and then when I wrote the story, she made me rewrite it. I was at the paper all day long—not that I mind that but it was incredibly frustrating. I felt like I was back in high school with a sadistic English teacher standing over me."

"Did you finish the story?"

"Finally. My second draft still had mistakes in it but Kate said that she would edit it and that it would do. It's going to be in tomorrow's paper."

Steve got up, came over and gave me a kiss. "That's wonderful news, DeeDee. You should really be proud of yourself. You're an honest-to-God newspaper reporter on a real newspaper and you did this all on your own. I'm proud of you."

"It's awfully hard," I told him. "Much harder than I expected it to be. I don't know if I want to be a reporter."

Steve sat back down. "Give yourself a little time. You're brand new at the game and it sounds like the newspaper is a pretty tough nut to crack. Do you have another assignment?"

I nodded. "Yes. I'm going to the new bakery downtown tomorrow to interview the owner about the new cupcake they're introducing. I gave him a call when I got home to make sure he'd be there in the morning." At least I'd learned that much as a result of my fiasco with Meryl. "Apparently they've designed a cupcake to celebrate the upcoming 50th anniversary of the local strip club. Those should be interesting."

"See what I mean? You're getting there, DeeDee. You'll do fine. Just take it one story at a time."

Not quite believing him, I returned to my now cold plate of pasta. Steve has always had faith in me. Always. When I decided to be a Girl Scout leader for our daughter Jane's troop and had go on my first camping trip ever, Steve told me what to do and assured me that I could do it. Then he helped me plan the entire weekend and shadowed us from a campsite he set up two hundred yards away. When I started my own catering business, Steve drummed up clients for me from his co-workers at the college and even though my venture as a business owner had ended fairly quickly, he'd been there for me throughout it all. I didn't want to disappoint him if my job at the newspaper turned out to be a flop but if I kept on messing up the way I did today, I didn't see how Kate could *not* fire me. She didn't seem to be too long on tolerance or even basic civility for that matter.

You've worked at the paper for all of three days. Give yourself a break! Listen to your husband. It will *get better once you know what you're doing.*

It was good advice and I decided to take it. All it took was practice. Feeling better, I asked Steve, "How about some dessert?"

"Sure. What have we got?"

"Let's see...ice cream or ice cream."

"I'll take ice cream."

Steve carried his plate to the dishwasher and put it in. "Say, did Jane get in touch with you?"

I cleared the rest of the table and got a tub of ice cream out of the freezer. "Not today. Why?"

"We had lunch together and we talked about that weight loss product her company has come up with. I worked on her a bit—told her how you'd keep your source confidential and how much it would mean to you."

"Oh, Steve, you're wonderful!" Putting down the ice cream scoop I went to hug him. "I really want to write that story. I think it could be huge."

"Well, I think you should write it too. After a little persuading on my part, Jane agreed."

"I don't want to get her in trouble," I said.

"I asked her to introduce you to that Fritz guy she told us about. How could that get Jane in trouble? Besides, I'd like it if you met him. I think Jane's interested in him and you know what lousy taste she has in men."

"I'd like to meet him too," I agreed. "Jane sounded very interested in him to me and I wouldn't mind checking him out either."

I wriggled out of Steve's embrace and went back to scooping ice cream into two bowls. "I'll call Jane after we have dessert and see what she has to say."

As if on cue, my cell phone rang. It was Jane. "Mom," she said when I answered. "How about lunch tomorrow?"

"At Kutrate Kemicals?"

"Why not? I can't see how it would do any harm for you to look around a little. After all, I've worked here for almost a year and you haven't even seen my office yet."

"That's because you haven't invited me," I pointed out.

"I've been busy," Jane replied. "Besides, it seems very childish to have my mommy come and see how I decorated my office, but after a year I guess it's okay.

I'll tell you what: come over when you're done with work and I'll treat you to a salad in the employee cafeteria. Then I'll introduce you to Fritz *if* you promise not to write a word until I tell you that you can. All right?"

"Of course!" I quickly agreed. Truthfully, story or not, I wanted to talk to Fritz and not just to see if he was suitable dating material for my daughter. I wanted to hear more about his invention. I'd love to get my hands on a spray that melted fat without any kind of exercising or dieting involved. "I'll see you tomorrow around 12:15."

"Park in the visitor's lot," Jane instructed, "and wear those black slacks and that tunic top I gave you for Christmas."

"Which shoes I should wear?" I asked a touch tartly. Jane has never had much confidence in my ability to choose my own outfits.

"Use your best judgment," Jane said, not hearing my sarcasm. "Just nothing with too high heels. You always walk funny in heels."

"Jane, I don't own any shoes with high heels," I reminded her. I do tend to totter in heels. "I'll see you tomorrow and thanks, honey." Picking up my bowl of ice cream, I joined Steve in the family room. "It's all set," I told him. "I'm meeting Jane and Fritz tomorrow."

"I'll keep my fingers crossed, hon," Steve said. He was reading the *Kemper Times*. "As soon as your interview is in tomorrow's paper I'm going to cut it out and taped it to my office door."

"Oh, Steve, that's not necessary."

"Are you kidding me? I'm going to save all of your articles and put them in a scrapbook."

"You're crazy."

"About you, you bet I am. Look at that."

I looked. Steve was pointing at a full page ad for Kutrate Kemicals in the newspaper. "I bet that cost a pretty penny," I observed.

"I've noticed that the *Kemper Times* doesn't write a whole lot of stories about Kutrate, not even when there were all those layoffs there a few years back. They seem to have a hands-off policy when it comes to them."

"Kutrate Kemicals is the biggest employer in town. I suppose they must spend a bundle on advertising and the paper doesn't want to bite one of the hands that feeds it."

"Still, that's not right. News is news, isn't it? The newspaper has a responsibility to print anything that's newsworthy."

"That's what Mrs. Silber said back in high school journalism. But I'm sure the paper would be thrilled to run a story about Kutrate Kemicals if they've come up with a new weight lost product. That could only be a win-win situation for both sides."

"Absolutely," Steve agreed before turning on the television. "Hey, *Send Me No Flowers* is on and then *Lover Come Back.* Looks like our evening is set."

Happily, we settled down with our ice cream to watch a Doris Day-Rock Hudson marathon.

Chapter Seven

"Don't be surprised if Fritz is a little cranky," Jane warned as she led me down spotless hallways toward the very back of the gleaming glass tower that housed Kutrate Kemicals. We'd had our salads in the cafeteria and so far I was impressed with everything I'd seen at Kutrate Kemicals—the food was good, the buildings were lovely and the people were friendly. Maybe I should look for a job at the chemical company since the ambiance was far more pleasant than the one down at the newspaper.

"Why is he cranky?" I asked.

"He's run into a little trouble with his invention." Jane paused. "You know, Mom, I'm glad that you're going to talk to Fritz. You have a way of making people see the bright side of things."

"I do?" I adore my daughter but she isn't big on handing out compliments so I knew that she meant what she said.

Jane nodded. "You do. Maybe you'll be able to cheer Fritz up."

"You really like him, don't you?" I asked.

Jane blushed. "Yes, I guess I do. He's not like anyone I've ever been interested in before. He's just so…intelligent. And quite attractive."

It sounded like our daughter was finally over her married ex-boyfriend and that was very good news. I already liked this Fritz person if he could get Jane to forget about that unfortunate chapter of her life. "He sounds wonderful," I said warmly.

Jane and I stopped in front of a door with a brass plate that read *FRITZ SCHEIDER*. Jane's knock was answered almost immediately. "Come in!" a deep voice barked from the other side of the door. Jane pushed open the door and I followed her into the room.

A tall, thin man with dark hair sat behind a desk. Jane was right; he *was* attractive. Fritz looked quite a bit like the Atticus Finch version of Gregory Peck although at that moment it was the upset edition of Atticus Finch. Actually, Fritz appeared more than upset; fuming seemed like a better description. Fritz was older than I expected, probably in his late thirties. Well, that was okay. Jane was in her late twenties so a ten year difference wasn't too much. "Fritz," Jane said, "I'd like you to meet my mother, DeeDee Pearson. Mom, this is Fritz Scheider."

Fritz's face lightened after Jane spoke and I could see that he was making an effort to control the anger that seemed to be seeping out of every pore of his body. "It's a pleasure to meet you, Mrs. Pearson." He had a slight German accent.

"Please, call me DeeDee. I'm sorry to barge in on you—perhaps this isn't a good time?"

"No, no, of course not." Fritz gave his head a hard shake. "I'm the one who is sorry. It's just that I'm a little angry right now. No, that isn't true. I'm furious. It's that pig of a boss of ours. He treats me like someone who comes in here to deliver the mail instead of a scientist."

"Mr. Morton is tough on everyone," Jane pointed out.

"Perhaps, but he's been especially obnoxious lately. If only there was some way that I could quit working for this joke of a company before—" Fritz broke off, looking at me out of the corner of his eyes.

"I hope you don't mind but I told my mother about what you're working on," Jane said. "She's very discreet and she won't tell anyone, but she's fascinated by the idea."

"It is an amazing idea," I agreed. "Imagine, a spray that makes people lose weight. You'll make this company millions."

"Billions," Fritz said dryly. "I don't mind that you know, DeeDee. I'm very proud of 'Fat Off'."

"'Fat Off'?" I repeated. *What a horrible name,* I thought.

"I thought of the name myself," Fritz said proudly.

"Very direct," I said.

"That's what I thought. Why call it something that it isn't? But our idiot boss doesn't agree. He thinks we should call it something else, something pedestrian like 'Feather Lite.' He's so stupid that I can barely stand to think about him."

"Then don't," Jane advised.

"But I must. I'm close to changing the smell of 'Fat Off' from its current dead skunk scent to something that is much more akin to a meadow full of wildflowers. I'm sure that once 'Fat Off' smells good, I'll be able to put my final seal of approval on it."

"Um, what about the pollution issue?" Jane questioned.

Fritz looked perturbed. "I'm working on that also. I'm hoping that once we change the scent, we'll also reduce the toxicity of production. Our boss, naturally, wants me to fudge the statistics so that no one will ever know how toxic the process of making 'Fat Off' truly is."

I had a sudden stabbing pain of conscience. “Hold on, Fritz,” I said, putting up my right hand in the *Stop* position. “There’s something I need to tell you.”

“And that is?” Fritz questioned.

As much as I wanted him to continue talking about his miracle fat loss formula as well as all the behind-the-scenes machinations at Kutrate Kemicals, I couldn’t allow that to happen until I let him in on the fact that I was a journalist. “You should know that I’m a reporter for the *Kemper Times.*”

“You are?” Fritz’s eyes boggled a bit.

I was getting a little tired of the incredulous stare that accompanied that question. “Yes, I am. Of course, everything you’re saying is off the record since I didn’t tell you that I was a reporter right away. I wouldn’t want you to tell me anything that you don’t want to.”

Fritz eyed me for a few moments, his intensely blue eyes studying me like a pair of sapphire opera glasses. Then he looked at Jane. “Your mother might be a big help to us.”

“Really? How?” Jane asked.

“The moment ‘Fat Off’ hits the shelves, this company is going to start making money hand over fist. Everyone knows that the entire world wants to lose weight without doing anything drastic like sweating or cutting out Doritos.”

“True enough,” I agreed.

“And where will that leave me? Getting a tiny share of the profits while our idiot boss drives to the bank in his Maserati to shovel dollar bills that *I* earned for him into his already bloated bank account.”

“But how can Mom help you?” Jane asked.

“Yes, how can I help?”

“You can be my Deep Throat—figuratively speaking,” Fritz quickly added.

A vivid memory of Robert Redford playing Bob Woodward in *All the President's Men* popped into my mind. As I recalled, he met his Deep Throat in a parking garage in Washington, D.C., but I presumed Fritz and I could meet someplace a little nicer, like maybe the McDonald's over on the highway. I smiled at Fritz. I had told Steve that being a reporter would be like watching *All the President's Men* and I was right. "I'd be happy to be your Deep Throat," I said but then I remembered something. "But didn't Deep Throat *provide* information for the *Washington Post* reporters? I wouldn't have anything to tell you."

Fritz waved an impatient hand in the air. "My bad. I would be *your* Deep Throat. How does that sound?"

"Definitely intriguing," I assured him. "A little scary but intriguing for sure."

"Mom," Jane said softly, "are you sure about this? I mean, we're talking about a major story and you're still wet behind the ears."

"Your mother strikes me as a bright woman," Fritz announced. "I'm sure that she'll do a swell job. I also suspect that by the time we reach the end of this story, she will no longer be wet behind the ears and I assure you that I will do nothing that might endanger her life."

Jane still looked doubtful. "It's just that she's never really done anything," Jane explained. "She's just, you know, a *mom*."

"Jane, my dear, mothers are the people who keep the world moving. Didn't you know that? If you're unaware of how much your mother has done for you and your father and your family for all these years, then I guarantee you that she'll be ideal for sharing my story with the press. Unobtrusive people are almost always the smartest people of all." I watched as Fritz's lips thinned. "This isn't right and it isn't fair and it isn't going to happen. 'Fat Off' is mine. The time has come to pay back our employer for at least some of the pain that he has caused the rest of us." Gone was the attractive scientist and in his place was something a little more menacing. Glancing over at Jane, I saw that she caught the change in Fritz also.

"I need to think about what I want to tell you," Fritz said. "We need to tread very carefully because we don't want any legal entanglements. Agreed?"

"Absolutely," I assured him. The last thing I wanted was any legal entanglements of any kind.

"Mom, are you sure you want to do this?" Jane asked sounding a little nervous.

"Of course I do!" I knew that with Fritz's help I was going to land a story that would knock the socks off of everyone down at the paper. Although I had the feeling that Fritz might be using me as a pawn for his own agenda, I didn't care.

"Good," Fritz said and for a second I thought I saw an odd glint behind his eyes. "Then it's agreed," Fritz said. "The owner of Kutrate Kemicals, Bernard Thornton, is now known as our enemy and what does one do when confronted by the enemy?"

Jane and I exchanged nervous glances. "What?" I asked.

"Why, one annihilates him. And we're going to help each other do just that."

"Mom, I don't know about this," Jane said as she walked me out to my car. "Fritz seems to be working on a vendetta with a capital *V*. The whole thing seems way too big for you to work on. I don't want you to get into trouble."

"Honey, what kind of trouble could I possibly get into? You're the one I'm worried about. If it comes out that you're my daughter after I write the story, it won't take a genius to figure out the connection between the two of us."

"If what Fritz is saying is the truth, that shouldn't matter. The board of directors would have to get rid of Bernard Thornton and then what would it matter?"

"Whistle blowers seldom get to keep their jobs," I reminded her.

"If Kutrate Kemicals is doing something totally illegal then I don't want to work here. And if Fritz really wants you to write about 'Fat Off,' then I guess it will be okay. You just need to be careful."

"Of course, I will be careful," I said before climbing into my car. "I'm the mom who made you wear lifejackets when you went into the wading pool, remember? I'm always cautious." I paused. "Fritz seems like a very dedicated person."

"He is," Jane assured me. "He's also *not* married. I checked."

"So you're thinking of dating him?"

Jane shrugged. "I'm thinking about it. Other than his vengeful streak, he seems like an interesting guy."

I laughed. "Thanks for introducing me to Fritz, honey. I'll see you later."

"Be sure to tell Dad everything you're up to," Jane called after me as I began to back out of my parking spot. "He needs to be kept apprised of what's going on!"

Shaking my head, I waved at my worrywart daughter and drove away, my mind spinning with ideas of how to write my feature on 'Fat Off,' the weight loss in a spray. Once I got the green light, that is.

Chapter Eight

The next morning, after vacuuming the newsroom, making fresh coffee and wiping down the refrigerator in the break room, I was hunkered in front of my computer, scrolling through diets again while I waited for my next assignment. *Really*, I thought as I read yet another movie star's tips on losing those annoying last ten pounds, if I could come up with a diet that worked, Steve's and my retirement fund would be positively overflowing.

"What is the matter with you people?" Kate's squeaky voice interrupted my research. Looking up, I watched as she stormed into the newsroom, her small eyes looking even smaller behind her enormous glasses, circa 1984 and covered with so many smudgy fingerprints that I didn't see how she could possibly see out of them.

"What now?" Ren muttered next to me as he leaned back in his chair to watch our boss too.

"I want to see some initiative! I want to see some creativity! Some drive!"

Caroline was the first one to speak up. "What's the matter, Kate?"

Kate whirled around and lunged at her, pushing her tiny little face up next to Caroline's like a kid looking in a toy store window. "What's the matter? The *matter,* Miss Osborn, is that we are putting out a daily newspaper that stinks! There is absolutely no local content in it or am I the only one who's noticed that?"

Initiative, creativity and drive were all things I wanted to display but it seemed to me that every time I—or any of the other reporters—tried, we were shot down in flames. "What kind of local coverage do you want?" Ren asked mildly.

Kate hit herself dramatically in the head. "That you would even have to ask that tells me how far I have to go to turn this paper around."

I decided to speak up. "So you want us to go out and find our own stories?"

Big sigh. "Yes, DeeDee, that is precisely what I want you to do."

"But I thought all of our assignments were supposed to come from Jeff or from you."

"And I'm telling you to figure a few things out on your own. Jeff and I aren't your mommy and daddy."

"Thank God for that," Ren muttered.

"Go out into the community and do some digging! Don't just sit on your butts waiting for assignments." She turned and gave me the stink eye. "Just make sure you don't take all day to do it."

I thought about my potentially enormous story at Kutrate Kemicals and smiled a tad smugly at Kate. Wouldn't she be surprised when I presented her with the story on 'Fat Off'? "I'll do my best," I assured her.

Kate laughed like a barking seal. "You'll have to do far better than that. Do you have any assignments for today?"

"Um, not really."

Kate looked pained. "That isn't an answer. 'Yes' or 'no' is an answer. 'Not really' is vague and inconclusive. Is it necessary for me to edit your speech as well as your copy?"

"No," I said clearly. "I don't have an assignment for today."

"Then find one and run it past me for my okay!" she snapped. Looking past me, Kate spotted Ren and her eyes narrowed. "And you, mister," she barked, "I've been looking for you. We have a few matters to discuss. Pronto."

I looked over at Ren. He had slumped down until he was sitting on his tailbone with only the top of his head showing over the edge of his desk. "Oh?" he asked politely.

"Did you have a chance to check out the toilet yet?"

"Not yet," Ren said. I could see that his jaw was clenched so tightly that it looked as if he might break off a molar or two at any moment.

"You know it's your job to do any extra plumbing jobs around the building," Kate practically trilled. "That toilet has been clogged all morning long. What am I supposed to do? Walk down to the gas station every time I have to tinkle?"

I could hardly believe my ears. Ren had to do plumbing in addition to writing stories and editing an entire section of the newspaper?

"I said I'd get to it," Ren sort of hissed. "I've been a little busy putting out my section of the newspaper."

Kate used the super slow voice on Ren that she so often used on me. "It's called multi-tasking," she told him. "I think a bright boy like you can handle it. We expect our employees to be multi-faceted."

Multifaceted was one thing. Slave labor was something else. After glaring at her, Ren turned away and buried his head in the mountain of papers on his desk. Apparently satisfied, Kate looked over at the rest of us. "Now get to it," she snapped. "I want to see at least one new story idea from each and everyone one of you and I want to see it *today!*" Kate turned on one of her worn heels and walked swiftly out of the newsroom.

I waited until she was safely back in her office before I spoke. "Uh, Ren?"

"What?" he growled and then caught himself. "Sorry, DeeDee, but that woman always puts me in an instant bad mood. What is it?"

"Do you really have to take care of the plumbing around here?"

"Yep."

"That's honestly on your job description? How is that possible? You're a journalist, not a plumber." I was unconsciously echoing what Caroline had said to me on my first day when she'd caught me cleaning out the coffee pot, but in Ren's case, I could see her point. He'd gone to journalism school for heaven's sake. Why on earth would he have to handle plugged up toilets too?

"No kidding although I wish I was a plumber. As a professional plumber, I'd be doing one hell of a sight better than I'm doing here. I might even be able to retire before I die."

I felt sorry for Ren. Although he was only in his early thirties, he had the exhausted air of someone in their late sixties. "Doesn't the paper have a maintenance person?"

"Nope." Ren glanced around to see if anyone was within eavesdropping distance but everyone else was hunched over in their cubicles too, presumably searching for some local story that would satisfy our boss. "A few years back, management decided to scale down on costs so they canned the janitor and the building superintendent and farmed their work out to the rest of us. I'm stuck with making sure all of the plumbing is in working order, Caroline's in charge of the boiler, Frank has recycling duties and Bob has to take care of all the computer stuff."

"But Caroline told me not to clean the coffee pot!" I said, remembering how irate Caroline had been when we first met. "She said it wasn't our job."

"I'm not sure why she said that because *everything* is our job. You know that line that management always tacks on to a job description? 'Other duties as assigned'? Well, the *Kemper Times* takes a little bit of advantage of that line. Make that a whole lot of advantage. They've got us all over a barrel and they know it. Worse, I honestly think that they enjoy it."

"That's terrible. Does management do extra things too?" I tried to picture Jeff taking out the garbage or Kate sweeping the bathroom when I remembered something Bob had said on my first day about the cleaning people working on Sundays. "Bob Meredith said there were cleaning people who come in on Sundays."

"That would be Natalie, our customer service representative, and her son," Ren said. "And no, management doesn't take on any extra duties. Rank has its privileges, in case you hadn't heard that yet."

"I've heard."

Ren looked at me with something close to pity in his tired brown eyes. "Have you seen your job description yet, DeeDee?"

Actually, I hadn't even thought to ask to see it. "No…"

"If I were you, I'd ask to see it and when you do I suggest that you read it very carefully. That woman has a way of slipping things in that you'd never dream could be part of your job."

"Kate does job descriptions? I thought Human Resources would take care of that."

"Kate *is* Human Resources."

"But she didn't interview me—Jeff did."

"They take turns interviewing people, not that we've had many new hires lately. You're the only person who's been hired in I don't know how long. I keep telling myself that I'm lucky to have a job and once in a while I can get myself to believe it but those moments are coming fewer and further between. I'm hoping that if I stay here for another year or two, I'll be able to land something in a bigger market. If I can stand it that long," he added.

"I hope you do find something else." Ren seemed like a truly nice guy and I hated to see him look so miserable. I didn't want to see *anybody* look so miserable.

"I do too. I just hope that I can get away from here without killing anyone first." He sighed and pushed his chair back from his desk. "I'd better go find the plunger and take care of that clogged toilet before Kate has to tinkle again. That woman needs to cut down on her coffee intake. She uses the bathroom more than anyone else on the paper."

"I'd better get going too."

"You have an idea for a story?"

"I think so," I said, thinking about Fritz and his amazing fat loss spray. "It could be big."

Ren looked at me a little pityingly. "I remember when I used to be excited about starting a new story," he remarked a touch wistfully. "Have fun and remember what I said: ask for your job description and read it very carefully."

"I'll do that," I promised. Leaving Ren, I grabbed my purse and headed for the newsroom door, anxious to get out into the fresh air. Everyone who worked at the *Kemper Times* seemed so unhappy and discontented that it was starting to make me feel like I was suffocating. It had been more than thrilling to see my interview with Meryl Cunningham in the paper but I was beginning to think that a fleeting moment or two of egomania wasn't worth working for someone like Kate.

"How the hell am I supposed to come up with a story?" I heard Caroline say to Frank as I walked past.

"Sucks to be you," Frank responded. "I already have a story. I heard the head hockey coach over at the college is jumping ship if he doesn't get a raise. I'm going to cover that one."

"No one cares about hockey coaches," Caroline informed him.

"They care more about hockey coaches than anything *you* could come up with," Frank responded. I hurried out of the newsroom before I could hear Caroline's answer.

In the lobby I paused to talk to Natalie. Out of everyone I'd met at the paper, Natalie seemed to be the happiest but that was most likely due to the fact that she worked by herself and didn't have to interact with Kate too often. Then again, Kate did seem a little obsessed with Natalie's bathroom breaks and the amount of time that she spent away from her desk so perhaps Kate's micromanaging tentacles stretched all the way down to the newspaper's sole customer service rep/receptionist/weekend cleaning person too apparently. "Hi, Natalie," I said when I reached her desk,

Natalie looked up from her computer screen, her dark eyes shining. "Well, hi there, DeeDee! How are you on this beautiful day?"

"Not bad," I told her and it was the truth. I already felt better now that I was out of the newsroom.

"How are things upstairs? Exciting as always?" Natalie was a very pretty woman who looked a lot like a young Diana Ross. In addition to being attractive,

Natalie also displayed an enthusiasm for her job that far outshone that of any of the reporters.

"Hmmm…well, I don't know that I'd call it *exciting.*" Nerve wracking, exhausting and frustrating might be better adjectives to describe the third floor of the paper. "How do you like working at the newspaper?"

"I love it. I don't know what it is but I have journalism in my blood. I can't write worth a darn so I know I can't be a reporter, but I have to work for a paper. It's the only job I've ever really wanted. I think it's the most exciting place to work, even a small paper like this one."

Natalie had a great attitude and just talking to her cheered me up. "That's good to hear. Most of the people upstairs seem pretty down."

Natalie laughed. "Understandable. You guys are all crammed into one room with barely room to breathe. And then there are the other people up there—" Natalie broke off, her eyes darting upward and I assumed she remembered about the microphone. It was like something out of the Cold War. "Never mind," she said.

"Well, I should be going. I'll see you later."

"Have a wonderful day, DeeDee."

After leaving the building, I climbed into my mini-van and sighed as I thought about how I'd really believed that I'd be able to inject some sweetness and light into the newsroom when I'd first started there all of four days earlier. What a dope I'd been. Mary Poppins wouldn't be able to inject any sweetness and light into that newsroom. The air was so thick with toxic feelings like anger, frustration and resentment that the whole building probably needed a priest to come and exorcise all the evil spirits.

I'll give it three months. Then we'll see.

A lot could happen in three months such as winning the lottery or hitting the jackpot in the Publishers Clearing House sweepstakes. Or writing a news story that would knock Kate and everyone else on their collective ear, land me a byline and secure me a job at the *Kemper Times* that would last me the rest of my life, if that was what I wanted. At that moment, I wasn't at all sure of what I wanted. Sighing one more time, I put the car into gear and steered toward Kutrate Kemicals. Time to see what I could get out of Fritz and maybe get him to agree to let me write *something* about his fabulous creation.

"DeeDee, how lovely to see you again." Fritz was all smiles when he ushered me into his lab twenty minutes later.

"Thank you for letting me drop in like this. I wanted to chat with you a little more about your product." I also wanted to ask him when I could write about 'Fat Off' but I knew that I was going to have to be a little patient.

"Of course," Fritz said. He shut the door of his lab firmly behind us and gestured toward a high lab stool.

"Is it all right to talk here?" I asked in a quiet voice.

"Do you mean is my lab bugged?" Fritz shook his head. "No, I check every morning with electronic equipment given to me by a friend. So far I've found nothing but one can never be too careful."

"Why do you think anyone would bug your lab?"

"Because they know that I'm a genius," Fritz replied. He spoke calmly, far more calmly than he had the other day. His whole attitude was more relaxed and I wondered if something had happened with 'Fat Off.'

"Did something happen with 'Fat Off'?" I was getting better at the pushy thing.

"As a matter of fact, yes." A wide smile covered Fritz's face. "I believe I've had a true breakthrough on the smell problem."

"Just how does 'Fat Off' work?" I asked.

Fritz waved a hand in the air. "It is quite complicated. How are you at chemistry?"

"Pretty bad," I admitted.

"Then let's just say that my invention inhibits certain parts of your brain while activating certain parts of your metabolism. Does that make sense?"

"Sort of. Is it safe?"

"As far as I know it is. Of course, we must have many months, probably years, of clinical trials before 'Fat Off' can be put on the shelves but we're getting closer and closer to that day." Fritz's eyes lit up. "How would you like to experience 'Fat Off'?"

I gulped. I mean, I knew I could stand to drop a few pounds but the thought of inhaling some chemical compound that would kill my appetite while messing with my brain and my metabolism was more than a little scary. "Now?"

"Why not?"

"What if someone catches us?"

"This is my lab and 'Fat Off' is my invention. Besides, it isn't illegal, DeeDee. I'll have you smell the first version and then the second one. You'll be amazed by the difference between the two. It will just be a couple of whiffs. Nothing to become alarmed over."

I felt a flutter of butterflies in my stomach. I've never been good with smelly things and I didn't have the strongest stomach in the world either. What if I threw up in front of Fritz? But I was a journalist. I was going to have to do challenging things every so often to get a story. "I guess so," I said slowly.

"Wonderful!" Fritz reached into a cabinet and pulled out a plain white aerosol can. He spritzed it once. Instantly the air was filled with the most putrid scent I'd ever had the misfortune to experience. It smelled like a combination of dead skunk, garbage and a pig sty. "Oh my gosh, that's awful!" I said as I covered my mouth and nose.

"Yes," Fritz said sadly, "it is. Now smell this one." He pulled out another can and spritzed the air again. "It's all right," he told me. "You can take your hand off your mouth and nose. This one smells much better."

Hesitantly, I removed my hand and sniffed the air. I smelled lemons and mint and none of the disgusting scent. "That's lovely," I said. "Are you sure they're the same product?"

"Quite sure."

"And I'm going to lose my appetite?"

"Are you hungry?" Fritz asked.

I thought about it and realized that even though it was closing in on eleven o'clock and all I'd had to eat that day was coffee and a piece of toast and by all rights should have been starving, I wasn't hungry. Not in the least. "No, I'm not. Does it work that fast?"

"Are you usually hungry at this time of day?"

"Starving," I admitted.

"Then there's your answer."

"How long will the lack of hunger feeling last?"

"Depends on the individual. It could last up to three days."

Three days! I'd drop at least five pounds if I didn't eat for three days! "Fantastic," I said. A sudden thought hit me. "Will there be any weird side effects?"

Fritz pulled in his lower lip and bit it. "None that I'm aware of," he said in a tone of voice that made me a little nervous. “But be sure to call me if anything…odd happens.”

“Such as?” I pressed.

“You know. The usual. Sudden swelling of the lips. Rapid breathing. Your heart feeling funny.”

Oh, wonderful! Being able to fit into size ten jeans again didn’t seem so important after all. “Do you know when these side effects might occur?” I questioned, hoping they wouldn’t be in the middle of the night. Bad things always seem to happen in the middle of the night and Steve would kill me if he found out that I gave myself fat lips, panting and a major heart episode just because I wanted to have thin thighs, something I hadn’t had since the seventh grade. “Is there an antidote?”

Fritz threw back his head and laughed heartily. A little too heartily. “Oh, DeeDee,” he said once he got hold of himself, “you are priceless. I didn’t poison you. Would Fritz do that? No, I gave you a release from your appetite for a few days, that is all—a release that your tummy will probably appreciate, no?” He eyed my blue jeans a little judgmentally. “As we age, it gets harder to lose weight.”

Since Fritz was around fifteen years younger than I, as well as a skinny as a bean pole—although he did have a bit of a paunch—I thought it was mighty generous of him to say “we.” “Yes, it does,” I agreed.

“You just go home and relax. Let’s get together in a few days and then I’ll give you the background of ‘Fat Off’ and we can begin our own strategy on how to introduce my product to first the community and then the world, one fatso at a time. I haven’t forgotten about our deal. I am writing my notes for what Deep Throat will tell you.”

"Will I be able to use those notes in a newspaper story immediately?"

Fritz nodded. "I think so. I have stories about this company that will curl your attractive hair."

"Won't your boss know where the information came from?"

"I think not. Much of what I'll tell you are things I heard from other sources. I won't be a suspect."

No, but the other sources would be. This all seemed far too convoluted for me and while I could understand where Fritz was coming from, I didn't really want to present a lot of rumors to Kate as rock solid story leads. "I'd really rather write about 'Fat Off'," I insisted.

Fritz pursed his lips. "How? Let me think on that one."

I continued. "Wouldn't it be easier for you to tell your boss that you aren't happy with the deal the two of you have? Can't your rewrite your contract or do whatever needs to be done?"

"DeeDee, you are obviously a babe in the woods when it comes to business," Fritz said. "I have been painted into a corner by the reprehensible Bernard Morton and I have no option other than to fight back through the media."

It pained me to say what I was going to say next but I knew that I had to do it. "You know, Fritz, I'm extremely small potatoes when it comes to the media. You would be much better off approaching a larger newspaper or someone higher up the chain of command on my newspaper, don't you think?"

Fritz studied me for so long that I began to feel like a specimen under a microscope. "I think not," he finally announced. "You serve my purpose very well, DeeDee. You see, you do not have the one thing that I truly cannot abide."

"What's that?" I asked, a little afraid to hear his answer.

"You are not jaded. Although you aren't a spring chicken by a long shot, you have an innocence about you that tells me that you don't know how to lie and you don't know how to manipulate. I trust you and that, my dear, is worth ten reporters from the *Chicago Tribune* or CNN or even the next person up the ladder at your newspaper."

I was flattered, sort of, but also a little worried. Fritz was putting a lot of trust in me and I wasn't at all sure if I merited it. No, I was positive that I didn't merit it. I wasn't even a true journalist, I was just a mom and a wife and a Christmas letter writer. "I'll do what I can," I said after swallowing hard.

"I knew that you would. Our little talk has given me an idea. You're right—writing about some of the other detestable things that are happening at Kutrate Kemicals would be counterproductive. I think it would be much wiser to focus on 'Fat Off.' Our first step should be a diary. You will write a diary for your newspaper about your amazing weight loss but you won't name any names. That will whet your readers' appetites for my product." Fritz chuckled over his joke. "After a few weeks of that, we will have an in-depth interview with me, the inventor of 'Fat Off'."

"Couldn't that get you into trouble?"

"What will happen? I will get fired? My severance package will be better than what I will get from 'Fat Off' the way things are right now," Fritz snarled.

"But what good is it in letting everyone know about your product if it's not for sale?"

"Don't you see? The public demand will be so great that it will force that pig Bernard Morton to hurry up and put 'Fat Off' on the shelves. He will have to abide by my rules and play ball the way I want to play."

"But what about all those clinical studies?"

"Government red tape. I assure you 'Fat Off' is perfectly safe. Just wait until the next time you get a whiff of it and you move into Stage Two."

"What's Stage Two?"

"Your appetite will return with a vengeance and you will want to eat everything in sight. And you will eat everything in sight only you won't gain any weight. That is the beauty of 'Fat Off.' If you maintain your usage you can have every banana split, every turkey sandwich with extra mayo, every double fudge brownie that you want and still stay slim."

"Wow," I breathed. If all that was true, I could see why Fritz wanted to get his hands back on his patent. 'Fat Off' was going to be huge.

"So you see what I mean? We must start getting the word out to the overweight public. It's imperative."

"All right," I agreed. "I'll start a diary and see if I can get it in the newspaper although I'll probably have a little trouble getting my editors to publish it."

"I doubt that," Fritz said. "You're going to start dropping pounds immediately. They'll let you print your diary. I suggest you blog it and Twitter it as well."

My face lit up. This would be perfect for me to blog and Twitter about! "You're right and that's part of my job description!" At least, I was pretty sure that it was. "I'll get started as soon as I get home." I stood up and I swear my pants felt looser. Maybe 'Fat Off' did work! But so fast? "I'll talk to you soon, Fritz."

"Very soon," he promised me. "We'll meet in three days for your second session. And remember, call me or head for the nearest emergency room if you have any side effects."

With Fritz's warning ringing in my ears, I walked out to the parking lot and got into my car. It was eleven thirty and I wasn't the least bit hungry. If anything, the thought of eating made me kind of sick. *Was that a side effect,* I wondered? The only times in my life when the thought of eating has ever made me sick was during my first trimesters when I was pregnant with Jane and Tyler. It was going to be interesting to see how long the 'Fat Off' spray lasted. It was also going to be interesting to see how loose my jeans got over the next three days, hopefully with zero side effects.

Chapter Nine

The newsroom was buzzing with activity when I arrived the following morning. Moving toward my cubicle some of the other reporters nodded at me as I walked past them and Caroline Osborne gave me a friendly wave and I felt the happy glow of belonging. I also felt the happy glow of being one pound lighter. The 'Fat Off' spray was working. I hadn't felt like eating all evening long and breakfast that morning had been black coffee. Best of all, there hadn't been any side effects, unpleasant or otherwise.

"DeeDee!" Kate Weston's shrill voice cut into my good mood like a knife cutting into a steak. "I need to see you now!"

Taking five seconds to deposit my purse in the bottom drawer of my desk, I was in her office within moments. "Good morning, Kate," I said somewhat breathlessly.

"What took you so long?" she questioned.

I was starting to get a little bit smarter as to how to handle Kate and instead of responding to her attack, I turned the tables on her. "What did you want to see me about?" I asked pleasantly.

It worked. Instead of harping on my three minutes of tardiness, Kate asked, "What are you working on?"

"Well..." I hesitated for a long moment. "Actually, I'm on the verge of something pretty big."

Kate fixed her bug-like stare on me. "Such as?"

"I'd like to do a new feature for the newspaper on diets."

Kate almost spewed an entire mouthful of black coffee across the top of her paper strewn desktop. When she got control of herself, she said, "I assume you'll be going on one? Is that why you've been spending so much time surfing the web looking at different diet plans? Look, DeeDee, this newspaper hasn't been set up to arrange for you to do little pet projects of your own and then have us pay you to do them. We need real stories that have an impact on more people than just you."

"How did you know I've been looking at different diet plans?" I asked.

"I can check what everyone's doing on their computer from my computer," Kate said in a very smug tone of voice. "It would behoove you to remember that."

Although Kate's tone of voice was irritating in the extreme, I gritted my teeth and tried to remember the red hot story I had cooking on my stove. "Yes, I'll be going on a diet. I've stumbled upon a weight loss plan that seems pretty amazing. I just started yesterday and I've already lost a pound."

"Well, you've got more to go," Kate said snidely. She sighed deeply. "Oh, what the hell. Go ahead with your little diary, DeeDee. It might be cute but if we don't get positive feedback from our readers, I'm pulling it. I'll give you three weeks which is mighty generous of me."

"Thank you," I said.

"You're welcome. Be sure you blog about it and Twitter too. And don't let me catch you eating any Twinkies!" Kate laughed loudly at her own wit.

Back at my cubicle, I sat down and sighed to myself. Talking to Kate always made me sigh deeply. "Are you DeeDee?" a voice asked. Looking up, I saw Bob Meredith standing next to my cubicle.

"Yes, I am. We met the day I started at the newspaper," I began but stopped when Bob ignored me.

"I'm supposed to take you on my next assignment."

"Why?" Ren asked, his head appearing around the wall between our desks.

Bob didn't turn his head to look at Ren as he answered. "Because, apparently, I'm supposed to teach her how to conduct an interview, although why the bosses would hire someone who needs to be taught how to do an interview is beyond me."

My face turned a bright shade of red. "Did Kate tell you to take me along with you?"

Bob nodded. "Yep. So get your notebook and let's go."

"I just saw Kate and she didn't say anything to me about going on an interview with you."

Bob shrugged. "Go ask her if you don't believe me. I assure you it wasn't my idea."

I believed him as I remembered what Sam had said about Kate's m.o.—how she never did any dirty work herself. "I believe you," I said.

Bob shook his head. "Just my luck to get stuck with the mentor role," he complained. "Like I don't have enough on my plate?"

It was on the tip of my tongue to apologize but I stopped myself. After all, it wasn't my idea to be foisted off on Bob Meredith and it wasn't like I wanted to go along with him on his assignment, but if I was stuck, and it looked like I was, then I might as well make the best of it. I'd have to start working on my diary later. "I'm ready," I said as I got to my feet.

"Well, come on." Rolling his eyes, Bob led the way through the newsroom. I felt exactly like a struggling math student being tutored by the class brain. As we walked toward the staircase, I could feel the eyes of the other reporters following us and in spite of my forced courage, I wondered what they were thinking and what they'd say as soon as we were out of earshot. Most likely they would be clucking over the fact that I needed remedial help in Journalism 101 and I was sure that most of them were wondering along with Bob why the newspaper had bothered to hire me in the first place.

It was a question that I was beginning to ask myself more and more. Why had the newspaper hired me? Was it just because I was cheap? Or did Kate and Jeff really see a small glimmer of talent in the writing samples that I'd submitted to them?

I hoped that it was more the latter than the former. While I never expected to win the Pulitzer in Journalism, I wanted to make this job work and the only way to do that was to learn as much as I could about writing for a newspaper. If that meant spending time with socially maladjusted people like Bob Meredith, then so be it. Maybe if I looked at it like Kate was doing me a favor by criticizing me then it wouldn't sting quite so badly.

In the parking lot, I climbed into the cab of Bob Meredith's enormous Ford truck. It was quite a climb. "What story are we covering today?" I asked.

"Rumor has it that Kutrate Kemicals Industries is about to introduce a new product. We're going to find out what the scoop is. I'm going to show you how an expert does it."

"Where did you hear about that?" I asked in what I hoped was a nonchalant voice.

"Oh, around."

It had to be 'Fat Off.' That had to be the product he had heard about. "So what kind of new product is Kutrate Kemicals going to introduce?"

Bob shrugged. "Some new vitamin drink. That's big business these days with so many baby boomers getting old and finally starting to think about their bodies when it's probably too late."

My heart lifted. Vitamins! Bob didn't know about 'Fat Off'! My scoop was safe!

We got to Kutrate Kemicals and Bob parked his truck in a visitor's slot. "Let's get this over with," he said. "Keep your mouth shut and your eyes open and you'll do just fine."

That was exactly what I planned on doing.

Dog trotting behind Bob, I followed him to the entrance. It was on the tip of my tongue to remark that my daughter worked there but I managed not to share that information with Bob. Mainly because I was positive that he wouldn't be interested. Bob walked inside ahead of me, not bothering to hold the door open for me. If there was a Mrs. Bob Meredith, I pitied her. The moment he spotted the receptionist, he turned on the charm that had been invisible up to that point. "How's that back?" he asked. I hung behind, hoping the receptionist wouldn't remember me from my visit with Jane or my visit with Fritz. The woman looked up, a sour look on her face. The sour look vanished when she saw Bob Meredith standing in front of her.

"Well, hello, Bob! It's been too long!"

"I don't get up here nearly as much as I'd like," Bob said. "Kutrate doesn't seem to be doing anything newsworthy lately."

Wanna bet? I thought.

"No, it's been business as usual," the receptionist said. "And my back is much better. Those exercises you gave me did the trick!"

"Glad to hear it! If I come across any more, I'll be sure to send them on to you."

"Thanks, Bob!"

"I'm here to see Bernard about the new vitamin product you guys are putting out," Bob said.

"Mr. Morton is expecting you," the receptionist is. She glanced over at me. "Is this your assistant?" She still didn't recognize me which was just dandy with me. There's a lot to be said about being extremely average looking.

"Yeah," Bob didn't introduce me.

"You can go up to Mr. Morton's office. See you later, Bob."

"You know it," Bob said, winking at her.

I didn't get it at all but apparently the Bob Meredith charm was lost on me. Then again, he hadn't used his charm on me so far. Bob led the way to a bank of elevators.

"I did a story on back pain and she was one of my subjects," Bob explained to me over one shoulder. "Dynamite gal but really in agony over a slipped disc. I was able to find some exercises for her that apparently helped her out."

"That was nice of you," I said. "To go out of your way like that." Nice and completely shocking. Maybe I'd been wrong about my rapid fire assessment of Bob Meredith. He'd seemed so self-centered and more than a touch of a jerk but here he was helping someone with their back problems and researching exercises for her. I obviously didn't know Bob as well as I thought I did, which, to be fair, was not at all.

"One of the best parts of being a reporter, DeeDee," Bob informed me. "I like to help people. That and I wouldn't mind getting her between the sheets, if you know what I mean. I wash her hand, she washes mine, so to speak." This time he winked at me as he pressed the floor button in the elevator. What a pig.

We rode up in silence until the elevator doors opened on the tenth floor. Bob stepped out and walked along the hallway. "Now you just sit and observe the master at work," he said as he knocked on the door. "We'll be in and out of here in fifteen minutes. That's how it's done, DeeDee."

"Come in," a deep voice called. Bob and I stepped into the office. A large man with a florid face was seated behind an enormous desk. He rose and with difficulty made his way around the desk to where we were standing, his hand outstretched like a politician greeting potential voters. "Bob! Great to see you!"

They shook hands and then the man looked at me. "And who is this?"

Bob glanced in my direction. "DeeDee....uh, DeeDee," he finished lamely having obviously forgotten my last name.

"DeeDee Pearson," I said as I extended my own hand. "How do you do?"

Bernard Morton took my hand and gave me a handshake that was firm to the point of painful. Narrowing his bloodshot eyes, he looked at me quizzically. "Pearson? Are you related to Jane Pearson?"

"I'm her mother," I said proudly.

"Wonderful young lady," Bernard said. "We're very happy to have her as part of the Kutrate family."

"Why don't we get on with the interview," Bob interrupted, looking a tad irritated. "I know what a busy man you are, Bernard."

"Never too busy for a journalist, Bob. I don't know what this town would do without you."

Bob chuckled. "That's a question I ask myself every single morning, Bernard."

"And it's a good question. Young people today don't seem to realize that without freedom of the press, this country would be in deep doo doo. Now shall we begin?"

I perched on the edge of my chair and grabbed the moment to try and objectively study the CEO of Kutrate Kemicals. Bernard Morton was short and heavy with dark curly hair that was balding in a not too attractive pattern that left a large whorl in the dead center of his crown. He also had a five o'clock shadow à la Richard Nixon and arms that were hairier than an ape's. His physical attributes all adding up to someone who looked like he'd be more comfortable as a butcher or a longshoreman instead of the CEO of a successful company. All in all, he was very simian.

Bernard caught me staring at him and gave me the slightest wink. Blushing, I turned my attention to one of his degrees that was hanging on the wall about ten inches from my head. According to the framed diploma, he'd graduated from the University of Chicago in 1978. The University of Chicago was a top notch school. Somehow I couldn't picture Bernard Morton going there. He had much more of a community college air to him.

"I take it you're Bob's assistant, DeeDee?" Bernard asked.

"In a way," I replied demurely, not thrilled to be seen as Bob's assistant but not wanting to shout from the rooftops the real reason why I was tagging along.

"Let's sit at the conference table," Bernard suggested. "I can't wait to tell you about 'Vita Vapors.' We know it's going to be a huge seller."

On the table were several plastic containers. "That's our newest baby," Bernard said proudly. "It goes in one of those e-cigarettes. People will be able to inhale their vitamins and look cool as heck while they do it."

Bob pulled a reporter's notebook out of his back pocket and made a production of flipping through the pages until he reached a blank one. "Let's get this show on the road, Bernard. I know how busy you are. We should be able to wrap this up in a few minutes." That was clearly for my benefit. "Okay, let's see. When will 'Vita Vapors' be available in stores?"

"We're launching the line next month," Bernard replied. "I have a press kit for you that should answer all of your questions."

"Who thought up the 'Vita Vapor'?" The question popped out of my own mouth before I could stop it. I knew that I wasn't supposed to talk and I didn't mean to but I was curious to know if Fritz had anything to do with it which he probably didn't. Fritz had his hands full with 'Fat Off' but I still thought it was a legitimate question.

"That doesn't matter, DeeDee," Bob informed me. "It doesn't matter who came up with the product; what matters is that Kutrate Kemicals is marketing it."

"He's right, little lady," Bernard agreed. "It's our policy not to credit the little people with their big ideas. We're all part of one big happy family here and everyone is treated equally."

It didn't sound that way to me if Bernard Thornton was taking all of the credit for every new product Kutrate Kemicals produced. No wonder Fritz was in such a snit over 'Fat Off.' It sounded like he wasn't going to get any credit for his product at all. "I don't know," I ventured. "I've always thought that it's a good idea to give credit where credit is due. Doesn't that help keep people motivated?"

Bob moved his foot out and kicked me not very gently in the shins. "Excuse DeeDee," he said smoothly to Bernard. "She just started at the newspaper and doesn't quite know her place yet. DeeDee's a reporter in training but for now she's acting as my right hand woman."

Bernard's eyebrows rose and I could almost hear him thinking *Isn't she kind of long in the tooth for that?* Squaring my shoulders, I primed myself to remind Mr. Morton about age discrimination lawsuits but fortunately Bernard didn't say anything. Or maybe not so fortunately. An age discrimination lawsuit had to pay better than the newspaper. "I suppose asking questions is one way for people to learn."

"So is keeping your mouth shut and your eyes open," Bob said snippily. "Let's get back to our interview. Do you have any other exciting new products up your corporate sleeve?"

Leaning back in his chair, Bernard steepled his fingers and smiled much like a cat who not only ate the canary but doused it with barbecue sauce first. "As a matter of fact, yes, we do. We're working on a product that I guarantee will knock not only your socks off but all of the socks in the United States of America."

'Fat Off.' It had to be 'Fat Off'! I held my breath and hoped that Bernard Morton would clam up. I so didn't want Bob Meredith to get my scoop!

"Care to elaborate?"

Bernard pursed his lips and suddenly looked like an old woman who'd just discovered her married minister out on a date with a hot twenty year old. "Sorry," he said after several long, agonizing moments, "No can do. When the product is ready you'll be the first newsman I call, Bob. I promise you that. First you and then the *New York Times.*"

"Well," Bob slapped his notebook together and got to his feet. I rose too. "I can't ask for anything more than that. Thanks, Bernard. Always good to see you. I'm going to snap a photo of you holding your new product and then we'll be off. DeeDee," he barked, "take a picture of Mr. Morton holding the Vita Vapor."

Wonderful. Almost every picture I've ever taken has looked like it's been shot from the back seat of a moving car by a very short five-year old. "I don't take the best pictures," I began. Bob interrupted me.

"You'll never learn if you don't practice," he said while rolling his eyes with a look-what-I'm-stuck-with expression on his face. "I'll meet you downstairs." After shaking hands again with Bernard, Bob left the office. I was glad to see him go since I was sure my hands would shake even more if I had to try and take a picture with him hurrying me along.

I tried to look professional. "Why don't you hold the Vita Vapor?" I suggested. Bernard willingly picked one of the vials up and put it in the palm of his hand.

"Like this?"

"Perfect," I said and it would be a good shot—in the hands of a professional photographer. In my shaky hands it was more than likely going to look like a picture taken by someone coming off a three day bender.

Bernard didn't seem to notice my nervousness or if he did he was too polite to say anything. He willingly sat while I took approximately fifty pictures with my cell phone—I was going with the belief that if I took enough snapshots surely one of them would turn out. As I circled him he asked me a few questions about Jane.

"Your daughter is such a good worker," he remarked. "Smart, professional, trustworthy—is she dating anyone?"

That was a strange segue. "I'm not sure," I said. "You know how it is with kids—they never tell you anything." I began doing a crab walk toward the door. "Thank you and if none of the pictures turn out I'm sure you'll hear from Bob to set up another photo session."

"One of them will be fine," Bernard said confidently. He walked to the door with me. "It's been a pleasure meeting you, DeeDee, and tell that talented daughter of yours to keep her nose to the grindstone and not to let herself be derailed by falling in love or any other such foolishness. We have big plans for her. I'd hate to see our plans not come to fruition." With that oddly ominous statement, he showed me out the door.

Now what on earth was that all about? I asked myself as I headed for the elevator. It sounded as if Bernard Morton was trying to warn me to warn Jane to do something but what that something was I couldn't tell. Did Bernard know Jane was interested in Fritz? I pondered that thought as I rode back down to the lobby. That had to be it. Jane and Fritz were obviously the topic of some water cooler gossip and it had drifted up to Bernard Morton's office. Maybe Bernard planned on getting rid of Fritz so that Fritz couldn't make any claims on 'Fat Off.' This day was turning out to be too much for me with my being foisted on Bob for some on the job training and Jane's boss hinting that she was about to get herself into some kind of trouble if she dated the wrong man and my new shoes just about killing me. I couldn't wait to get home and tell Steve everything.

Chapter Ten

"Bob Meredith brought me along on an interview with Bernard Morton over at Kutrate Kemicals," I told Steve as I dished out tuna casserole that smelled positively delicious but that I had absolutely no desire to eat. I poured myself a glass of ice water and sat down next to Steve. "He wanted to show me how a real interview is done."

"He actually said that?" Steve questioned.

"Yep." I shrugged. "It didn't really hurt my feelings. I am a rookie at all of this and the more I can learn, the better."

"So what was the interview like?"

"It was fine. Bernard Morton complimented Jane and said she's a wonderful employee." I didn't add all of the borderline creepy stuff he'd said about her. Steve tends to be very protective of his only daughter.

"What did Bob Meredith ask him about?"

"Kutrate Kemicals is introducing a new product. A vitamin that you inhale from one of those e-cigarettes."

"Did he say anything about the weight loss spray?"

I shook my head. "Not a word."

"Well, at least he likes Jane. It's good to have your boss like you."

"I imagine it would be," I agreed, thinking of Kate and how she glared at me every time I saw her. Jeff seemed neutral when it came to how he felt about me.

"Your bosses will love you once they get to know you," Steve assured me. "It would be impossible for them to do anything else. Hey, aren't you having any dinner?"

"I'm not hungry," I said truthfully.

Steve set down his fork and stared at me. "Are you all right?"

"No, I feel great. Why?"

"You always have an appetite. I can't remember the last time you didn't have dinner. Are you sure you're okay?" Steve's eyes suddenly narrowed. "DeeDee, you didn't have any dinner last night either. You picked at your food. And this morning you had black coffee without the English muffin slathered in butter that you've had every morning for the past thirty years. What have you been up to?"

"I'm sure I don't know what you're talking about," I began but then stopped. I can't lie to Steve. "All right, Steve, I had a whiff of 'Fat Off' yesterday and it killed my appetite completely. I've lost two pounds already."

"What?" Steve shouted. "Are you insane? You smelled a chemical that hasn't been tested yet? Have you lost your mind?"

"Of course I haven't. Would you calm down please? Fritz assured me that 'Fat Off' is perfectly safe and he said I'll get my appetite back after our next session only—get this—I'll be able to eat anything I want. Isn't that fabulous?"

"Impossible is what it is," Steve corrected me. "I think we should go straight to the ER."

"What for? I told you, I'm fine. Don't make a production out of this, Steve. I'm perfectly all right."

Steve wasn't convinced. "Why on earth would you take a risk like that, DeeDee? You did something very foolhardy and dangerous."

While I knew why Steve was upset, I wasn't in the mood to listen to it. I was actually feeling a touch cranky which was unusual for me. "I'll be fine," I repeated. "I am fine. Eat your dinner and tell me about your day. I think we've talked this topic to death."

Reluctantly, Steve picked up his fork and began eating his tuna casserole. As I sipped my ice water and watched him eat, I thought how odd it was not to be hungry. Odd and a little bit boring. Food has always been one of the greatest pleasures of my life. It was going to be very nice when I entered the next phase of 'Fat Off.'

"How's the diary coming?" Kate asked me the moment I stepped into the newsroom the following morning. She stared at me. "You know, you do look a little smaller. What are you doing? Atkins?"

"No, something new and the diary is coming along. I'm almost done with my first entry."

"I want it before you leave today. But first I want you to go check out this graffiti artist and write up a story on him. He uses the walls at the train station as his canvas."

"How is that not just vandalism, plain and simple? Why hasn't he been arrested or ticketed?"

"Art is subjective, DeeDee. Everyone knows that. Now get me five hundreds words before you leave today. And a picture—you take it. We don't have a photographer available." Kate returned to her computer, her body language telling me that our conversation was over. I was getting slightly better at figuring out how she related to people and my conclusion was that she didn't relate to anyone very well. "And puh-leez let me see with your finished product that you learned something when you went with Bob the other day. I want to read professionalism in every single word of what you write. Now are you going to get to work or stand there all day long?"

I left without saying a word.

An hour and a half later, I was on my way back to the newspaper, my interview with Gilbert the graffiti artist—just Gilbert, no last name—completed. There was no doubt in my mind that not only was Gilbert a very strange young man, he was also a criminal. He saw nothing wrong with vandalism and had proudly informed me that he'd just been awarded a grant from some art league to continue his life of crime in train stations around the Midwest. Shaking my head over the confused state of the world, I slammed on my brakes. At least five police cars were parked in front of the newspaper building with their lights on. A small crowd of people were gathered in the empty lot next to the *Kemper Times*.

My stomach was suddenly filled with knots. Getting out of my car, I joined the people standing off to one side. "What's going on?" I asked a young woman dressed in jogging clothes.

"I don't know. I was doing my morning run when suddenly all these cop cars came screeching in here. The police ran into the newspaper building like they were chasing down a serial killer."

"When did that happen?"

The woman shrugged. "Maybe five minutes ago."

"Do you think it was an accident?"

"How should I know? I don't work at the paper. Ask one of the cops."

"It wasn't an accident." A tall man wearing a raincoat joined us. "Someone's dead in there."

"How do you know that?" I asked.

"I was listening to my police scanner." He pointed to an ear bud going in one of his ears. "I always listen to my scanner during my morning walk just in case there's a neighborhood I should avoid. Also, it's kind of fun listening in on the domestic calls. You'd be amazed how many people get into screaming arguments over their eggs and bacon."

"Who's dead?" I asked.

"Don't know. The police use codes and they used the code that basically means: dead body on premises."

"Oh, my gosh!" My hand flew up and covered my mouth. Someone in the newspaper building had died. Who could it be? I tried to picture my co-workers but knew that I had to be forgetting a good portion of them. I was too new to know everyone in the building. Maybe it was someone in the printing area. I had spied one man who was seriously obese. Perhaps he'd had a heart attack. "Can I go in there?"

The woman jogger stared at me. "Why would you want to go in there?"

"That's where I work."

"They haven't put up any yellow *Do Not Cross* tape," the man in the raincoat said. "Go ahead and see what happens. Worse thing they can do is tell you to get out."

He had a point. I took a few steps and then stopped. "You didn't hear anything on your scanner about there being a crazed shooter in the newspaper building, did you?"

The man shook his head. "Just a dead body. If there was a shooter in the area, we'd all be told to take off by now."

Walking up to the front door of the *Kemper Times*, I felt both afraid and anxious. I didn't want anyone to die but since someone I worked with obviously already had, I hoped that it was someone I hadn't met yet and that whoever it was had died from natural causes. The first person I saw once I was inside the building was Natalie. “Oh, DeeDee! Did you hear? Isn’t it terrible?”

“I heard that someone died but I didn’t hear who it was.” Natalie was alone in the small downstairs area that housed her desk and a run-down reception area. “Who was it, Natalie?” I waited breathlessly for her to reply, fear gripping my insides.

Delicately dabbing her eyes with a tissue, Natalie sniffed. “It was Kate.”

My limbs turned to ice. “Kate? Kate Weston is dead?”

Natalie nodded. “Yes, she is. She was found in the storage room.”

“But I was just talking to her a little over an hour ago and she was fine! What happened? Did she have a heart attack or a stroke or something like that?”

Natalie shook her head sharply. “No, it wasn’t anything like that. She was murdered.”

“What?”

“She was killed. Bob Meredith went into Kate’s office to ask her a question but she wasn’t there. Then he went into the break room but she wasn’t there either. He figured she was in the bathroom so he went into the storage room to get some printer paper and that’s when he found her.” Natalie shuddered. “Dead.”

“But how does he know that she was murdered? Was she shot or stabbed or what?”

Natalie looked at me with frightened eyes. “He found her with a plumber’s helper duct taped across her mouth but it looks like she was strangled.”

I immediately thought of Ren and how he’d been dispatched by Kate to unplug the toilet in the bathroom. He must have used a plumber’s helper to do that. Was it possible that in some kind of rage he had marched into Kate’s office, dragged her into the storage room and used the plumber's helper on her after choking her to death? No, no way. Ren was too quiet, too gentle to do anything like that. Besides, it was the middle of the morning. Surely someone in the newsroom would have seen something like that happen. Then again, the newsroom was usually pretty empty at that time of day. Maybe Ren could have gotten away with dragging Kate into the storage room and killing her. "How horrible," I said, hugging my arms to my sides. It was a pleasant day outside and the air conditioning at the newspaper wasn't set very low, but I still felt chilled to my bones. A woman I'd been talking to not very long ago was lying upstairs dead, never to speak to anyone again. How could such a terrible thing have happened?

"Hideous," Natalie agreed. "And to think that it happened while we were all at work. Any one of us might have killed her." Glancing up at the camera in the corner of the room, Natalie sighed. "Well, one good thing has come of this. At least I won't have to worry about Kate watching me anymore." She clapped her hand over her mouth immediately. "Oh, I'm so sorry I said that! Of course I never wished any ill on the woman. I didn't like her or the way she was always spying on me but I'd never wish any harm on the woman."

I believed Natalie. There was no way a woman like Natalie could ever attack another human being. *How do you know that? You don't really know anything about Natalie or anyone else who works at the newspaper.* I brushed the thought away impatiently. Maybe I hadn't known Natalie for too long but I'm fairly good at reading people and I knew instinctively that Natalie had a heart of pure gold. "I guess I'd better go upstairs," I said a little reluctantly. I didn't want to but I had to see if there was anything that I could do.

"Oh, DeeDee," Natalie said sadly, "when I woke up this morning I never dreamed that something like this was going to happen."

"Man, oh, man. Of all the ways to go." Bob Meredith shook his salt and pepper head, his hands crossed over his chest as he tilted back in his chair.

Needless to say, there wasn't much writing getting done in the newsroom for the rest of that day. I stayed while the police questioned everyone—since I wasn't in the building when Kate was killed they barely talked to me—and then the paper was put together by rote. It seemed rather cold to me to keep on working when someone had been murdered in my midst, but Ren explained that the newspaper had to be put out on time. "We can't miss putting out an edition. It's tradition that no matter what, the paper goes out and on time."

"Like 'The show must go on'?" I asked.

Ren smiled a little sadly. "Something like that."

Once all of the stories were completed, everyone sat at his or her cubicle. Jeff had told us that we could go home once we were through but the entire reporting staff, myself included, seemed reluctant to leave. I'm not sure why that was other than maybe feeling like there was a little safety in numbers.

"Look at it this way; she didn't suffer too much," Caroline offered.

"How would you know that, Caroline?" Ren asked. "Have you ever had a plumber's helper taped across your nose and your mouth?"

"No, but the police said it looked like she'd been knocked out so with any luck at all she died before she knew what was going on."

No one in the entire room was what I would have called broken up over Kate's demise but out of all of the reporters, Caroline was definitely the most blasé. She was filing her nails as she spoke and looked as unperturbed and unbothered as if she was discussing where to plant her petunias next spring.

"Kate lived for this place," Ren said. "Slept, ate and breathed the newspaper. It was really all she ever seemed to care about."

"I suppose if she loved it so much then she was one of the lucky ones," I said, tossing my two cents into the conversation for what they were worth. "Isn't that the goal? To find something you love to do and then figure out a way to get paid for it?"

"Sure, that's the goal but how many people ever reach it?" Bob asked. "I love what I do most of the time and I get paid for it but not very much."

"Kate reached it," I said softly. I really felt sick to my stomach. True, I didn't like Kate but maybe I would have grown to like her if I'd gotten to know her better. I wrinkled my nose. Then again, maybe not. I didn't want to speak ill of the dead but I was pretty sure that even if I had worked with Kate for fifty years we never would have gotten to be best friends or even casual friends. She really had been unlikeable. "I wonder who killed her. I wonder *why* someone killed her."

Bob snorted. "Are you kidding me?"

"I beg your pardon?"

"Kate must have had a list at least a page long single-spaced of people who wanted to see her dead. She wasn't exactly well loved around the newsroom or around town for that matter. She had the personality of road kill. Sorry to be so blunt but there's no use sugar coating facts. The woman was a witch."

Thinking what a suck up to Kate's face Bob had been, I said, "Maybe someone should have been honest with her about her shortcomings. If that had happened perhaps she wouldn't have been killed."

Bob snorted again. "Yeah, right. Tell your boss why everyone hates her and you'd be out on your ass so fast your head would spin. There was no telling Kate anything. I bet half the staff here wished she was dead at one point or another."

"There's a pretty big difference between wishing someone was dead and actually killing them," I remarked. It was time to go home. Hanging around the newsroom was only going to make me feel more depressed. Rummaging in the bottom drawer of my desk, I found my purse and slung the strap over my shoulder. "I guess I'll head off now," I said to no one in particular.

Ren looked up. "See you tomorrow, DeeDee." No one else glanced in my direction as I left the newsroom.

On my way downstairs I had to walk directly past Jeff's office. Jeff was seated at his desk, his head bent over a stack of papers, his hands firmly gripping the tufts of hair on his forehead. He glanced up sharply and caught me gawking at him from the hallway. "What is it, DeeDee?" he asked. His voice sounded terrible. Shocked and low and quite miserable.

"Nothing, really," I said. "I'm on my way home."

"Now?" Jeff glanced at the large clock hanging on his wall. "It's only one-thirty."

"I work until twelve and then I'm done for the day."

"Oh, right. You're part-time. I forgot." Wearily, Jeff rubbed the bridge of his nose. "This hasn't been a good day." He laughed. "That has to be the understatement of the decade."

"I'm sorry," I said sincerely. "I was truly shocked to hear what happened to Kate. I'm sure it must be a lot worse for you since I barely knew her and you've worked with her for so long."

"Fourteen years," Jeff replied. He threw the pencil he was holding down on the top of his desk. "I won't lie and act like working with Kate was always a walk in the park. She could be quite irritating but no one should die the way she died."

He didn't sound like someone who had just committed murder. Then again, if he was a sociopath, he'd be good at hiding his true feelings. "Violent deaths are the hardest to hear about, especially when they happen so close," I agreed. "Does Kate have any family?"

"A husband," Jeff said. "No kids. She always said that the newspaper was her baby and that was more than enough for her."

"Do you know when her service will be?"

Jeff shook his head. "No clue. I suppose in a few days. Man, this is some week. I never dreamed that at the end of it I'd be heading for Kate's funeral."

"We're all in shock. Please let me know if there's anything that I can do," I said.

"Do?" Jeff repeated. "What do you mean?"

"I imagine everyone's going to be especially busy around the newspaper with Kate…gone. If there's anything extra that I can do to help out, please tell me."

"For a second there I thought you were talking about helping with the funeral. Wow, work. I haven't really thought about that too much yet but you're right. We're going to be understaffed with Kate gone. She didn't do any reporting but I'll have to take over her editing duties for the time being. Maybe you can help out, DeeDee. What story were you working on?"

"I just interviewed a graffiti artist and I started a diary about weight loss. Kate said she'd run it in

Friday's paper. I'm going to start a blog too and a Twitter account." Whatever the hell that was.

"It would be a help if you'd do some extra filler stories. You know—stuff we can run at any time."

I perked up a little bit. It was a terrible way to get a new assignment but then again, as a newspaper woman, I was positive that Kate would have understood. Like Ren and I said, the show must go on and all that. "Of course I'll help."

"Thanks. I'll have your assignments tomorrow."

"Who is going to cover Kate's murder for the paper?"

"Bob will have to do it. Or Caroline. They do the crime stories, not that we have too many of those in Kemper, thank God. Ren has his hands full with his section and Frank can barely get the sports section done by himself." Jeff looked worried. "We might have to hire another reporter."

"I'll do all I can to help," I promised.

"Good. See you tomorrow, DeeDee."

"See you tomorrow, Jeff." Somberly, I continued my walk out of the newsroom, my mind still trying to grasp the fact that Kate was dead, gone forever. I hadn't like the woman but I certainly hadn't wished any harm on her.

Who could have hated Kate enough to kill her?

Shuddering, I looked around my shoulder but no one was behind me. It had to be someone from the outside, someone who came into the building to use the bathroom or perhaps to steal something. Maybe an escaped mental patient or convict. But how could someone from the outside have gotten past Natalie? Unless Natalie had been in the bathroom or taking a break. The front door to the newspaper building wasn't locked during business hours. Anyone could have walked in. Thank goodness for the camera system. If it was an outsider, they would have been filmed when they came in and the police would be able to find them almost immediately.

But in my heart of hearts I knew that an outsider coming in and killing Kate as some kind of crime of opportunity wasn't very likely. Kate had been a very unpleasant person who seemed to make enemies everywhere she went. Whoever killed her more than likely had meant to kill her. It hadn't been a crime of opportunity or a robbery gone badly. I was almost positive that whoever killed Kate had wanted her gone.

Permanently.

Chapter Eleven

"I can't believe this," Steve said as we walked down the street together on an evening stroll. The humidity level had been building all day long and now the air was heavy and I couldn't wait for our walk to be over so I could get back to the comfort of air conditioning at home. "You do realize that this is the second job that you've had where someone has gotten murdered?"

"Technically speaking, I didn't work for Eden Academy," I pointed out. "I simply catered a luncheon for them."

"Still, someone was killed the day of your luncheon," Steve said, as if I needed reminding. "It makes me nervous, honey."

"I know but it's just one of those weird coincidences," I reassured him. "I had nothing to do with Frank Ubermann's murder and I don't have anything to do with Kate's either."

Steve walked silently but I could practically hear his thought process. When you've been married for as long as Steve and I have, it's pretty easy to know what the other person is thinking. "Maybe you should quit. I think working at that newspaper might be dangerous."

I put a calming hand over his. "Honey, I don't want to quit. I promise you that I'm totally safe." I didn't want to quit, not now when I was going to get more assignments and more responsibilities. I also didn't want to quit until I knew who had killed Kate. My mother always told me that I was too curious for my own good and she was probably right but there was no way that I could leave the newspaper before learning who had murdered my boss. It would be like walking out of a mystery movie before the ending.

"Do you promise me that you won't try to investigate Kate's murder on your own?"

"I'm not a professional investigator."

"That doesn't answer my question and you know it."

"I won't put myself in danger," I promised.

"DeeDee," Steve began but I interrupted.

"You know I'll be careful, honey. Aren't I always careful? Besides, I'm not going to interrogate anyone. I just plan on keeping my eyes and my ears open at all times. I think it must have been an inside job. My money is on Caroline or Bob. Possibly Ren. They all hated Kate."

"Now that's just what I'm talking about! You can't keep on working there if you think your co-workers are capable of murdering someone."

"Oh, Steve, I don't really think one of them did it," I said soothingly. "It probably was some freaky case of manslaughter. Maybe someone came in to use the bathroom and Kate caught them. Believe me, she wouldn't have been shy about telling an outsider to get lost. Maybe the person snapped and strangled here."

"Leave it to the police," Steve instructed. "I don't want you putting yourself in harm's way. You've done that before and it scared the hell out of me, DeeDee."

Since I really wasn't in the mood to listen to Steve list the times when I'd acted first and thought later, I steered the conversation away from murder in general and Kate's murder in particular. "Did I tell you that Jane called? She's in Las Vegas for a convention. Doesn't that sound exciting?"

"Sounds like an odd place for a convention to me," Steve replied. "Too many distractions."

"Maybe, but I say good for her. I'd love to be sent anywhere for a convention. Maybe the newspaper will send me somewhere and you can come along and we can have a second honeymoon. Maybe someplace exciting like New York."

"Or even Milwaukee," Steve kidded. "DeeDee, I see right through you. You aren't going to distract me by dangling thoughts of a second honeymoon in front of me. I don't want you doing any kind of freelance investigating of Kate's Weston's murder, all right?"

"I won't," I promised. "But Steve, I work at the newspaper. It's going to be pretty hard to ignore hearing any rumors that might be floating around the newsroom. I mean, Kate is—was—our boss. Naturally we're going to talk about what happened."

"I don't expect you to suddenly develop a hearing loss," Steve replied, "I just don't want you sticking your nose where it doesn't belong. You could wind up in a lot of trouble that way. I mean it, DeeDee. Kate's death is a tragedy but it has nothing to do you. If you won't quit then concentrate on writing your stories and learning your craft, all right?"

"That's exactly what I intend to do," I said slightly huffily. Honestly, I adore my husband but there are times when he acts as if I'm the Lucille Ball of the twenty-first century.

"Don't be mad. You know I'm right."

Since I did know he was right, I said, "Let's go home. I'm getting all sweaty."

We were just stepping through the front door when my cell phone rang. Not recognizing the number, I let it go to voice mail, waited a minute and then called to hear the message.

"Mrs. Pearson—DeeDee—this is Fritz Scheider. Or should I say Deep Throat." Fritz's voice sounded almost as if he were whispering. "Could we possibly meet for coffee or a glass of wine? My treat, of course. Please call me as soon as you get this message."

"Who called?" Steve asked. "Your face lit up like you just heard from the Prize Patrol at Publisher's Clearinghouse."

"Almost," I said as I called Fritz back. Fritz answered immediately. "Hello, Fritz? I'm sorry I missed your call. I'd love to get together with you. When are you free?"

"Half an hour." Fritz said. "Let's meet at the Coffee Hut. I'll see you then." He hung up before I could respond.

"That was the chemist from Kutrate Kemicals?" Steve asked.

I nodded. "He wants to meet me at the Coffee Hut in half an hour. You don't mind if I head out, do you, honey? Or you can come with me if you want to." It would have been nice to have Steve along since he usually remembers things that I forget. I looked at him hopefully.

Steve shook his head. "No, thanks. You can be Girl Reporter and I'll stay home and grade papers. Just don't be out too late. Is he going to give you any more of that 'Fat Off' garbage? I'm not so sure I want you messing with that. You don't need to lose weight anyway and who knows what kind of side effects that crap might have?"

"He didn't say a word about 'Fat Off'," I said truthfully. I wasn't all that sure I wanted to move into the next stage of 'Fat Off' anyway. Like Steve said, I didn't want to deal with unknown side effects somewhere down the road even like the ones that are in those legal commercials all the time. While I'd love to be thinner, I didn't want to pay for it later. Besides, I missed eating.

Steve started to speak but I was halfway up the stairs and I kept on going. Honestly, my husband is a doll but sometimes he really does worry too much. It took about five minutes to drive to the Coffee Hut so I had a little time to change into something appropriate for meeting with my very own Deep Throat, although I had absolutely no idea of what I might have hanging in my wardrobe that would be suitable.

I couldn't remember the last time when I'd felt so excited, like I was about to open a great big present with my name on the gift tag. Well, I reasoned as I changed into a fresh pair of jeans and a casual yet chic top, I *was* about to open up a present with my name on the gift tag. The present was the story on 'Fat Off' and it was going to be a gift that kept on giving. If Fritz let me write about the new weight loss product and if my story was printed in the *Kemper Times* and then picked up by, oh, say, the *New York Times,* then Jeff was going to have to offer me a full-time job and maybe a column of my own. How wonderful would that be? Sure, I was excited about my diet diary but a story about how 'Fat Off' was invented would be so much better.

I was adding some fresh eye pencil when I suddenly remembered Kate Weston and how she'd been murdered that very morning. Sobered, I put my hand down and stared in the mirror at my reflection. It felt shallow and selfish to be thinking about my journalism career when there was a murderer on the loose, a murderer who had killed my boss and who might very well be sitting next to me, or at least near me, in the newsroom.

It would be nice if I could figure out who had killed Kate but I knew the odds of that happening were astronomical. I'd gotten lucky finding out who had killed Frank Ubermann but this was a totally different ball game. Frank's murder had been a crime of passion. I wasn't at all sure why anyone had killed Kate. True, she had a lousy personality but if people were killed because they had bad personalities the population on the planet would be down to about twenty-five.

I supposed it didn't really matter one way or the other. I didn't have a clue who'd killed Kate so it wasn't either shallow or selfish of me to focus on my job. Feeling better, I finished outlining my eyes, shoved my feet into a pair of flats and ran down the steps.

The interior of the Coffee Hut was dark and filled with lumpy couches and chairs next to rickety tables that wobbled when touched. There was the scent of mildew in the air along with freshly brewed coffee. Fortunately, the coffee scent won. I waited for a few moments for my eyes to focus in the gloom since I really didn't want to walk into one of those rickety tables and send an espresso flying into someone's lap. When my eyes adjusted, I looked around at the patrons, searching for Fritz Schneider. It didn't take long to spot him at a table in the back of the room. He still looked like Gregory Peck but an even more harassed version. I noticed that he was tapping his coffee cup with a spoon in quick staccato bursts and I could see that his feet were twitching as well. Fritz was obviously keyed up over something.

Taking a deep breath to calm myself, I wove through the tables until I reached him. "Hello, Fritz," I said a little breathlessly. I'd had to park five blocks away and had half jogged to the coffee shop since I didn't want to keep Fritz waiting.

I watched with a little amusement as Fritz sucked in his small paunch as he half stood to greet me. "Hello, DeeDee. You're looking quite lovely tonight." What is it about all men who feel the need to suck in their stomachs whenever they meet someone in a restaurant? I've noticed that they seldom do that at home. I sat down in the chair across from Fritz and ordered a concoction called Honey Do when the waitress scampered over. After she left, I spoke.

"I'm so glad that you called me, Fritz."

"I told you that we'd speak again soon," Fritz said. His voice was quiet but I sensed a tension that hadn't been there before.

"Yes, you did. I take it you're ready to tell me about how the magic happens?"

Fritz frowned. "Magic?"

"How you invented 'Fat Off.' If it works, it's going to seem like magic to a whole lot of people."

"Well, that wasn't what I wanted to talk to you about tonight but I'll give you a little bit of background since you're so interested."

"I'd like that," I said. "I'm interested. I think you've invented something that's going to go down in history."

Fritz looked pleased. "It was really a fluke, like so many brilliant inventions start out. I was experimenting with a spray that would keep dogs off furniture—my German shepherd is always jumping on the sofa and leaving dog hair behind. I have to constantly yell at poor Hans even though it isn't really his fault. So I created a spray that smelled offensive enough that Hans didn't want to be around it. All I did was squirt it around the sofa whenever Hans was about to jump up on it. Hans stayed off the sofa but I noticed that he also got extremely skinny. I thought he had worms but when I had him tested he was fine. I also dropped twenty pounds too without even trying. I deduced that it had to be the spray that I was using since neither Hans nor I had changed our diets. Further experimentation proved me right."

"You sprayed that awful stuff in your own house? How can you still be alive after smelling that disgusting scent?"

"It grows on you," Fritz replied. "Well, at least you get used to it enough not to notice it quite so acutely. Plus notice how skinny I am." He patted his small pot belly. "With the exception of this, of course. I can't seem to lose my tummy. You need to remember that there are trade-offs for everything—fat and nice smelling air or skinny and stinky air. Everything is about choice." He had a point. "But that is moot now that I've discovered how to make my product smell like a meadow in springtime."

"Was it difficult to make it smell better?"

"Extremely difficult. I've spent the better part of the past two years working on improving the smell. To tell you the truth, if it was up to me I wouldn't bother to make 'Fat Off' smell better since I believe people would do anything not to give up their Taco Bell and Big Macs and hot fudge sundaes and still be skinny. Oh, and let's not forget our wine and beer. Heaven forbid that Americans don't have their wine and beer." Fritz shrugged. "However, my opinion seldom matters at the sty where I'm forced to work."

"That's too bad," I sympathized. "Have you thought about taking 'Fat Off' to another company?"

"Yes, I have and I hope that will happen but that's not why I wanted to talk to you tonight. I have something to tell you about your boss."

"Jeff?"

"No, Kate Weston. The one who was murdered. There's a connection between her and 'Fat Off' and I need to talk about it to someone. Since you work at the newspaper, you seemed like the logical choice."

"What kind of connection?" I asked, unable to imagine any way that the handsome scientist sitting at the table with me and my late editor could possibly be connected.

"A, well, I suppose an odd connection. You see, I knew Kate Weston—"

"You did? How?"

A shadow fell over the table and Fritz and I both lifted our heads. "Well, hello, Fritz. Is this your date for the evening? Haven't we met before, young lady?"

Looking up, Fritz and I found ourselves staring into the grim features of the president of Kutrate Kemicals, Bernard Morton.

Chapter Twelve

Oh, boy. Time to do some fast tap dancing. I smiled up at my daughter's boss then glanced at Fritz to see how he was reacting. He wasn't reacting at all. Nodding curtly, he asked, "What are you doing here?"

"I came to meet a friend," Bernard replied. "I think the more interesting question is: what are the two of you doing here? Together?"

Fritz shifted uncomfortably in his seat and I could see that he was agitated as his face turned a deep shade of red. "I don't really see how that's any of your affair, Bernard."

Bernard laughed. "I disagree. You work for me and this charming lady's daughter works for me and I'd like to know what you're up to. This charming lady also works for the local newspaper. Are you telling her some trade secrets, Fritz?"

"My, my," I said in what I hoped was a light, teasing tone. "Isn't that a touch paranoid? We're having coffee, we aren't trading company secrets—not that I'd know if Kutrate Kemical had any, of course."

Looking as if he didn't believe a word I was saying, Bernard spoke sharply to Fritz. "Fritz, don't forget we have a meeting first thing tomorrow. I'll expect you to be there bright and early. And bring some pastries from the bakery downtown."

"Yes, sir," Fritz said in not exactly a meek tone but not like Superman either.

"And make sure you don't get any of those long johns without custard filling but no jelly. I hate jelly." Nodding at both of us, Bernard moved away. I tilted my head slightly so I could see who he was with but all I could see were a pair of long, slender nylon-covered legs sticking out of the corner booth. So there was a woman in the picture. I refocused on Fritz who was still red-faced and shaking with anger. "Are you all right?"

"That...pig!" Fritz spit out. "How dare he question the validity of the two of us being out together? How dare he act as if he can control our private lives?"

"Well, he is a pompous, self-serving jerk," I readily agreed. "But he's the boss—what do you expect?"

"What do I expect? I expect respect, I expect admiration and I expect gratitude."

"I think you're expecting way too much. Maybe you should start looking for another job. After all, if your fat loss product is a success, why should you let Kutrate Kemicals share in the glory with you?"

"Believe me, I'd love to do that but I'm unable to."

"Why?" I leaned closer.

Fritz hesitated. "Because of the contract Bernard Morton tricked me into signing."

"How did he trick you? And what's your connection to Kate Weston?"

Fritz shook his head. "Not now, DeeDee. Perhaps later, when the walls don't have ears. You come up to my apartment for a little schnapps and we'll talk frankly then."

I wasn't at all sure how Steve would feel about that scenario. I knew it made me a little nervous, not because I thought Fritz would hit on me but because I knew I'd be uncomfortable. "My husband is waiting for me," I said. "I don't think that would work. Come on, Fritz, tell me about your connection to Kate Weston."

"All in due time. Are you hungry?"

I realized that I was. "Yes, I am. I think my appetite is back." Phew! No more cooking meals and not feeling like eating them! After a few days of being on 'Fat Off,' I wasn't sure that being skinny was worth giving up eating.

"But the pounds aren't. Another whiff and you'll maintain your weight loss."

"No, thanks," I said. "I think I'd rather be a touch chunky than not eat."

"I told you that when you enter Stage Two of the 'Fat Off' plan you can eat all you want without gaining an ounce."

It was so tempting. Too tempting. In the name of science and research, I decided that one more little sniff couldn't possibly hurt me. "Well, I don't know," I said. "Maybe one more time but that's it."

"Smell this." Fritz held out a cotton handkerchief.

I held it to my nose and inhaled the faint lemon and mint smell. "Lovely," I said.

"Now let's order dessert," Fritz suggested.

Over pecan pie—that tasted even better than usual since I knew it wasn't adding unwanted inches to my bottom and thighs—I managed to pry a little more information out of Fritz. For a Deep Throat wannabe, he was frustratingly slow on telling me anything. Over his second piece of pie, he finally began to open up. "We're going to nail Bernard Morton to the wall," Fritz announced, a few pecan crumbs clinging to his chin. "We're going to hang him out to dry and watch him flap in the breeze. We're going to throw him under the bus and back up to make sure he's good and dead! The man deserves to have a vendetta against him. He's so rotten—almost evil! Why should he get even more money when there are so many people who deserve it more than he does? Like me? After all, 'Fat Off' is my creation! I'm going to change the name of the product and no one will know the difference!"

"How do you think you're going to make that happen?"

Fritz thinned his lips again. "I have my ways."

I really needed to steer him off the topic of 'Fat Off' and his boss and onto who murdered Kate Weston—not because I was abandoning 'Fat Off' or the story that I wanted to write on it but because Fritz got too crazed when he spoke about Bernard Morton. He needed time to cool off or distance himself and I needed to find out what he knew about Kate's death. "So Fritz," I attempted, "what did you want to tell me about Kate? Did you know her?"

Fritz's eyes glittered behind his glasses. "Quite well. Intimately, you might say."

I thought Kate was married but maybe I was wrong about that because it sure sounded like Fritz meant they did more than meet for checkers once a week. "Oh? You dated?"

"Of course not! She was my business partner until about six months ago when she dropped me. Quite unceremoniously, I might add. But I got to know Kate very well and I believe I have a good idea of who killed her."

"Okay," I finally said when Fritz remained silent. "Who?"

"One moment." Fritz held up a finger as he forked his last piece of pie into his mouth. Suddenly Fritz's eyes suddenly bulged outward in a most unattractive manner and his face turned a very unflattering shade of dark purple. "Grrrrggghhhhh," he muttered, clutching his throat with his hands.

"What's the matter? Are you choking?" Leaping to my feet, I ran behind Fritz and began whacking him on his back.

"Do the Heimlich!" a customer shouted. Fluttering my arms by my sides, I realized that I had completely forgotten how to do the Heimlich maneuver.

"Hug him! Give him the hug of life!"

I tried, I honestly did. I reached around Fritz and did the pull and lift up that I suddenly remembered from the CPR class Steve and I had taken together years ago. It was like hugging a whale. Fritz kept gurgling but nothing popped out of his mouth like it was supposed to. "It's not helping!" I shouted.

A waiter rushed over and pushed me out of the way. He was a lot bigger and stronger looking than me so I let him. He did the Heimlich too but it didn't help. In the distance I could hear the sound of sirens approaching the Coffee Hut. They screeched to a halt outside and a pair of EMT's raced in. I stepped back even further and watched as they worked over Fritz for several long minutes and as they loaded him into the back of the ambulance. "Is he alive?" I asked one of them as they rushed past.

"Barely," he replied.

Oh, boy. Fritz might die and if he did so would whatever knowledge he was about to share with me over who'd killed Kate Weston. Slowly I picked up my purse and headed for the cashier to pay our bill. As I moved I looked around the restaurant for Bernard Morton but he was nowhere to be found. Fritz's boss had vanished but I didn't know if Bernard had left before or after Fritz's attack and I had no clue whatsoever what had caused it.

Chapter Thirteen

"I guess it was a heart attack," I told Steve later that night when we were in bed. I shivered and cuddled up next to him. Seeing Fritz choke or have a stroke or a heart attack or whatever had happened to him had been horrible and a whole lot ickier and more graphic than anything I'd ever seen on any *CSI* show. If I shut my eyes I still saw his purple face so I kept them open. I might have to learn how to sleep with my eyes open.

"He just up and had a heart attack?" Steve asked.

"It happens," I said as I tried to snuggle even closer to my husband. He felt warm and alive, two things I desperately needed at that moment.

"Not usually in the middle of a conversation. There were no warning signs? He didn't complain of chest pain or that his arm hurt or seemed agitated?"

"Well, of course he was agitated and then we saw Bernard Morton at the restaurant and that only made Fritz more upset."

When Steve didn't answer me, I pulled back so that I could look up at my husband's face. He was wearing a serious expression that I usually saw around Christmastime when he told me to cut back on charging presents for the kids. "Steve?" I persisted. "What is it?"

"Let's go over the facts," Steve said. "Fritz tells you he knows something about Kate's death. He asks to meet you to discuss it. At the restaurant he tells you that he knows something about Kate's death but before he can tell you anything else he suddenly starts to choke, passes out and is rushed to the hospital. Doesn't that seem highly coincidental to you?"

"Well, not *highly* coincidental but a little convenient, yes." Sinking back into Steve's arms, I thought hard. It was a shame that Fritz had started to choke before he told me who he thought might have killed Kate but I wouldn't say it was anything other than really bad timing on his part. After all, even if he had been poisoned, whoever poisoned him couldn't have known that he'd drop dead right after he'd given me a tiny little bit of information about Kate's murder, so tiny that it really barely helped me at all. So they'd been business partners. So what?

"What did Fritz eat at the restaurant?"

"Let me think…two slices of pecan pie and about seven cups of coffee."

"Black?"

"No, with cream and sugar. Four sugars in each."

"My gosh, it's amazing he didn't fall into a diabetic coma at some point!"

"I know. I was pretty amazed just watching him consume all that sugar and fat. He's skinny though—although he does have a bit of a pot. See? 'Fat Off' does work."

"That doesn't mean it's safe. Did you take any more of it?"

"Just a tiny sniff."

"DeeDee!"

"I had to, Steve, for my article. Fritz has been using it for a couple of years and he's fine." I stopped talking and began thinking. Hard. Why would Kate dump Fritz as a business partner when he was on the verge of getting what was going to be a blockbuster product onto the shelves? Had Kate gone into business with Bernard Morton? Were Kate and Bernard trying to gaslight Fritz or completely cheat him out of any profits from his own invention? If that were true, I didn't blame Fritz for hating Bernard. Or Kate for that matter.

"I can hear the wheels spinning inside your head, DeeDee," Steve remarked. "It sounds like a hamster wheel going ninety miles an hour."

"I was just thinking about what I have to do," I said.

"And what would that be?"

"Well, I really don't know but I'd like to talk to Fritz again to find out more about his connection to Kate. So they were business partners. How could that have anything to do with her death?"

"Maybe you should talk to the police."

"I can't do that."

"Why not?"

"Because of 'Fat Off'! Jane would kill me if I told the police about her company's new product. It would be much better if I did a little sleuthing on my own."

"No, it would not," Steve said firmly. "A little sleuthing on your own could lead to a whole lot of trouble. For you, mainly."

I didn't respond immediately because in my heart of hearts, I knew Steve was right. However, I didn't want him to be right. I wanted to do my own private investigating because, well, because I am a nosy woman and it would have been very rewarding to figure out who the murderer was and *then* go to the police. But it wasn't meant to be and I knew it. "I won't do anything dangerous," I said. "I promise."

"I'm going to hold you to that, DeeDee. Man, I can hardly keep my eyes open. Good night, honey."

"Night," I replied. Steve rolled over and within a minute or two I could hear him softly snoring. I wasn't that lucky. For at least two hours, I lay on my back, staring up in the dark at the ceiling, trying to figure out the connection between Fritz, Kate and 'Fat Off' and who could have killed Kate and possibly poisoned Fritz so that he started choking. Finally, sleep took over around one in the morning, but I tossed and turned all night long as my brain processed the mystery that I found myself thrust into.

I woke up stiff, still tired and not very rested. I was on my third cup of coffee when Tyler surprised me by joining me at the breakfast table. "Wow, you look terrible," he told me with the candor that children always use with their mothers.

"I don't feel all that wonderful either," I told him. "I didn't sleep very well last night."

Tyler poured himself a bowl of cereal that would have been the right serving size for Paul Bunyan. "Thinking about that guy who passed out in the restaurant last night? Jane heard about it too. She texted me around three in the morning wanting to know what happened."

Oh, my. Jane. I'd totally forgotten to tell our daughter about Fritz. "How did she hear about it?"

"Everyone at Kutrate Kemicals knows that Fritz dude is in a coma. Jane heard it from the big boss."

"Fritz is in a coma?"

Tyler nodded. "I guess the boss sent a text out to the whole company."

"Is Jane upset?"

"Naturally but she was more upset when she found out you were with him last night. Sounds to me like she's got a thing for him."

"How did she find that out? Surely that wasn't in the text message."

"Well, I told her," Tyler admitted. "I didn't think it was a secret."

"How did you know?"

"Dad told me when I got home last night and asked where you were. No offense, Mom, but you don't go out much by yourself so it seemed kind of odd."

"I would have told her myself if I hadn't been so upset last night. Why didn't Jane text me?"

"She knows you and Dad go to bed early. She didn't want to bother you."

"I'll call her," I said, getting to my feet so I could go and find my phone.

"Not necessary," Tyler informed me. "She's coming over here before she goes to work. She should be here any second now."

As if on cue, Jane's silver Prius pulled into the driveway. I watched as she parked behind my car and then walked swiftly to the back door. "I think I'll finish my breakfast in my room," Tyler said. "I'm not really in the mood to hear Jane grill you over my Cap'n Crunch."

"She's not going to grill me," I said with a laugh.

Tyler shot me a wry smile. "You may be her mother but you don't always know her that well. Good luck, Mom."

Tyler was barely out of the room before Jane opened the kitchen door. "Mom!" she rushed across the room and hugged me. "What happened? Are you all right?"

"I'm fine. Get yourself a cup of coffee and I'll tell you everything." I held out my mug, the one with *BEST MOM IN THE WORLD* written on its side. "Hit me again while you're at it."

Jane got our coffee and then sat down in the chair Tyler had just vacated. Steve had left for work already so I knew we wouldn't be interrupted. Seeing the determined look on my daughter's pretty face, I realized that Tyler was right: I was in for some pretty heavy duty grilling. Not that I could really blame Jane.

She had worked with Fritz and I had been with him when he had his attack or choked or whatever had happened to him. Of course she was curious. "Now what happened?" Jane asked after we had our cups of coffee in front of us.

"Fritz called me and said he wanted to talk. We decided to meet at the Coffee Hut."

"What did he want to talk about?" Jane asked.

"At first I assumed 'Fat Off' but then he said that he had information about Kate Weston and who murdered her."

Jane frowned. "Who's Kate Weston?"

"My editor at the newspaper. She was killed a few days ago. Someone strangled her and then taped a plumber's helper over her nose and mouth."

"Eeew," Jane said, making a face. "When did that happen?"

"Tuesday. You were at your convention so I didn't tell you about it. It's not like there was anything you could do about it. When did you get home anyway?"

"Yesterday. My gosh, how awful for you, Mom! But how would Fritz know anything about who killed your editor?"

"That's what I wanted to know. Fritz was quite angry over Bernard Morton and how he was handling the whole 'Fat Off' situation. Then who should walk in but Bernard Morton himself! He came over and said hello."

Jane blinked. "Bernard Morton was at the Coffee Hut?"

"Yes."

"That's odd," Jane muttered.

"Why is that odd?"

"Well, for starters Bernard hates coffee but even if he was the biggest caffeine addict in town I just can't picture him at the Coffee Hut. He's something of a snob and that dive is beneath him."

"It's a cute place," I said, "and the coffee is great."

"Believe me, it's not the type of place where Bernard would normally go. Okay, go on—Bernard saw you two sitting there and said hello. Then what happened?"

"He left and Fritz was upset. He said how Bernard was ruining 'Fat Off.' He calmed down a little and told me that he and Kate had been business partners until six months ago when he suddenly turned purple and began choking or having a heart attack or whatever it was. Do you know?"

Jane shook her head. "The doctors don't think it was a heart attack or a stroke and he didn't appear to be choking on anything."

"Then what happened to him?"

"I don't know." Jane leaned back in her chair. "Wow. This is absolutely surreal. I saw Fritz right before I left for Vegas and he was fine! He was super healthy. He was into stair climbing, working out, taking care of himself—"

"He ate two large pieces of pecan pie and had seven cups of coffee with cream and sugar," I informed her. "Not exactly health food."

"But he also had 'Fat Off,'" Jane reminded me. "He can eat anything he wants because he knew that it wasn't going to stay on him."

"Maybe it was a side effect of 'Fat Off,'" I said. That did it. I wasn't smelling any more of Fritz's wonder product.

"I don't think so. 'Fat Off' has been through a lot of tests already and there have been no side effects."

That was good news. "Did you know that Fritz and Kate Weston were business partners?"

"Mom, I'd never heard of Kate Weston before. Why would Fritz need or want a business partner?"

"Maybe they were going to start their own company once Fritz got the patent for 'Fat Off' back."

"Like that's ever going to happen. Fritz is going to have to accept sooner or later that he *might* be able to get a percentage deal, but Kutrate Kemicals is never going to give him the patent back." Jane frowned.

"It must have something to do with the *Kemper Times.* That has to be the connection. Kate must have been planning on doing a story on 'Fat Off' and was killed to shut her up."

Jane looked doubtful. "Do you really think the *Kemper Times* was going to do a story on Kutrate Kemicals? You know they never touch anything even remotely controversial. The most touchy subject they've ever covered is what color to paint the outdoor bathrooms at the county parks."

Jane sadly had a point. My new place of employment wasn't known for hard-hitting news stories. "What other connection could there be?"

"I don't know but if your boss *was* killed to keep her quiet, then the murderer had to be someone from Kutrate. Who else would go that far?" Jane drained her coffee cup. "You'll have to figure that one out, Mom. I should be going. I'll let you know if I hear anything else about Fritz."

I walked Jane to the back door and watched as she got into her car and backed down the driveway. Jane was taking the news of Fritz's accident like a trooper although I detected a lot more emotion under the surface than she was allowing herself to show. She liked Fritz and I didn't blame her. He was handsome, smart and seemed like a nice guy when he wasn't boiling mad over the whole 'Fat Off' debacle. Maybe if he pulled out of his coma, calmed down and acted reasonable the two of them might have a future together. I hoped so because I was really looking forward to a grandchild or two.

After Jane left, I finished my coffee. I needed to get going too since it was undoubtedly going to be a busy day at the newspaper. But my mind lingered on Fritz and Kate. How had those two ever gotten together in the first place?

Chapter Fourteen

"Why were you with that Fritz guy last night?" Bob Meredith asked me before I had my jacket off. Bob had jumped up from his cubicle the second I walked into the newsroom and come over to where I was standing like an extremely aggressive kiosk worker at the mall. I half expected him to grab one of my hands and start buffing my nails.

"I beg your pardon?" I asked, stalling for time. How had Bob Meredith found out that I was with Fritz?

"I said, why were you with that Fritz guy last night? You bopping him?"

"What?"

"You heard me. You fooling around with him?"

Bob was the absolute limit and while I knew that there was no reason on earth for me to answer him, I did anyway. The manners my parents drummed into me as a child have been a handicap ever since. "No, I'm not fooling around with him! I'm married!"

"So?"

"So I don't bop or fool around with anyone but my husband!"

Bob smirked. "You look like a nice housewife type but you never know, DeeDee. So if you weren't bopping him, what were you doing with him?"

To my relief, Ren stood up. "Bob, shut your sewer before someone does it for you."

Bob stared at him, his jaw hanging open. "Huh?"

"Go away," Ren said. "DeeDee doesn't have to answer your vulgar questions."

Bob looked offended. "I was only *asking*," he said huffily. "That's my job, remember? It's your job, too, Ren." With that, he stalked off toward his own cubicle.

"Excuse Bob," Ren said in his soft voice. "He doesn't know how he comes off most of the time but that doesn't make him any easier to take."

"Thank you for getting rid of him," I said. "I suppose I'll learn how to do that in time."

"You will," Ren agreed. "It gets easier and believe it or not, his bark is worse than his bite."

I sat down at my cubicle and looked up at Ren. "So I suppose the whole newsroom knows I was with Fritz Scheider when he collapsed?"

Ren nodded. "Pretty much. It was on the news this morning."

"You're kidding me! Why would the local news station cover that?"

"Fritz is a pretty big deal over at Kutrate Kemicals. If he dies, he's going to be an even bigger deal. You want to talk about it?"

I shifted uncomfortably in my chair. "There really isn't all that much to talk about," I said uneasily. "We were having coffee when he suddenly turned purple and started making weird choking noises. I tried to do the Heimlich but it didn't help. Thankfully, the EMT's arrived and took him to the hospital. My daughter told me that he's in a coma."

Ren was looking at me curiously. "Are you two friends?"

"More like acquaintances," I said. Brand new acquaintances but I didn't see any point in sharing that. One thing I'd already learned working for the newspaper was to keep most of the good stuff to myself. While I didn't think Ren would try to scoop me, you never knew. "I guess he knew Kate too," I threw out and watched to see if Ren's expression changed.

It didn't. "Kate had a lot of friends, surprisingly. Until they got to know her, that is." Ren disappeared back into his cubicle and under the ever present mountain of work that was waiting for him. I really didn't know how he managed to put out an entire section of the newspaper without any help plus take care of any number of maintenance duties assigned to him.

That reminded me of something. Leaning back, I said, "Excuse me, Ren?"

He reappeared. "Yes?"

"Um, now that Kate's, well, gone, are you still stuck with taking care of the plumbing?"

Ren looked at me quizzically. "Why wouldn't I be? We still have bathrooms here, don't we?"

"I just thought that maybe things would change since she isn't around any longer."

Ren shook his head. "As long as we work here, we'll always have 'other duties as assigned.' Accept it, DeeDee. Things are easier once you accept them."

"DeeDee, could you come to my office, please?" Jeff's voice rang out.

"Our master's voice," I said to Ren.

I heard Ren laugh as I headed for Jeff's office. "You've got to admit that he's easier to take than Kate," I heard him say. Although I felt a little guilty, I silently agreed with him.

Jeff was in his usual position hunched over a computer. "Hi, Jeff," I said. "What can I do for you?"

"Just a second," he said, holding up one finger. "Let me finish this thought." He pecked for a few more moments. "All right, that's my editorial for tomorrow," he said, rubbing his temples wearily. "Damn but it's going to be hard without Kate here. I'm going to have to write three editorials each week instead of one. So I hear you were with Fritz Scheider last night?" Jeff inquired.

"Yes," I said.

"What were you doing with him?"

"Having coffee."

"Just the two of you?"

"Yes…" I still had no idea of what Jeff wanted from me.

"Suppose we could get a story out of this?"

"A story?"

Jeff leaned toward me, his face more excited than I'd ever seen it. "Yes, an eye witness account of what happened. You know, that Scheider guy is a pretty big wheel over at Kutrate Kemical. Might make a nice write up to describe how he went down right in front of you."

"Well, I don't know about that," I began as I desperately tried to figure out a way to get out of writing the story Jeff was describing. I couldn't tell him that it was not only tacky; it was also disturbing and definitely not anything I'd want to write about. "It all happened so quickly."

"But you were there," Jeff said, "and we need filler. Write it like a column. If it's any good, who knows? It might lead to some regular kind of column."

"I'm already doing the diet column," I said, stalling for time.

"No, you're not. I thought about it and I don't like the diet column anymore. It's boring. Write about Fritz instead."

"I don't know…I'm not really comfortable writing about Fritz Scheider and what happened to him. It was awful."

Jeff stared at me as if he was seeing me for the first time. "I still don't get what you two were doing together."

"Having coffee," I repeated firmly.

"And?"

"And nothing," I said. "Just coffee."

Caroline Osborn poked her head into Jeff's office. "Hey, Jeff, I'm heading out to cover a fire on the other side of town. Do you still want me to do the story on the old lady who got mugged too?"

"Yeah. And drop by the police station too. See what's going on with that hit and run."

Caroline sighed elaborately. "Want me to pick up your laundry or any groceries too, Jeff? You need to hire someone ASAP." Her heavily mascaraed eyes fell on me. "What about DeeDee here? Why don't you make her full-time?"

Jeff looked like Caroline had just suggested that he name me Prom Queen of the newspaper. "Her?" he said, somewhat ungraciously I thought.

"Why not? You hired her part-time and we need more warm bodies. And she doesn't out and out suck at writing."

It wasn't the greatest compliment I'd ever had but it wasn't the worst either. "I'd love to work full-time," I said although I wasn't sure if Steve would be thrilled. But maybe things would be better if I was at the paper forty hours a week. I'd be more of a team player, more of a real journalist. Plus I'd make more money, always a good thing.

Jeff looked at me doubtfully. "I don't know…I was kind of thinking we could eke by with what we have. Besides, Kate hired her, not me."

"Well, we can't eke by," Caroline informed him. "Give her the fluff pieces so I don't have to do those on top of everything else. Hire DeeDee or I'm walking and I mean that, Jeff," she said in a threatening tone. "This is ridiculous. The paper has more money now that Kate's gone so you can afford to hire DeeDee full-time on what you're paying her. If it bothers you so much, make her job temporary in case she doesn't work out."

It was like I wasn't even in the same room. I cleared my throat. "Don't either one of you want to ask me if I want to work full-time?"

Both Jeff and Caroline turned and looked at me. "Why wouldn't you?" Jeff asked. "You're always asking for more assignments. If you were here full-time, I guarantee I'd keep you busy. Here's your first story: write about Fritz Scheider and make it snappy."

"That's right, I heard you were with Fritz last night." Caroline tilted her head and looked at me doubtfully. "You certainly get around, DeeDee."

"Do you know Fritz Scheider too?" I asked.

Caroline winked at me. "I get around too," she said. "Fritz is a doll. I hope he doesn't croak."

Oh, what the heck. If Jeff was going to look at me as a temporary employee, why couldn't I look at him as a temporary employer? "All right," I agreed. "I'll work full-time but let's definitely make this on a trial basis. If it doesn't work out then no hard feelings and I can go back to being part time, right?"

"Sounds like a plan to me," Jeff said.

"Will I make more money?"

"You'll be working twice as many hours so obviously you'll be making twice as much money," Jeff pointed out.

That wasn't what I meant. I opened my mouth to ask if I'd be making more money per hour but Caroline beat me to the punch. "She means will she get a raise. She'd better, Jeff. What you're paying her is pathetic."

"You want me to make her salaried?" Jeff sounded horrified.

"No, but give her at least twelve bucks an hour! Good grief, no one can live on what you're paying her."

"Our customer service gal makes the same and she lives on it quite nicely," Jeff said piously. "Perhaps she just has better money management skills than DeeDee."

"Or perhaps she has a rich boyfriend, which she does," Caroline corrected.

"DeeDee has a rich husband."

"I do not!" This talking about me like I wasn't in the room was getting irritating.

"Isn't your husband a college professor?" Jeff asked. "They make out like bandits. What do they work, twenty hours a week for some ridiculous salary? You're doing fine."

I knew that I should have gotten up and walked out the door but I didn't. I wanted that full-time job and even though it was neither Jeff's nor Caroline's business how much money Steve made, I found myself correcting their delusional thinking. "Steve works for a small, private college that isn't known for paying big bucks," I said hotly. "We aren't rich."

Jeff looked at me speculatively. After a few moments he said, "I can do twelve an hour but that's it. And don't expect a raise next year."

Again, I should have walked out his office door but I didn't. In addition to wanting the full-time job, I also wanted to do some sleuthing and find out who killed Kate Weston. The best way to do that would be to remain an employee at the newspaper. "Deal," I agreed. I didn't know how long I'd last at the paper but for the time being it was obviously the best place to be if I wanted to solve Kate's mysterious death.

"Then get to work," Jeff ordered. "Fifteen hundred words on your dinner with Fritz."

"It wasn't dinner—it was coffee and dessert."

"Whatever, DeeDee! Just write about it and get it back to me pronto!"

Caroline and I left Jeff's office and as we moved back toward our cubicles, Caroline patted me somewhat patronizingly on the shoulder. "You don't have to thank me, DeeDee. I would have done that for anyone. Now don't disappoint me and show me what a *real* journalist you can be. You go, girl!" With a final little ta-ta wave, she took a left toward her desk. I sat down at my own desk, my head spinning. Had that really just happened?

Ren leaned back. "You look like you're in shock. Everything okay?"

I nodded. "Jeff made me full-time."

"Good for you! Now you're really a part of the jungle."

Although Ren was joking, I sensed that there was a lot of truth in his statement. The newsroom did feel like a jungle much of the time and I was either the newest animal or the fresh meat. Only time would tell which.

Chapter Fifteen

It wasn't easy to write about what had happened to Fritz but after struggling over the piece for an hour or so, I came up with something that I didn't think was too horrible. I still didn't think it was a good idea or tasteful at all for the newspaper to feature an article on what it was like to sit with someone as they collapsed but since it was Jeff's newspaper, I figured that it was up to him to decide what he wanted. I thought the diet idea was better but, again, it wasn't my call. I sent the piece to Jeff and then just sat for a few minutes staring at the grey fabric walls of my cubicle. What had Fritz been about to tell me before he passed out? Why were Kate and Fritz business partners? How could I find out?

What I needed to do was find out more about Kate. I really knew precious little about my late boss. I knew she was married and I knew she had an obnoxious personality but that was about it. Maybe I should pay a condolence call on her husband and see what I could discover.

I frowned over the thought of doing that. It seemed so cynical, so self-serving to visit Kate's husband paying condolences that I didn't really feel. On the other hand, I was sure that Kate's husband would want to know who killed his wife just as much—if not more—than everyone else did. But how could I find out where Kate's husband lived? I couldn't ask Jeff or Ren or anyone else in the newsroom without raising a whole lot of uncomfortable questions.

Natalie. The receptionist/customer service representative/whatever the heck else was on her job description would be able to tell me who Kate's husband was and where he lived. Plus I wouldn't be afraid to ask her because there was nothing intimidating about Natalie, something that most definitely couldn't be said about the majority of the rest of the employees at the *Kemper Times.* Ren didn't scare me but I did sense a lot of frustration emanating from Ren that made him seem on edge more often than not. He didn't strike me as the violent type, but he really did seem like he was about to blow and I didn't want to be the one to trigger that volcano.

After Jeff approved my story on my meeting with Fritz, he gave me another assignment: Eden Academy's school board was meeting to introduce their new director. Yikes. "I had a rather unfortunate experience at Eden Academy," I told Jeff. "I was there when their previous director died."

"Craig Grey? He didn't die. He got canned."

"The one before Craig. Frank Ubermann."

Jeff waved his hand dismissively. "Ancient history. No one will even remember you. Besides, if you want to be a reporter you're going to have to get used to going to places where you might not be totally welcome. I need about four hundred words and get it to me before five. Thanks, DeeDee."

Grabbing my purse, I walked carefully down the narrow flight of stairs that led to the front reception area. As usual, Natalie was seated at her desk. "Hi, Natalie," I said, pausing on my way toward the door.

"Well, hello, DeeDee! I was just thinking about you!"

"You were?"

"The oldies station played something by Steve and Eydie Gorme and I remembered you said your husband's name is Steve. Am I right?" I nodded, knowing what was coming next. "That makes you Steve and DeeDee! That is so cute!"

It was cute, the first thousand times I'd heard it. However, I hadn't heard it lately since Steve and Eydie aren't exactly household names anymore. "I'm surprised you know who Steve and Eydie are," I remarked.

"Oh, I love the oldies," Natalie said. "Besides, I'm fifty-four so I remember them, sort of."

"Those were the days," I agreed. I changed the subject a little awkwardly. "I was thinking about Kate just now," I said.

Natalie's smile faded. "I think about her a lot," she admitted.

"She was married, wasn't she?"

"Uh huh. Her husband used to work on the newspaper but he left a long time ago."

"Is it true that they didn't have any kids?"

"No, it was just the two of them."

I shivered at the thought of being left alone if Steve died before me and was grateful for Jane and Tyler and that Steve has them too if I predecease him. "Where did they live?" I asked in what I hoped was a casual tone.

"Over on Claremont. Do you know that big white house with the white lions in front of them and the dolphin fountain?"

Everyone in Kemper knew the White House as it was called. The owners had ripped out the lawn and replaced it with shiny white rocks that were surrounded by a six foot high white metal fence. It was positively blinding when the sun hit all the white just right. "Yes. That's Kate's house?" Somehow I had pictured her living in a one bedroom apartment with cracked plaster and a hot plate instead of a real stove but that might have been because I was mentally projecting her *Kemper Times* office into her private life. "That's a mighty big house," I added. Either Kate was paid at least ten times what everyone else was paid on the newspaper or her husband had a very good job.

"It is," Natalie agreed, "and you should see the inside. You think the outside is white? Wear sunglasses if you ever stop over there. Every single thing inside is whiter than white. It's like someone had a fixation with Mr. Clean. Kate had the office Christmas party there once and I spent the entire evening petrified that I'd spill my glass of red wine on all that white shag carpeting."

"Shag carpeting? I didn't know anyone still had shag carpeting."

"I know. I didn't really like it but Kate was so proud of it." Natalie's large eyes welled with tears. "You know, I never liked Kate but no one should die the way that lady did. I can't imagine what kind of person would do that."

Neither could I. "It's awful," I agreed. "What's also awful is that whoever did it is still walking the streets. As far as I know, the police haven't found a suspect."

"Well, at least it's not one of us," Natalie said.

"How do you know that?" I questioned.

"If it was one of us, the police would be hanging around here a lot more," Natalie pointed out. "They questioned everybody, did all their evidence stuff and we haven't seen anyone in a blue uniform since. Doesn't that tell you that it can't be one of us?"

"I certainly hope you're right," I said soberly. "It scares me to death to think that someone who works for the newspaper might have killed Kate but on the other hand, it was such a bizarre crime that it almost seems like it would have had to have been an inside job, doesn't it?"

"What do you mean?"

"She was suffocated by a plumber's helper."

"So?"

I waved my hands helplessly in the air, not wanting to come out and say that if anyone chose a plumber's helper as a murder weapon, it seemed to me that they had to work for the newspaper. It was too fitting that Kate's irritating voice and horrible laugh had finally been silenced by such a utilitarian and apropos object. "It just seems odd to me," I finally said.

"Not to me. I'm guessing that whoever killed her grabbed the first object they found to do her in," Natalie surmised. "They probably whacked her on the head and then grabbed the plumber's helper and taped it to her mouth in case she came to and started screaming. It's very likely that they didn't even intend to kill her."

Natalie was speaking calmly, as if she was talking about a new recipe for pineapple upside down cake that she wanted to try. A sneaking suspicion crept into my mind. Was it possible that *Natalie* might have killed Kate? Kate was always spying on the poor woman and listening to her conversations. But could Natalie have a connection to Kutrate Kemicals? "But she was strangled," I said. "That's what killed her. The plumber's helper was like a bizarre afterthought."

Natalie considered my statement. "Maybe," she finally said. "Or maybe not. Who knows what the killer was thinking? The end result is the same. Now where are you off to, DeeDee?"

"Eden Academy to cover the school board meeting. Then I might go over to Kutrate Kemicals to see my daughter." And to learn if there was any news about Fritz.

Natalie looked interested. "Oh, really? I used to work there too."

Another connection to Kutrate Kemicals? "What did you do there?" I asked.

"I was Bernard Morton's secretary for about a year before I quit. Too high pressure and, believe it or not, the pay was about as bad as it is at the newspaper." Natalie laughed. "At least for the hourly staff. I hear the salaried staff does pretty well. Someone needs to tell the employers of this town that people cannot live on what they pay."

"That's for sure," a voice said from behind me. Caroline came down the steps and joined us. "I hope you appreciate how I stuck up for you, DeeDee," she added. "I know that you'd never ask for more money." She glanced over at Natalie. "I got DeeDee a full-time job on the newspaper and a raise," she bragged, snapping her fingers between Natalie's and my heads. "It happened just like that!"

"A temporary full-time job," I clarified. Caroline's attitude was annoying, like I was incapable of doing anything for myself, which might have been true but it was still irritating. "If it doesn't work out, it's not going to last."

"You're a bit of a Negative Nellie," Caroline remarked. "You need to lighten up, DeeDee. Being a downer is going to get you absolutely nowhere."

"Well, I should be going," I said, holding up my reporter's notebook. "I've got a story to do."

"Thanks to me!" Caroline said. "Tell you what—you can take me out to lunch next week. How does that sound?"

I laughed and did a semi-nod and shake of my head as I walked away. True, Caroline had spoken up to Jeff and I suppose had been the one to cinch my promotion for me but she was acting like she'd just given me a winning lottery ticket, something that I wasn't at all sure my new job at the newspaper would turn out to be.

I got into my car and headed for Eden Academy. As soon as I was through I planned to drive past Kate's house and see if her husband's car was in the driveway and if I had the nerve, I was going to knock on the door and introduce myself.

I swallowed a bit nervously, not at all sure what I was doing but at the same time knowing that I had to do *something.* Kate was dead, Fritz was in a coma and somehow or other the two events were connected. I was sure of it.

"Welcome to the White Elephant!" Kate Weston's husband opened the door widely and gave me a smile that was positively dazzling. He wasn't at all what I had expected. If I'd thought about the kind of man who would marry someone like Kate—which I hadn't—I would have imagined someone just as nerdy and geeky as Kate had been. Someone short and skinny with thick glasses and hair that needed cutting. The man I was looking at was none of those things. Tall with dark hair and stunning blue eyes, he looked a bit like Paul Newman in his prime—not that Paul Newman had ever been out of his prime. How on earth had Kate ever managed to bag this guy? "Do I know you?"

"Hello," I said as I realized that I didn't know Kate's husband's name. Some reporter I was! "I work at the *Kemper Times* and I was in the neighborhood and wanted—"

"To stop by and tell me how sorry you were about Kate's passing," he finished for me. "How kind of you. What's your name?"

"DeeDee Pearson."

Throwing back his head, Mr. Weston laughed. "The newbie!" he said. "Kate talked about you quite often right before she died. What did she call you? Her 'latest lamb to the slaughter.' Would you like to come in?"

"Just for a minute," I said. "I don't want to disturb you."

"You aren't disturbing me at all. I'd welcome the company, actually." He gestured for me to come in the house. Mr. Weston was dressed in a peacock blue silk bathrobe that had lots of gold embroidery all over it and silk pajama bottoms along with a pair of Ugg slippers. I knew they were Uggs because I'd gotten the same slippers for Steve last Christmas.

Oh, boy, Steve. My husband wasn't going to be pleased at all when he heard what I was doing but I was sure that the end would justify the means. Taking a deep breath, I stepped into the front hallway of the White Elephant.

I could see what Natalie meant about needing sunglasses. The glare off the white walls made me squint and although it didn't seem possible, the inside of the Weston house seemed brighter than the sunshine outdoors. "Wow," I said as my eyes teared up.

"I know," Kate's husband said sympathetically. "It's blinding, isn't it? What can I say? Kate loved white. Never wanted any color in the house. It was a thing of hers. One of her many 'things.'"

"Quirks, you mean?"

"Or affectations. Six of one, half a dozen of another. Let's go in the kitchen. I've started doing a little something there about this hideous color scheme—if you can call it that. Lack of a color scheme might be more accurate."

is robe flapping at his sides like a huge, oversized bird, Mr. Weston led me down the wide hallway to the back of the house. It was silly but as we walked I put my hand in my sweater pocket and found my phone. If he tried anything funny I'd be able to dial 911 faster than the speed of light.

"I'm Lou Grant, by the way," he said over one shoulder.

I couldn't have heard him correctly. "What?" I asked as I struggled to keep up with him. Even though he was wearing slippers, Kate's husband walked like he was racing to catch a bus.

"Lou Grant," he repeated. "Do you remember the old *Lou Grant* show or the *Mary Tyler Moore Show*?" We had reached the kitchen, a sparkling room filled with, naturally, white cupboards, walls and a floor that looked like a sheet of ice. Lou Grant—really?—hadn't been kidding when he said that he was doing something about the unrelenting tidal wave of white on white. Fortunately, there was relief from the snowy landscape on the other side of the room where a huge table was covered with a rainbow striped tablecloth. On top of the table was a box from Macy's. The box was open and I could see that it was filled with Fiestaware in every color offered.

"Of course, I remember *Lou Grant*," I said with a laugh. "That show is why I always wanted to work for a newspaper."

"Me too. I was born with the horrible name of Rudolph Fenton Weston but I legally changed it to Lou Grant in 1979 when I was eighteen. After my hero of the newsroom."

"Why didn't you change it to just Lou?" I asked.

"What fun would there be in that?" Lou Grant questioned. "Besides, no one remembers *Lou Grant* anymore, of course, just dinosaurs like us, DeeDee. Coffee? Or a glass of wine?"

"Coffee would be fine but I really didn't mean to take up a whole lot of your time. I just wanted to stop by and tell you how sorry I am for your loss."

Lou Grant looked at me quizzically before comprehension dawned in his sky blue eyes. "Oh, right, my loss! You mean Kate?"

"Well, yes," I said feeling slightly idiotic. Lou Grant most definitely wasn't acting like the grieving widower. If anything, he seemed quite chipper.

"How do I put this diplomatically? I guess there's really no way to do that although I should know that by now—I was married to the woman for thirty years. I'm going to be blunt with you, DeeDee. Kate and I got married because I had health insurance and she didn't. We were never romantically involved. We started out friends and that's what we remained, more or less, throughout our marriage."

I sat down on a white kitchen chair with a thump. I'm not completely naïve but I still always register a large degree of surprise when I hear about people having a marriage of convenience. Steve is my best friend in the entire world but he's also my husband and I can't imagine being in any other kind of marriage. What's the point? Why would anyone want a marriage of convenience? "Didn't Kate get health insurance when she started working at the newspaper?"

"Of course she did, although it was never a very good policy. As you will undoubtedly learn, DeeDee, the *Kemper Times* does everything on the cheap. My insurance policy was always better."

"I heard you once worked at the *Kemper Times.*"

"Yes, I did, about a million years ago. I'm actually the one who got Kate her job. I lobbied for her and since no one else applied, she got it. She owed me for that as well as for so many other things it created something of an imbalance in our relationship. There were times when I felt quite strongly that she resented me."

"Then why did you stay together?"

Lou Grant shrugged. "It was easier than splitting up. Maybe that tells you how lazy the two of us were but it's the truth. Besides, Kate came from a very wealthy family and once she came into her inheritance there was no way that I would leave her. Once and for all, I balanced our relationship by doing exactly what I wanted to do."

"What was that?"

"I became a househusband and let her decide just about everything while I got to do just about everything my little old heart desired." He cocked his head as he studied me. "You strike me as a nice, normal woman so I'm sure this is all very bizarre to you."

"Just a little," I admitted. "So Kate was the one with the white fetish?" I asked as I looked around the kitchen again.

"She certainly was. Now that she's gone I'm going to either sell the White Elephant or spend a whole ton of her money making it something I like. Who knows? I might even go hog wild and paint the living room red. Kate would be rolling in her grave if I hadn't had her cremated."

Wow, this guy was possibly thrilled to pieces that his wife was gone. Kate probably had a nice, fat life insurance policy on top of all of the family money that Lou Grant was now going to inherit. It wasn't surprising that he was so giddy. "I wonder who would have wanted to hurt her," I ventured, "although I suppose she might have interrupted a robbery in the newspaper building."

Lou Grant laughed loudly. "You are a babe in the woods, aren't you? Why would there ever be a robbery at the newspaper? There's no decent equipment in that building, not even a semi-decent coffee maker. I'm sure there's less than a hundred bucks in petty cash. There's nothing to steal in that dump. And who would want to hurt her? How much time do you have, DeeDee, because I could give you a list about half a mile long of people who would like to have killed my wife. She wasn't exactly a well-loved figure in Kemper. Everyone disliked her."

"Did you?" I asked feeling like the rudest person on the planet.

Lou Grant considered my question. "Sometimes," he admitted, "although I understood her. Not many people did. Let me put it this way; I appreciated her. Kate let me live my life exactly how I wanted to, no questions asked, and I did the same for her."

"Huh," I said, confused. Was Lou Grant talking about both of them having relationships outside of their marriage? He had to be. Well, that made sense since it didn't sound to me like they had any kind of marriage at all. "So what did Kate get out of being married to you?"

"Other than the insurance at the beginning of our relationship, I gave her respectability and freedom. Kate needed a husband to hide behind but she didn't want a real husband. I didn't ask her where she went or who she was with or what she was up to." He smirked. "I especially didn't ask who her current boy toy was."

I felt my eyes boggle inside my head. Of all the people I'd ever met, Kate Weston was about the last one I ever would have expected to have a 'boy toy.'

"Oh?" It occurred to me to wonder—briefly—why Lou Grant Weston was being so forthcoming with me, a complete stranger. Then I spied the almost empty bottle of vodka on the gleaming white counter and I had my answer. I could smell a faint whiff of alcohol emanating from him but he wasn't slurring his speech and he walked like he was perfectly sober. Perhaps alcohol had the effect on him of loosening his tongue.

"You look shocked. I know, it is surprising since Kate was so, well, unattractive. However, even the most unattractive people are able to attract attractive people if they have plenty of money. Which my dear, late wife most definitely did."

"Um, who was she seeing?" Whoever her latest boy toy was might provide a very big clue as to who killed Kate Weston.

Lou Grant picked up a Fiestaware coffee cup and took a large swallow, a smile tugging on the corners of his Paul Newmanesque mouth. "Her latest? He worked at Kutrate Kemicals. I do believe his name was something like Tex or Rex. Tex, I think."

It wouldn't be hard to track down someone named Tex working at Kutrate Kemicals. I had what I'd come for and now I wanted nothing more than to scoot down the white carpeted hallway and out the white front door and into the safety of my own car. I didn't feel unsafe with Lou Grant, but I didn't feel exactly comfortable with him either. I had one last question for him. "If you loved newspapers so much that you changed your name to Lou Grant after a character on a TV show about newspapers, why did you stop working at the *Kemper Times*?"

"I wasn't a reporter at the *Times,*" Lou Grant explained. "I was the newspaper's accountant. I got a much better paying gig at Kutrate Kemicals, actually, with far better insurance coverage."

"Why weren't you a reporter?"

"Because, my dear, I can't write worth a damn and I hate interviewing people. That's a lot harder than I bargained for. I contemplated changing my name back to Rudolph but I like Lou Grant. It has appeal. Lou Grant Weston. It has panache, just like me."

It did although it was something of a mouthful. "Well," I said, "I should be going. Thank you for talking to me and again, I'm sorry for your loss."

"Very kind of you," Lou Grant said as his cell phone started to chirp. "How about that coffee?"

"No, thanks. I've taken up enough of your time. I'll see myself out."

Walking out of the kitchen, I lingered for a moment to see who was calling Lou Grant.

"Hey," Lou Grant said, "I've been waiting on you...yeah...I'll be there. Give me an hour to clean myself up and then you'd better come over here because I'm half in the bag and the last thing I need is to get popped by the police. See you soon, Caroline."

Caroline?

I scooted down the long hallway and out the front door like I was being propelled by a giant catapult. Of course there was more than one person named Caroline living in Kemper but it was highly possible that the Caroline Lou Grant was talking to was none other than Caroline Osborn, ace reporter at the *Kemper Times.*

I got into my car and considered my next move. I wanted to go out to Kutrate Kemicals and see if I could track down Tex or Rex although if I did manage to find him I wasn't at all sure how I'd broach the subject of Kate with him. I also wanted to stay in my car and stake out the White Elephant to see who drove up and parked in the driveway in an hour. Well, there was no reason I couldn't do both. I knew what kind of car Caroline drove. I'd go out to Kutrate and then swing past Lou Grant's house on the way back home. Steve and I were going out to dinner so it wasn't like I had to rush home and throw something on the stove. I glanced at my watch. Almost four. Steve had a meeting until seven. I had plenty of time to drop by the paper and type up my story and then head out to Kutrate Kemicals. Putting my car into gear, I pointed it in the direction of the *Kemper Times*.

Chapter Sixteen

After finishing my story and leaving the paper for the day, it occurred to me that my best source of information about what was going on at Kutrate Kemicals was probably Jane but I seriously doubted that Jane would cooperate. After all, it was her job on the line. My second best source of information probably would have been Fritz Scheider but he was in a coma. Maybe this Tex or Rex would come through.

After parking in the visitors' lot, I walked to the main entrance. This was my fourth visit to Kutrate Kemicals in less than ten days and it was starting to feel familiar to me, almost like *I* worked there. An idea occurred to me as I entered the lobby area and smiled at the receptionist. "Hello," I said in a very mom-type voice, "do you remember me?"

The redheaded receptionist shook her head. "Not really."

I hesitated as I tried to choose between jogging her memory as Bob Meredith's assistant or Jane's mom. I decided to go with the role that made me much happier—Jane's mom. I'm Jane Pearson's mom."

"Oh, right, now I remember," the receptionist said. "You two don't look anything alike. Jane's so pretty. And thin."

I smiled. "Jane asked me to come in and pick up something from one of her co-workers. His name is Rex or Tex." I giggled in what I hoped was an absentminded middle-aged kind of way. "I can't remember which," I confided.

The receptionist looked sympathetic. "Don't worry about it, Mrs. Pearson. That happens a lot to people when they get older. My grandmother forgets things all the time."

No doubt about it; I didn't like young people.

"Jane must have meant Rex Folsom. He's the caretaker for her floor."

"The caretaker?"

"That's what Kutrate Kemicals calls custodians," the receptionist explained. "It sounds more PC than janitor."

Not seeing what difference the title made as long as the person was treated with the same respect as everyone else, I asked, "Do you know where I could find Rex?"

"Probably up on Jane's floor. He comes in at three o'clock so I imagine he's already started working."

"Is it okay if I just go up there?"

"Sure. You're practically family, Mrs. Pearson. Here at Kutrate Kemical, we treat our family well."

"Thanks…" I looked down at the receptionist's faux wood nameplate. "…Elizabeth."

"My pleasure. Just take that elevator to the seventh floor and you'll find Rex. You can't miss him."

I smiled my thanks at her again and walked toward the elevator. Elizabeth seemed happy working at Kutrate and Jane was usually happy with her job. Fritz, however, wasn't the least bit happy but that appeared to have more to do with his boss than the job he had. I'd have to see if Rex felt like he was part of the Kutrate Kemical family too.

Stepping off the elevator on the seventh floor, I glanced quickly in both directions but didn't see a single soul. Everyone must have quit for the day. I was trying to decide what to do next—flying by the seat of my pants often results in, well, flying by the seat of my pants—when a burly young man came around the corner pushing a cart full of cleaning supplies. He was on the short side but well-built with broad shoulders, a flat waist and muscular thighs that I could see through his very tight blue jeans. He had curly blond hair and was maybe twenty-five years old. If this was Rex I could see why Lou Grant had called him Kate's boy toy. He was practically an infant.

"Hey," he said when he spotted me. "Can I help you? Everyone's gone for the day."

I thought fast. I was tempted to lie and tell Rex that I was doing a human interest story on custodians but Elizabeth might tell him that I was Jane's mother and then I'd be in trouble with Jane. The next time I had a murder case to solve I was going to make sure that none of the members of my family had even the remotest of connections to it. "I hope so," I said brightly. "My daughter is Jane Pearson. I left something in her office and I'd like to get it. Could you open it for me? Elizabeth sent me up." I added that so Rex wouldn't think I was some crazy woman who'd wandered in off the street.

"Sure," Rex said agreeably. "I can see the resemblance between you and your daughter. Both beauties. When is Jane getting back from Vegas?"

This was one young person I liked. "She's back. She was in today but I imagine she's at the hospital now checking on Fritz." I mentally patted myself on the back for bringing Fritz into the conversation so neatly. My goal was to get as much out of Rex as fast as I possibly could without looking like I was pumping him and then get the heck out of Kutrate Kemicals.

"Oh, man, Fritz," Rex said as he swiped an electronic key over the lock on Jane's office door. "Bummer."

"You know him?"

"Sure. I used to be in his part of the building. We got tight, old Fritz and me. I hope he's going to be all right."

I plunged onward. "Our little town has had quite a few tragedies lately," I said somewhat inanely.

"I guess," Rex said. He opened the door and took a step back so that I could enter Jane's office.

"Like Fritz and that terrible murder at the newspaper. Kate Weston."

The expression on Rex's face morphed from pleasant to something I couldn't identify. Shocked? Upset? Angry? Possibly a combination of all three. "Did you know Kate?" he asked.

"Actually I work at the paper," I said. "Kate was my boss."

Rex sat down in a chair, a stricken look on his face. "I knew her too."

"You did?" I asked innocently. "How? Were you friends?"

"You could say that." Rex shook his head. "Phew, this still gets to me whenever I hear her name."

"I'm sorry. I didn't mean to upset you," I said gently. I really hadn't. What I'd meant to do was pump him but that seemed somewhat callous to me now. Rex was truly distraught. Maybe there was more to their relationship than I'd suspected since what I'd suspected had been shallow, cheap and vulgar.

"It's okay," Rex said, brushing a big hand across his eyes. Good grief, was he crying? The guy looked like he ate bricks for breakfast and washed them down with tequila. My guilt increased. I hadn't expected this kind of reaction.

"I take it you two were close?"

"We were more than close, Mrs. Pearson," Rex said in a husky voice. "I was in love with her."

"Please, call me DeeDee," I urged. I paused for a second as my mind tried to unscramble what he was telling me. How could a good looking and apparently nice young man like Rex ever be in love with someone like Kate? Not to speak ill of the dead but Kate was rude and nasty and not at all attractive. What had Rex seen in her? Besides all that, she was married. True, in name only, but she was still a married woman. "Um, would you like to talk about it?"

Rex considered for a second or two before saying, "Yeah, I would. I don't have anyone I can talk to. My mom lives in Honolulu and my grandma's dead. Would you mind if I did tell you about it?"

Although I didn't mind being compared to his mother, the grandmother allusion was a little annoying but I brushed it aside. Rex was about to open up to me in a big way so he could compare me to Lucretia Borgia for all I cared. "I'd be happy to listen," I said sincerely. I sat down in the chair next to his and opened my ears wide. I thought about taking notes since my memory can be a tad sketchy but decided against it. "Go ahead, Rex."

"Well, it all started about four months ago," Rex said, his eyes taking on a faraway gleam. "Kate and I met when I went down to the newspaper to put an ad in the classifieds. I was going to do it online but I didn't have a credit card. I don't have any credit cards. I don't believe in them."

Thinking of my stack of unpaid credit card bills, I wished that I could make the same statement. "All right, so you went down to the newspaper to put in an ad. How did you meet Kate? She works—worked—upstairs."

"I went to the wrong door and she opened it for me. I didn't know I wasn't supposed to use the back entrance. I was pulling on it and cursing up a storm when she opened it and stepped outside. I swear, DeeDee, I felt like I was looking at an angel when I saw her. The light hit her in exactly the right way and she had a kind of glow all around her, like an ember."

I swallowed as I remembered my late boss with her oversized glasses, mousy features and prominent upper teeth. Whoever said love is blind sure knew what he or she had been talking about. Well, maybe Kate behaved differently with Rex. She must have or he wouldn't be so broken up. "I'm sorry," I said.

Rex nodded. "Thank you. We started talking and I told her how I work here at Kutrate and she asked me out for a drink. One thing led to another and…" his voice trailed off leaving me to fill in the blanks. I did. Yuck.

"Excuse me for asking but you did know Kate was married, didn't you?" I asked gently.

"She was going to leave her husband. She told me that the first night we met."

I wondered if she meant it or if she'd just been telling Rex that to keep him interested. This was a more peculiar story than I'd expected. On the surface it sounded like love at first sight and that in itself was downright unbelievable from Rex's point of view but it was also pretty unbelievable that someone like Kate would be interested in someone like Rex. True, he was handsome and had a nice body but Kate struck me as something of a snob and not the kind of person who would date a janitor no matter what kind of job title was used to describe his line of work. "How long were the two of you together?"

"Right up until the end. As a matter of fact, we were talking about going on a vacation together when she died." Rex's eyes filled with tears. "We were going to go to a resort in Cancun where we could sit on the beach and sip Mai Tai's together. It was all-inclusive."

"I wonder who killed her," I said, watching Rex closely to see his reaction.

"I wonder that every second of every day," he answered fiercely. "If I ever find out, they're going to pay for taking my darling Kate's life, I promise you that."

Yikes, he sounded like he meant it. "Did Kate ever visit you here at Kutrate?"

Rex blushed. "Funny you should ask. This was our favorite trysting spot. Right after we met, Kate asked me to show her around the whole place. She was especially interested in the labs. I think it was that incredibly brilliant mind of hers that wanted to know everything about everything, you know?"

"Sure," I agreed. "Did Kate know Fritz Scheider?"

"I'm not sure but she seemed to like his lab the best. Especially his secret lab."

"His secret lab?" I sure hoped Rex never got kidnapped by some enemy government. He wouldn't have to even be tortured to spill his guts. The guy apparently had been born without any kind of filter.

"Yeah, it's way down in the bowels of the building. He used to work on all his top secret inventions down there. Kate really liked to see that."

"I wonder why?"

"Who knows? Like I said, just incredibly curious in addition to being brilliant and beautiful."

Oh, this poor delusional man! He needed to get back to reality as quickly as possible. I only hoped he met a nice woman who could snap him out of his fantasy world. "That must be it," I agreed. "I'll have to ask Jane about Fritz's secret lab."

"I doubt she knows about it. Not many people here do."

"So Kate never said that she knew Fritz?"

Rex shrugged. "I don't think so. Why?"

"Well, I'm an acquaintance of Fritz's and he told me that there was a connection between Kate's death and Kutrate Kemicals although I'm starting to wonder if maybe the connection isn't between the newspaper and Kutrate." Maybe it was stupid of me to share that with Rex, a man I'd known for all of ten minutes, but I didn't see much point in keeping the information to myself. I suppose I should hope that I never get kidnaped by an enemy country since I don't seem to have a filter either.

"Come to think of it, I guess they did know each other. I'd forgotten about it until you said that." Rex looked a little alarmed. "It was like the second time we came over here for a visit and we ran into Fritz in the vending machine room. I was buying Kate a king-sized Snickers bar and I bought myself some sweet and sour beef jerky." He sighed deeply over the memory.

"How did they hit it off?"

"What do you mean?"

"Well, did they act like they knew each other?" Truly, I didn't know what I was searching for but there had to be something memorable about the meeting. Fritz had said that they used to be business partners. "Like they'd met each other before?"

"Let me think. She said she liked his tie and he said he liked her thin ankles. She did have cute ankles. Does that help?"

"I don't know. How did Kate react when Fritz said that about her ankles?"

Rex thought for a moment. "She laughed and said, 'you would.' I didn't know what she meant so I asked her about that later. She said that Fritz struck her as the type of man who liked his women very thin and very rich. Then she said, 'like all men.' I didn't get that because I personally don't care how much money a woman has and I also like girls who are a little on the hefty side. Kate was beautiful but she would have been even more beautiful if she'd added a few pounds. We ate out constantly but she never gained an ounce."

"She didn't?"

Rex shook his head. "I had to work out to compensate for all the rich meals we had but Kate stayed mean and lean."

It sounded as if Kate might have had access to a can of 'Fat Off' of her own. "How interesting," I said. Suddenly we heard footsteps in the hallway and we both jumped up as if we'd been doing something immoral or illegal.

"I should be getting back to work," Rex said.

"Thanks for talking to me, Rex. Just one more question."

"Sure."

"Do you know what kind of business connection Kate and Fritz had?"

"I don't know. We never talked about business." Rex blushed. "We just talked about life and how much we loved each other."

Poor Rex. While it was possible that Kate wasn't as loathsome as I thought, I still had a hard time convincing myself that she returned his feelings quite as sincerely. Rex continued. "Thank you for listening to me, Mrs. Pearson. I needed to talk about Kate."

"It was my pleasure," I assured him. We left Jane's office together and Rex pulled the door shut behind us, giving the handle a good tug to make sure it was locked. He nodded at me before heading back toward his equipment cart and I started for the elevator. I was almost there when I practically ran into Bernard Morton. *Rats,* I thought as I looked at my daughter's boss. I had almost been home free.

"Well, if it isn't Mrs. Pearson!" Bernard said in a loud, hearty voice. "Fancy running into you again. You know, we've really got to stop meeting like this. People are going to start talking about us pretty soon."

"I was just getting something from Jane's office," I said lamely, shoving my empty hands into the pockets of my jacket.

"What?" Bernard asked.

Feeling around for something, I detected a piece of gum, what felt like a crumpled lottery ticket and my car keys. Deftly pulling off the *BEST MOM EVER* keychain Tyler had given me on Mother's Day when he was ten, I held it out for Bernard to see. "This. I dropped it in here the other day. At least I *thought* I dropped it in here—I've been searching for it for days when I remembered that I'd visited Jane and maybe it was in her office. Rex was nice enough to let me in and I found out."

Bernard stared down at the inexpensive keychain. "You spent days looking for that?"

"It has a lot of sentimental value to me," I told him. "My son gave it to me. I'd be very upset if I lost it."

"What is it?"

"A keychain."

"How did you get home if you left your keys in your daughter's office?" Bernard asked in a very triumphant tone of voice.

"I had another set in my purse."

Bernard raised a bushy eyebrow but dropped the subject. "Did you have a nice chat with Rex?"

"He just opened Jane's office for me," I lied. I didn't want to get Rex in trouble and I had the feeling that a janitor or caretaker or whatever term Kutrate Kemicals used for the hired help talking to an outsider on company time was not going to go over too well with the Big Boss.

"Oh?" Bernard said, that one eyebrow still cocked like a furry comma in the middle of his forehead. "I happened to be glancing at one of our security cameras when Rex let you into your daughter's office and I noticed that you were in there for a good five minutes. You didn't talk at all during that entire five minutes?"

"We chatted a bit," I relented.

"About what?"

My father always used to say *N.O.Y.D.B.* whenever I asked a question he thought was None of Your Damn Business. I hadn't heard that expression for years but I longed to say it to Bernard at that moment. "Just things."

"Such as?"

"I can't really remember," I said. "Now I've got to run. My husband is home cleaning out his gun closet and he gets quite upset if I don't have dinner on the table at precisely six o'clock on gun cleaning day." Steve doesn't even own a pellet gun but Bernard Morton didn't know that.

Bernard didn't look scared or impressed. "Are you sure you have to go?" he semi-snarled. "There are a few things I'd like to discuss with you, DeeDee."

No more Mrs. Pearson. Not that I minded that too much—Bernard and I were roughly the same age and it always made me feel old when someone around my age called me Mrs. Pearson. Especially when they said it in a snotty, sarcastic tone like the one Bernard Morton was using. "Perhaps some other time," I said sweetly. "My husband can be a real bear if I'm not home on time."

Bernard put out a hand and put a firm grip on my lower right arm. "I can be a bear sometimes too, DeeDee. Especially with my employees. Did you know that Jane's annual review is coming up? I'd certainly like to give her the best review possible."

That sounded like a threat to me, a threat that if it came true would result in Jane not only losing her job but never speaking to me again for the rest of my natural life. "I guess I could find a few minutes to talk to you," I said.

"Then let's go to my office," Bernard suggested, his iron grip still on my arm. "It's two floors up. I'm sure you remember that from your visit here with Bob Meredith."

We rode up to the top floor of Kutrate Kemicals in a strained silence. I was desperately trying to figure out what I was going to tell Bernard about my conversation with Rex and also how I could gracefully get out of his office and off the Kutrate Kemicals grounds as quickly as was humanly possible.

Bernard walked purposely toward his office while I trailed a step or two behind, glancing into every office we passed, desperately hoping to see another human being but I didn't see a soul. Maybe Rex would appear to vacuum or another caretaker would show up.

"Have a seat," Bernard said after he pushed open the heavy mahogany door of his office. "Want a drink?"

"Oh, no," I demurred although I could have really gone for a nice big glass of wine at that moment.

Bernard shrugged and went to his bar and poured a tumbler full of scotch. He added a single ice cube and the tiniest splash of soda I'd ever seen. It was like a Barbie-sized splash of soda. Carrying the glass to his desk, he sat down. "Now," he said after taking a long gulp. "Let's chat. I'd like to know exactly what you and that lame brain Rex were talking about for seven minutes and forty-three seconds."

"How do you know how long we were talking?" I questioned.

Bernard pointed at his computer screen and touched his mouse pad. The screen lit up and I saw that it was focused on Jane's office. Rex came into view pushing a vacuum cleaner. The noise from the cleaner was horrendous, a hundred times louder than it was in reality. "That's how I know," he said.

"If you were listening, you must know what we were talking about."

"I couldn't hear everything. When you went into Jane's office I couldn't hear a thing. Rex was mumbling and you've got a very soft voice, DeeDee. You should really work on that."

"To make it easier the next time a private conversation I'm having is being listened to by a third party?" I asked.

"Well, yes," Bernard agreed. "That wasn't thoughtful of you at all, DeeDee, and you strike me as a very thoughtful person. The kind of woman who bakes cookies for new neighbors and takes care of lost puppies. Am I right?"

"Pretty much." I made a show of looking at my watch.

"Tell me what you and Rex were talking about and I'll walk you to your car."

"Why are you so interested?" I asked although I already knew the answer. Bernard obviously had a paranoia complex working overtime inside his head, hence the cameras and microphones. Just like Kate Weston had.

"Because I'm interested in every facet of what is going on in my company," Bernard replied. "Take, for instance, your daughter. Jane is obviously a go-getter and could go quite far at Kutrate Kemicals. Provided there aren't any roadblocks thrown in her way."

Not being a complete idiot, I was able to read between the lines of what Bernard was saying. Either I told him what Rex and I had discussed or he'd start sharp shooting Jane. Great. I was going to get Jane in trouble without even trying. For a split second I vacillated between coming up with some big fat lie or telling Bernard the truth. The truth won since it was so much easier. I don't think that fast anymore and I've always been a lousy liar. "Rex and I were talking about Kate Weston."

Bernard flinched like I'd just slapped him. "Why?"

"Because we both knew her. She was my boss at the newspaper and Rex was her…friend."

"But why would you be discussing her?"

"I just told you. We each had a connection to her and she was murdered. It's shocking when someone you know dies but it's even more shocking when they're murdered. And then what happened to Fritz—"

"Fritz Scheider choked or had a stroke or something. Once he pulls out of that coma he'll be fine."

"We don't know that," I replied. "He might have been poisoned for all we know."

"He choked on whatever he was eating," Bernard insisted. "I was there and I saw the whole thing."

"I was there too," I reminded him. "I was sitting at the same table as Bernard but I don't know for sure that he choked and neither do you."

"What's your interest in all of this? What do you care if Fritz was poisoned or not?"

"I'm a journalist," I reminded him. "Of course I'm interested!"

Bernard squinted at me for several long and uncomfortable moments. I had the feeling that he wanted to grill me some more but I also had the feeling that he didn't think he'd learn much. "Why don't I walk you to your car?" he finally said.

"That isn't necessary in the least," I told him as I got to my feet. "I'd prefer to walk by myself. If it's all right for me to leave, that is."

Putting a butter-wouldn't-melt-in-his-mouth expression on his face, Bernard looked at me innocently. "You were never being held here against your will, DeeDee. I simply wanted to talk to you in private."

Right. And I'm constantly being mistaken for Angelina Jolie. "If you'll excuse me," I said stiffly. "My husband is going to be wondering where I am."

Bernard followed me to his office door, too closely for my taste, and put a large, sweaty hand on my arm as I reached for the door knob. "It's been pleasant talking to you, DeeDee, but I have a brief word of advice: don't bother wasting your time trying to figure out who killed Kate Weston or if Fritz was poisoned. People like you should stick to things you know—baking and cleaning and taking care of that husband of yours."

Although he might have had a point, I didn't appreciate his comment or the patronizing tone he used to deliver it. "Thanks for the advice," I said curtly, biting my tongue to make sure I didn't add anything else. After all, this creep was Jane's boss and I'd done enough to jeopardize her job. But one thing I knew for sure: as soon as I got home I was going to start a campaign encouraging Jane to start finding a job someplace—any place—else. Bernard Morton was not the kind of person I wanted my daughter, or anyone else's child, to work for. The guy was a jerk through and through.

Safely in the hallway, I half walked, half ran to the elevator that would bring me back into the world and away from the oh-so-slimy Bernard Morton. Thankfully, the elevator doors were open and I slid inside and pushed the *L* for *Lobby* button quickly. The doors shut and for the first time since arriving at Kutrate Kemicals a half an hour or so earlier, I felt the tension in my shoulder muscles relax slightly although they still felt as tight as steel cords. That man was unbelievable! He was either the most paranoid person on the planet or he had something to hide. Something shady that involved not only Fritz Scheider but the murder of Kate Weston and more than likely Kutrate Kemicals.

It has to be 'Fat Off.' That's the connection, only how?

Thinking hard, I hit the lobby running and within about thirty seconds was behind the wheel and headed straight for home, completely forgetting about going back to Lou Grant's to spy on his mystery guest. All I wanted was to get home as quickly as I possibly could.

"DeeDee, this is too dangerous," Steve said. We were sitting at the kitchen table an hour later over a meal that I'd thrown together from boxes, mixes and whatever I could find in the freezer. Although I'm sure the end result was unbelievably high in sodium and chemicals, it tasted pretty good but that might have been because of my chat with Bernard. Near death experiences often ignite a person's appetite. "I forbid you to do any more investigating into either your boss's murder *or* what happened to Fritz."

I helped myself to some more macaroni and cheese. "Since when have you ever *forbidden* me to do anything? We don't have that kind of marriage, Steve."

"Maybe we should," he said darkly. "I don't like this, DeeDee. I don't like it one little bit."

"Well, neither do I but we can't just let it go. Jane works for that man, remember? It's our moral duty to find out if he was involved with Kate's death. I'm pretty sure he had something to do with Fritz's."

"But how can *you* do anything?" Steve persisted. "Leave it to the police. That's what they're paid to do. You're not a detective or anything resembling any kind of sleuth, honey. You're a wife and a mom and a journalist. Stick with the things you know."

Although I was happy that he'd remembered to include journalist in the list, I wasn't about to let anything go. "Steve, Jane works at Kutrate Kemicals. She works for Bernard Morton. Something stinks in that whole set up and I'd bet my last dollar that it's directly related to 'Fat Off' and that man. I think Kate found out about 'Fat Off' and was planning to do an expose on it. Bernard must have found out and killed her. Maybe Fritz knew about it and that was what he was going to tell me at the Coffee Hut the other night."

"People like Bernard Morton don't go around killing people. They hire other people to do the killing for them. Besides, why would he kill her when he could just buy her off?"

"Maybe Kate wasn't interested in being bought off. Maybe she was shooting for the Pulitzer. She was plenty rich on her own, remember. Her house is extremely tacky but it takes some mighty big bucks to be *that* tacky. Besides, everyone has been saying that all she cared about was her job at the paper. It makes sense that she was planning some kind of expose that would make her famous."

"And that's another thing," Steve said. "I don't like you going to strange men's houses by yourself. Kate's husband could have been some kind of weirdo who might have attacked you when you started asking nosy questions."

"He's weird but he isn't a weirdo. I can tell the difference."

"I'm sure you can but you didn't know that until you were inside his house. If he'd been a weirdo instead of weird, it would have been too late for you to do anything about it."

"And what about that thing Fritz said, about Kate being his business partner? Maybe she owned a piece of 'Fat Off.'"

"Then why would she write an expose?"

"I don't know. Maybe Fritz decided to freeze her out and that's when she decided to write something up."

"That's a whole lot of maybes."

"I have another one for you."

"What?"

"Maybe you could help me out," I suggested.

Steve snorted. "How could I possibly help you out?"

"I'm not sure yet but I know we could think of something. You were a huge help when we were trying to figure out who killed Frank Ubermann."

"I'd never describe what I did as a 'huge' help but if there's something I can do, just say the word. You're sticking your nose into places where it doesn't belong and if I can't stop you, I'd like to be around to make sure you don't get into any trouble."

I smiled. "Thanks, honey. You're one in a million."

"So are you and that's why I'd like to keep you alive until we retire. I'm too old to find another wife."

"You smooth talker," I laughed. "Now let's figure out our next move."

"That's up to you," Steve responded. "Just tell me where to be and what to say and I'm good. Now if you don't mind, that new cable channel is rerunning *The Dick Cavett Show* and I want to watch it."

"Have fun," I told him. "I'll clean up in here. I'll join you in a few minutes."

Steve's offer got my mind running and as I cleaned the kitchen I tried to figure out what was going on. It was clear that Bernard Morton was up to something but what that something was I couldn't quite see. After loading the dishwasher, wiping down the counters and getting the coffee ready for the morning, I sat down at the kitchen table with a legal pad and a sharp pencil. On the pad I wrote:

Who killed Kate Weston? Why? Was Fritz poisoned?

Chewing the eraser end of the pencil, I decided that Kate might have been killed by anyone. Her fellow employees hated her and her husband didn't seem all that fond of her either but my money was on somebody Bernard Morton hired to permanently shut her up. That had to be the connection between Kate and Fritz. Fritz knew that Bernard had hired someone to kill Kate and he was going to spill his guts to me, the only person he knew who worked for a newspaper. Bernard stopped that from happening by somehow poisoning him. Maybe he paid off someone in the kitchen at the Coffee

Hut, gave him or her a thousand bucks to slip some kind of poison into Fritz's slice of pecan pie. Bernard had to have access to all kinds of chemicals since he was the head of his own chemical company.

Of course, I reminded myself, I didn't know for sure that Fritz had been poisoned. He might have had a heart attack or a stroke but the timing of his attack did seem mighty coincidental to me.

Who is the most likely person to know about the business connection between Kate and Fritz?

Again, pencil chewing time. I stared at the sheet of paper and tried to pinpoint someone who had a connection to both Fritz and Kate. Jane? No, she didn't know Kate. Me? I barely knew Fritz and my relationship with Kate was almost brand new. I thought some more but couldn't come up with anyone. Fritz knew the most and at the moment he couldn't tell me a thing. Frustrated, I crumpled the paper up and threw it in the recycling basket. The problem was that I didn't know what I was doing, a problem that had often plagued me throughout my entire life. I didn't know enough about the newspaper or Kutrate Kemicals or Kate or Fritz or Bernard Morton to figure out what the heck had happened.

So find out. You're a journalist now. Start asking the hard questions. Do some digging. Research. Sitting at the kitchen table feeling sorry for yourself isn't going to solve anything!

All true. I got up and headed for the family room. Time to pull out my laptop and see what I could discover.

"This is great," Steve told me when I sat down next to him. "Dick Cavett is talking about Watergate. I'd forgotten most of this stuff."

Looking at the television set, I watched a young Dick Cavett talk about the Watergate scandal. As he talked, I remembered how Carl Bernstein and Bob Woodward had broken that scandal. They had been newspaper reporters assigned to cover the break in at a hotel named the Watergate. The result of their coverage had been the resignation of the President of the United States and an entire country changed forever. But they had a Deep Throat to help them. My Deep Throat was in a coma. I was on my own.

Chapter Seventeen

"I know what you can do," I told Steve excitedly, shaking his shoulder to wake him up. It was almost three in the morning and Steve had to get up at seven but I couldn't wait until then. If I waited, I might forget my idea and once I forgot it I knew that I'd never be able to retrieve it. There's something about hitting fifty that makes remembering things, even important things, an often impossible task.

"What is it?" Steve bolted up and reached for his glasses. "What's the matter? Is it one of the kids?"

"Everything's fine," I quickly assured him. "But I had an idea of how you can help me figure out who killed Kate and Fritz!"

"DeeDee," Steve moaned, put his glasses back on his nightstand and fell back on his pillow. "Can't this wait?" He pulled the pillow over his face.

"It could but I'm afraid I'll forget. Just listen, Steve. This will just take a minute. What if we did the same thing we did when we were trying to figure out who killed Frank Ubermann? Remember how you pretended you wanted to buy a piece of pottery from Jack Mulholland so you could question him?"

Steve's voice was muffled. "Yes. I also remember that I ended up paying eighty bucks for four of the ugliest mugs on the planet. Didn't we wind up giving them to Goodwill?"

"That's beside the point," I said impatiently. "The point is that you could do the same thing at Kutrate Kemicals."

Steve pulled the pillow off his face and lifted his head to glare at me. "How could I do that?"

"You could pretend you were a salesman and tell them that you heard about a new weight loss product and you want to get in on the ground floor."

"And how would that help you find out who killed Kate or Fritz?"

"Well," I elaborated, "if you talked to Bernard Morton and he got all upset and nervous, we'd know that he was involved."

"I hardly think a salesman would talk to the president of the company," Steve said. "Especially a fake salesman. Besides, I don't know anything about sales or diet products or chemicals or anything remotely related to Kutrate Kemicals."

He sounded a little irritated and I knew that I should drop it but I was too wound up to stop. "Then you could pretend you want to work there," I suggested. This was my Plan B and while I knew the odds were extremely low that Steve would go for it, I was willing to give it a shot.

"Doing what? I'm not qualified to do anything at Kutrate Kemicals other than clean at night after everyone has gone home."

"That's it!" I said, bouncing up and down. "I knew you'd think of something! That would be perfect, Steve!"

"DeeDee," Steve said, "I have a full-time job that takes up all of my energy. How would I ever be able to do another job at night?"

"You wouldn't have to do it forever," I pointed out. "Plus you have a vacation coming up. You could do it then."

"I didn't plan on spending my vacation working as a custodian at Kutrate Kemicals. Why don't you suggest your idea to Tyler? He's not doing anything. Although I doubt Kutrate will hire him," Steve added grumpily. "Your son doesn't have the most stellar work history."

"That's a great idea! I'll talk to Tyler in the morning. Now go back to sleep," I told him, lying down myself. "You're keeping me up."

A few minutes later, I heard the deep, even sound of Steve's breathing and knew that he'd fallen back to sleep. I also knew that I wasn't going to be so lucky. My mind was racing but in a good way. Tyler working at Kutrate would be perfect. Now I had to find out if there were any openings and what Tyler needed to do to apply. Who knew? Maybe he'd like working there and might be able to get benefits like health insurance and PTO. It had to beat his current job of doing exactly nothing.

I finally fell asleep around four after setting my mental alarm clock for seven. I wanted to talk to Tyler as early as I possibly could. Leave it to Steve to give me a great suggestion. Whoever said that marriage was a two-part invention sure knew what they were talking about.

"I'll do it," Tyler said immediately. "I've always wanted to work the night shift. I don't know why I didn't think of applying there myself."

"It's not a glamour job," I cautioned. "Being a custodian is hard work and it doesn't pay very well." I had already looked up openings at Kutrate Kemicals and there were several custodial positions available immediately. They didn't pay well at all but on the other hand, whatever they paid was more than what Tyler was currently making which was whatever I gave him.

"I know that but it's honorable work," Tyler said. "Where would the world be if people didn't clean it up at night? I think it might be a very cool job. Plus I could sleep all day without Dad having a hissy fit."

"If you don't like it, you can quit. This is just to find out some information for me about Kutrate Kemicals."

"I can do both," Tyler said with a wave of his hand. "I don't want anyone to know that Jane is my sister or that I'm spying so I'll keep a very low profile. After all, if I like it I don't want the bosses to know I'm a snitch."

"You aren't a snitch. You're an investigator."

"That sounds good," Tyler agreed. "How do I apply?"

After showing Tyler the website, I left for work. I had an interview lined up for later that morning but before I left I wanted to do a little sleuthing on my own. First on my list: another chat with some of my co-workers. Everyone seemed too casual about Kate's death to me. While I didn't expect anyone to be all that broken up—the woman hadn't exactly incited sympathy in anyone—I did think that there should be some kind of emotions cropping up around the newspaper. My gosh, we were a bunch of reporters, but no one seemed interested in figuring out who killed Kate. Or why. Shouldn't there be at least some professional curiosity about her death?

At work I went into the break room to start a fresh pot of coffee, a job that seemed to be permanently mine. I was okay with that although I did always take a fast look around to make sure Caroline wasn't within striking distance when I was brewing coffee. Even though I knew it was her problem and not mine, I still didn't want to deal with it.

The coffee was almost ready when Bob Meredith came into the room. "Ah, the fair DeeDee!" he exclaimed. "Our Coffee Queen! Our Earth Mother of the Humble Coffee Bean!"

"Hi, Bob," I said. "You're just in time."

"I planned it that way. Did you know that it takes exactly nineteen minutes from your arrival to a fresh pot of coffee? I've been watching you. And timing you."

"How observant," I said.

"I am an award-winning journalist," Bob reminded me. "It's my duty to be aware of the details."

"I see." Here was an opening if ever I'd heard one. "So what do you think about Kate's death? What kind of details have you observed about that?"

Bob almost spilled the mug of coffee he was holding all over the front of his blue jeans. "What?" he asked in a hearty voice—a little too hearty voice—after setting the mug down and shooting me an ingenuous glance. "I for one don't know who offed that crazy woman. Nor do I care."

"You just said that it's your duty to be aware of details," I said. "Don't you think someone getting murdered in this very building would require a little investigation from the rest of us?"

"It's a touchy scenario, DeeDee. Kate was our boss; she was killed on site and nobody wants to do the digging and then discover that it was one of us. Especially since none of us really care who killed Kate. We're just glad she's gone."

"That's terrible," I said.

"But true. You didn't know her well, DeeDee, but I think you'd been around Kate Weston long enough to have realized that the woman didn't exactly inspire admiration in her employees. Or underlings, as she preferred to call us."

"That still doesn't mean that we shouldn't be trying to figure out who killed her."

Bob shrugged. "Maybe you're right. I know it looks pretty bad that a bunch of reporters aren't investigating a murder that hit so close to home. I really am sorry about that and I suppose it just shows how burned out we all are. Now I have a question for you."

"What?" I asked a little warily.

"Haven't you noticed how much nicer it is to be at work without Kate here?"

"Well, sure, but—"

"See what I mean, DeeDee? What's done is done. Let the police figure it out and when they do, I'll write up another prize-winning story. Until then, if I were you, I'd let it go."

Maybe it was sound advice but it didn't seem like good advice to me. It seemed heartless and cold and cruel. But I had a strong feeling that it was also going to be the advice I'd get from everyone else at the *Kemper Times.* "I don't know," I began. "I can't let it go. It seems wrong to me that no one around here cares."

"Suit yourself," Bob said shortly as he turned to leave the break room. He was almost through the door when he tossed over his shoulder, "But if you're determined to keep on 'investigating,' I suggest that you don't look too far from your very own cubicle."

"What does that mean?" I called out, but Bob had already vanished. Was Bob talking about Ren? I'd suspected Ren myself but I still couldn't square the nice guy who sat next to me with a cold-blooded killer. I poured myself a cup of coffee and then on a whim fixed one for Ren. I usually brought Jeff coffee in the morning but Bob's words were sticking in my head. Ren was right next to my cubicle. Was Bob implicating Ren in Kate's murder? He seemed like an unlikely suspect but everyone knows that the least likely suspect is usually the guilty one. Jeff could get his own coffee this morning.

I found Ren in his usual hunched over position in his cubicle. "Good morning," I said cheerfully. "How about a fresh cup of coffee?"

Ren lifted his head and looked at me bleary eyed. "You're a life saver, DeeDee," he said as he reached for the cup. His hands were trembling and he looked like he hadn't slept for a week. Noting the stubble on his chin, his bloodshot eyes and his clothes—the same clothes he'd been wearing the day before—I asked, "My goodness, Ren, have you been here all night?"

Ren took a long gulp of coffee. "Yep. My feature for Sunday crapped out on me. I had to work double time to fill the front page."

No one so dedicated could be a killer. Still, I had to do some fishing. "I was just talking to Bob about who might have killed Kate."

Ren looked at me from over the rim of his coffee cup. "Oh, yeah? Any insights?"

"None at all. How about you? Who do you think did it?"

"Frankly, I don't really care. Sorry if that sounds cold but I've got bigger fish to fry. I've got two more stories for the Sunday Lifestyles and I'm still short a column."

"I thought you wrote the Sunday column yourself."

"I usually do but my mind has gone completely blank. It's weird, DeeDee. Totally shot. I feel like someone erased my brain at some point over the past twelve hours." Ren's gaze suddenly sharpened. "Hey, DeeDee, you could do me a huge favor."

"Name it," I said.

"Would you be able to write this week's column for me? You could be my guest columnist."

"What?" My heart pounded with excitement. "I'd love to do that! What should I write about?"

"Your pick," Ren said magnanimously. "Seven hundred and fifty words and I need them by five o'clock Friday at the latest. Think you can handle that?"

"Of course I can!" A dark thought hit me. "What will Jeff say? Don't we need his permission?"

"Who cares?" Ren responded a little sharply. He reeled himself back in. "He won't remember if he gave his permission or not. I'm sorry, but I'm more than a little tired of waiting to get the green light from Jeff to do anything other than the most boring, formulaic crap that this paper regularly turns out. Let's make this a real newspaper again."

"I'm not exactly the person you want to use if you're trying to make this a real newspaper again," I reluctantly said.

Ren shook his head. "Don't sell yourself short, DeeDee. I've read the stories you've written and you have a nice style. I'm betting that you'll give me a great column. Just do me one favor."

"Name it!"

"Don't make it too cute and momsy or all about your hubby. That kind of stuff makes me gag. I want something fresh and different. Shock me."

"Shock you?"

"Shock me," Ren repeated. "This paper and its readers need some shaking up. Are you game?"

"Totally," I assured him. I turned to my computer. Now my hands were shaking. Writing a column was going to be completely different from doing a story on a local theater group or any of the other fluff pieces that I'd been doing. While I was thrilled that Ren had asked me, I was also more than a touch nervous. What did I know about writing a column? Worse, what did I have to write about if I couldn't write about being a mom or Steve or anything else cute in my life? I was basically a cute kind of gal. I didn't know anything else.

Still, if fresh and different was what Ren wanted, then fresh and different was what he was going to get. Staring at my computer, I thought long and hard about something that I hadn't seen in the *Kemper Times* before. Finally, after twenty intense minutes, I got an idea and began to write. As I worked at my computer, a stray thought popped into my head. Had Ren asked me to write a column because he really needed my help or was he just throwing me a bone to get me to stop asking him about Kate's murder?

Now who's paranoid? I asked myself. Still, it was a little strange. Well, strange or not, Ren had asked me to write a shocking column for him and that was exactly what I intended to do. Shock him.

"Mom? I got the job!" Tyler's voice was excited.

"You did? What happened, did they hire you on the spot? You just had the interview today!" I was home, in my kitchen where I belonged. Dinner—cheeseburgers, a tomato salad and chocolate cake for dessert—was ready and I was enjoying a well-earned glass of sauvignon blanc. Writing a column was much more demanding than I'd anticipated. How had Erma Bombeck churned out two a week for years and years and years?

"Yeah, they did," Tyler said proudly. "They asked me if I could start tonight. I work seven to three. Kind of sucky hours but I can still see friends after work."

"At three in the morning? Who do you know who's still up at that hour?" I forced myself to stop talking. Sometimes I sound like such a mom that I don't know how Jane and Tyler stand me. "Never mind. You're an adult. You can see whomever you want whenever you want."

Tyler laughed. "Thanks. Hey, listen, if this works out I'm going to get an apartment of my own. I think I could get into working for Kutrate Kemicals for the rest of my life."

As a custodian? I bit my tongue. Like Tyler had said, any job was an honorable job and in Tyler's case, any job was a good job. Although I had dreamed of my only son being a lawyer or a doctor, I'd be happy to have him working steadily. "Good for you," I said warmly.

"Now what exactly do you want me to do?"

"Where are you?" I asked.

"About three blocks from home."

"Come home and have dinner," I instructed. "We can talk then."

"All right. See you in a few."

Tyler hung up and I put the finishing touches on dinner. Steve had a meeting that night and while I usually miss him when he doesn't come home for dinner, I was glad that he was going to miss tonight's meal. I didn't want him to hear Tyler and me scheme. When Tyler breezed through the back door five minutes later, I was setting the table. "Hi!" I said. "Congratulations!"

"Thanks," Tyler said. "You know, I'm really glad you steered me in the direction of Kutrate Kemicals. I never would have thought of applying there since Sister Dearest is also employed by them."

"Did you tell them that?"

"Yeah, I had to. They ask on the application if you have any relatives working there but since we'll be in completely different areas it doesn't matter. Jane is white collar while I'm strictly blue."

"Nothing wrong with that," I said.

"You've got that right. I think that's been my problem, Mom. I've been thinking I needed to have some kind of management job when really I'm probably going to be a whole lot more comfortable being a custodian. This way I can use my body and work and let my mind wander. It's going to be ideal for songwriting."

"It does sound ideal," I agreed. "Now let's eat. We have some planning to do."

Over dinner Tyler and I came up with a very bare bones plan on how Tyler could find out about the business connection between Fritz Scheider and Kate Weston. I was treading very lightly because I didn't want to get my son fired before he'd worked a full week. Or even a full day. "Now, if you feel the least bit uncomfortable, don't do anything," I warned him.

"Don't worry," Tyler said. "I'm fine. I'll ask around about Fritz and keep my ears open about your dead boss. No problemo."

Since Tyler didn't seem worried, I tried to follow suit and discovered that it wasn't all that hard. After all, Tyler was going to be legitimately employed by Kutrate Kemicals as a custodian. It wasn't like he was going to be doing anything illegal. And if I really wanted to put my Pollyanna glasses on, he was also going to be employed, something he hadn't been in quite some time. "It's kind of fun being detectives, isn't it?"

Tyler laughed. "I wouldn't say what either of us is doing is really detective work, Mom. Columbo would probably laugh at us."

"No, he wouldn't! Columbo was always kind, even to amateurs although I don't think it would be smart to tell Jane about our sleuthing," I suggested.

"Can I tell her I'm working at Kutrate?"

"Well, of course you can! She's going to notice sooner or later. You know she's always working late and you'll probably run into each other."

"How about Dad? Can I tell him?"

"Sure but let's emphasize your new job and de-emphasize our detective work, okay? Dad and Jane tend to get a little..." I searched for the right word.

"Hysterical," Tyler supplied.

"Exactly," I agreed. "We don't need to get them all worked up while we do some research. It's pointless."

"No problem, Mom," Tyler said. "I don't want Princess Janie stroking out on me and there's no sense in getting Dad all worked up either. We'll just do our thing and not say a word in front of either of them."

Is it any wonder why Tyler is my favorite child? I adore Jane but Tyler and I have always been very simpatico. "So I think you need to go to work, learn your job and start casually asking about Fritz and Kate. But give it time," I urged. "There's no rush."

"Don't worry," Tyler assured me. "I'll find out what you need to know and I'll be so smooth about it that no one will even know they're being interrogated. Piece of cake. And speaking of cake, I could really go for something sweet. What do you have?"

"Chocolate ice cream or peanut butter cookies."

"Homemade?"

I shook my head. "From the grocery store. I haven't had much time to cook or bake lately."

"Maybe you need to stop working," Tyler said. "I liked it better when you were always home making stuff."

"I did too, honey, but I like earning a paycheck. It feels good."

"You got that right," Tyler agreed. "I can't wait to start getting paid again. It sucks being broke all the time. I guess I'll have the ice cream if you're sure Dad won't mind."

"He won't even notice," I said, rising to my feet and heading for the freezer. Steve wouldn't notice because I wasn't going to tell him that Tyler finished the ice cream. Steve can be quite territorial about two things: me and ice cream. After fixing Tyler a generous bowl and covering it with chocolate syrup, I returned to the table. "All I ask is that you be careful. I couldn't stand it if anything happened to you."

"Mom," Tyler said with his usual confidence, "are you kidding? I'll be fine. You know I can take care of myself."

I did know that but I also knew that someone had killed Kate Weston and it was looking as if someone might have wanted to kill Fritz Scheider as well. This wasn't a game Tyler and I were getting involved in. It was much more serious than that; it was murder.

Tyler left for work at six thirty after promising me that he'd text me if he learned anything. I was on pins and needles all evening while I waited to hear from him. Sometimes I'm so grateful that I wasn't a parent during the 1970's when young people hitchhiked all over the country and cell phones weren't around yet. I would have gone mad not knowing where Jane and Tyler were all the time and I never would have been able to stand the thought of them hitching a ride with anyone. I always thought I'd worry less when Jane and Tyler were older. Another thing I was wrong about since I seem to worry about them even more now that they're adults and make their own decisions. After checking my cell phone every five minutes, I finally gave into my urge to text Tyler right before I went to bed.

"What are you doing?" Steve questioned although it should have been fairly obvious. "Who are you texting?"

"Tyler."

"Now?" He looked at the bedside clock. "It's almost midnight."

"He's at work and I want to hear how it's going," I explained. Tyler had texted Steve earlier to tell him that he was starting a new job but neglected to say where his new job was. Steve had neglected to ask since he was so happy that Tyler was working anywhere. "You know me—the original mother hen."

"He's lucky to have a mom like you," Steve said sleepily. "Tell him I hope everything's going good for him and then turn out the light. It's late."

I turned out the light and then texted in the dark. *How's it going?*

Tyler texted back almost immediately. I will never know how that kid can text so fast. *Wow! Just wow! Do I have some dirt for you! I'll tell you when I get up tomorrow afternoon.*

I hadn't considered that part of Tyler's new schedule. He wouldn't be getting up until the afternoon when I was at work. How would I be able to stand waiting so long? *Can't you tell me now?*

Again, his response was lightning fast. *Let's just say that Kate's fingerprints are all over this place. Tell you more tomorrow.*

The phone went silent and I knew Tyler wasn't going to text anymore. When he's done with a conversation, texted or otherwise, he's done. How frustrating, I thought as I plugged my cell phone into its charger for the night. What could Tyler possibly have to tell me? Laying back on my pillow, I stared up into the dark. What had Tyler meant about Kate's fingerprints being all over Kutrate Kemicals? Not that I was totally surprised by that. Kate had been a journalist by trade so naturally she was curious about everything. And nosy. But how could she have possibly gotten her fingerprints all over when she hadn't worked at Kutrate? What had Tyler meant?

Well, I obviously wasn't going to find out until the next day and since I had two interviews lined up for the following morning, I really needed to get some sleep myself. I'd find out soon enough what Tyler was talking about and hopefully one more piece of the puzzle would fall into place.

Chapter Eighteen

Work passed with glacial slowness the next day and even the interviews I did didn't help make the day go any faster. It was interesting how old hat doing an interview had become. Ask a few leading questions and then sit back and listen while your subjects talked about their favorite topic—themselves. Even though I was brand new to the newspaper biz, I had already learned that most people leap at the chance to talk about themselves. It was kind of sad in a way—didn't any of these people have friends or relatives who listened to them? But it was also relaxing. All I had to do was say, "Tell me about yourself," and my story was all but written. I was putting the finishing touches on an interview I'd done on a local pediatrician who moonlighted as a magician when Ren poked his head around the wall of our adjoining cubicles. "Hey, DeeDee, did you hear?"

"Hear what?" I asked.

"The police are holding a person of interest in Kate's murder."

My head jerked upwards. "Are you serious? Who?"

"Guess," Ren said.

"Ren, don't tease me! I don't have a clue who killed Kate and it's driving me crazy!"

Ren looked slightly surprised by my heated response. "I didn't know you were all that enthralled by the case," he said.

"Well, I am. Kate was murdered right here. Of course I'm enthralled. I haven't been able to understand why everyone else on the newspaper doesn't seem all that interested."

Ren shrugged. "I guess it's a mixture of ennui and exhaustion. Working here tends to suck your spirit right out of you. We all want to know who did it but no one has the energy to do more than sit back and let the police do their job."

"So who are the police holding?"

"You really aren't going to guess?"

"Ren!"

"All right, I'll tell you. They've got her husband. Oldest story in the book. Follow the money."

"You're kidding me!" I truly hadn't suspected Lou Grant at all. Yes, he stood to inherit quite a bit and their marriage seemed loveless, but murder? That takes a whole different kind of personality than the one I saw the other day at Kate's house—the free spirit in the peacock blue silk robe and the Fiesta plates. "Do they have any evidence?"

"They must have something if they brought him in for questioning," Ren said. "I'm not all that surprised. They had a weird marriage from the get go. Any guy who'd legally change his name to Lou Grant because of some old TV show," Ren shook his head in disbelief, "well, I think that speaks volumes, don't you?"

"I always loved that show," I said a little wistfully.

"I used to see the reruns when I was a little kid," Ren said. "It was pretty good but changing your name because of it? That's plain bizarre. Their whole marriage was bizarre."

"What do you mean?"

"For starters, Kate dated other people and he dated other people. Why be married if you're still going to date? Most husbands and wives wouldn't tolerate that. I know my wife wouldn't and neither would I."

"I guess it was pretty popular back in the 1970's. Open marriages." I was only a child then but I remembered whispered stories about neighborhood couples who had open marriages. "So did everyone know about their open marriage? Everyone on the newspaper?"

"Sure. It wasn't a secret. What puzzled all of us was who in their right mind would ever date Kate. She wasn't exactly a beauty and her personality would never be described as sparkling but she kept finding guys who wanted to go out with her. It had to be her money."

"There are a lot of people who will do anything for money," I agreed.

"Even date someone like her." Ren shuddered. "I was brought up never to speak ill of the dead but Kate has to be the exception to that rule since it would be hard to say anything nice about her, dead or alive. The woman was a horrible human being."

"She wasn't too pleasant," I agreed, "but I can't believe her husband killed her. He would have had to come into the newspaper and done it here."

"Why is that surprising? It would make sense to kill her here instead of at their home. That would have been incredibly stupid. Have you ever seen that place? It's all white. The crime lab technicians would have had a field day there. This way it looks like some disgruntled employee whacked her."

It might have been my imagination but Ren's eyes seemed to have taken on an odd glint and for a second I felt almost frightened of him. He looked possessed or obsessed or simply totally pissed off even though Kate was never going to order him to fix the plumbing or a sentence in one of his stories or anything else ever again. "True," I agreed, "but why? I met him the other day and he seemed quite distraught. Maybe distraught is the wrong word but he did seem to be a little sad over losing her."

"Yeah, right. So sad that he won't be able to enjoy spending the money she left behind that's all his now? I don't think so, DeeDee. Most murders are committed by family members and spouses are high on that list. He did it."

"Hmmm...." I said. "I guess we'll have to wait and see."

Ren leaned forward into his cubicle and I leaned into mine but my mind was no longer on the interview with the pediatrician magician. It was on Ren and the pure hatred I saw in his eyes when he talked about Kate. She had picked on him and he did seem on edge much of the time when Kate had been alive. Now he was a lot mellower. Maybe he had killed her. The plumber's helper taped to her mouth seemed like a sure indicator that whoever had done the deed had an axe to grind, although it did strike me as a bit obvious if Ren had done it since everyone knew that he was the building's on-call plumber. It seemed more likely to me that someone was trying to frame him but the police had talked to Ren and as far as I knew nothing had come of it.

Glancing at the wall clock, I saw that it was almost time to go home and find out what Tyler had learned. One thing was certain: I was getting closer to finding out who killed Kate although I still had absolutely no idea of who the murderer was.

"Ren," I said before I left.

"Yes?"

"How did you hear that Kate's husband was being questioned?"

"Bob Meredith told me. He heard it on the police scanner and went down to the police station to get the story. It'll be in tomorrow's paper."

"See you tomorrow," I said to Ren as I left the newsroom.

"How's the column coming?"

"I'm getting there," I assured him.

"I can't wait to read it. Remember, Friday at five is the deadline."

"You'll have it."

"Tell me everything," I instructed Tyler a little while later. As soon as I'd gotten home I prepared a huge meal of eggs, sausage and hash browns for Tyler, operating on the theory that the smell of the sausage cooking would wake him up. I'd been right. He'd stumbled down the stairs just as the toast popped out of the toaster. I have to say that I couldn't blame him since everything smelled delicious. My sniffs of 'Fat Off' must have worn off because not only was I back to my old appetite level, I was also no longer losing weight but I was more than okay with that. I'm not much of a gambler and the risks of taking 'Fat Off' and getting skinny were too high for me. Grabbing a sausage off Tyler's plate, I asked, "What did you learn?"

"I learned that Kutrate Kemicals is a freaking awesome place to work," Tyler told me. "I love it there!"

While that was definitely good news, it wasn't what I wanted to hear at that moment. "That's great, honey; I'm really happy to hear that but what about Fritz and Kate? Did you learn anything about them?"

"I sure did. Is there anymore toast?"

"I'll get it for you." Tyler's been eating like he's half-starved ever since he turned ten and I knew that he'd be a much better source of information on a full stomach. After putting two more pieces of toast into the toaster, I turned and looked at my son expectantly. "Well?"

"Well," Tyler said, "did you know that Kate stole some of Fritz's top secret stuff and was blackmailing him?"

"No! Are you serious? How did you find that out?"

"One of the other custodians told me. Apparently everyone knows about 'Fat Off' even though it's supposed to be top secret. Kate was doing an expose on it and on Kutrate Kemicals and she was using Fritz to help her."

"Did he know that she was using him?"

"I don't know," Tyler said. "Maybe."

"Did you hear anything about them being business partners?"

"No. Were they?"

"I'm not quite sure what they were to each other." Leaning back in my chair I thought hard as I watched Tyler eat. So Kate *had* been doing an expose on Kutrate Kemicals. A sour thought hit me. Kate had been mighty curious about Jane and her job at Kutrate. Was *that* why she hired me? It made sense—a lot more sense than the far-fetched notion that I was hired because of my yearly Christmas letter writing samples I'd submitted along with my resume. A wave of disappointment washed over me but I got over it pretty quickly. Maybe that was the reason I'd been hired but my job had morphed into something full-time and I was getting better at it every day.

"What are you thinking?" Tyler asked. "You've got that million miles away look in your eyes."

"Just wondering about a few things." I shook myself out of my fog. "Do you think you can find anything else out about how Kate was going to blackmail Fritz?"

Tyler shrugged. "I'll keep my ears open. I'm sure I'll hear something sooner or later."

"You really liked working there last night, didn't you?"

"Why do you sound so shocked?"

"Well..." I smiled, "you've had quite a few jobs in your twenty-some years on this planet."

"Not that many," Tyler replied, "and most of them sucked. This one isn't rocket science but I did like it last night. I like moving my body, keeping busy and it was nice not to have to deal with a lot of people, you know?"

"Yes, I do. I like people but they can get exhausting."

"You've got that right." Tyler finished his coffee. "Time to take a shower. Thanks for the breakfast, Mom. It was great."

"Thank you for all the information you found out."

"Did it help?"

"It gave me some idea of what direction to go in."

"Yeah? What direction would that be?"

"I have absolutely no idea," I told him. "Hopefully Fritz will come out of his coma and will be able to shed some light on this whole thing. He was about to tell me something big right before he passed out."

"Is Jane still interested in him?"

"I think so. She's been at the hospital every night."

"Well, I hope he's a good guy. She's had her share of losers." Tyler got up from the table and carried his plate over to the dishwasher. As I watched him, I thought about what he'd just said, about Jane having more than her share of losers. It was true enough but did I really want her to get together with Fritz—provided he came out of his coma? True, Fritz had a good job and if he could get a better deal with Kutrate Kemicals over 'Fat Off' he was going to be a very wealthy man, but I wanted more than just a good provider for my only daughter. Jane could provide for herself. What I wanted for her was love, the same kind of love that Steve and I had for each other. Would she be able to find that with Fritz Scheider?

My cell phone rang and I picked it up. It was Jane. "I was just thinking about you," I said.

"Mom?" Jane sounded excited. "Fritz came out of his coma! He's going to be all right and he wants to see you!"

Chapter Nineteen

"You gave me one heck of a scare," I gently scolded Fritz from my chair next to his hospital bed. Fritz was ghostly pale which made his black hair look even darker. He had an IV going into one arm but other than that he looked all right. Tired with huge circles under his eyes, but all right. "How are you feeling?"

"Like I was hit by a truck," Fritz said weakly. "My stomach hasn't felt this bad since I had botulism poisoning when I was nine years old."

"Was it—were you poisoned?" I asked, eyeing the IV. "I thought you were choking on something." Fritz gestured toward the open door and made a motion for me to close it. After it was shut, I went back to my seat. "What is it?"

"It was poison," Fritz whispered. "Bernard Morton poisoned me."

"How do you know it was Bernard Morton?" I whispered back.

"Who else could it possibly be? Bernard knows that I'm unhappy with his handling of 'Fat Off.' If I'm out of the picture permanently then he no longer has to deal with me."

"But murder? Isn't that a bit extreme?"

"Not when it comes to money. I believe he killed Kate Weston too."

"Why?"

"She was blackmailing him. She knew about 'Fat Off' and she knew about the potential problems with it. She threatened to do an expose if he didn't pay up."

Wait a second. I figured that Kate had been blackmailing Fritz, not Bernard. Then again, it would make a lot more sense for her to go after the big bucks. "And what would those be?"

Fritz lifted a weak hand and waved it back and forth in the air. "A whole lot of environmental impact problems. They'll be solved eventually but Kate wanted a piece of the action or she was going to spill the whole story in the *Kemper Times.* She said it would earn her a Pulitzer. I suspect she was going to take money from Bernard and still write the story. Kate wasn't weighed down by too many scruples."

"Wow," I breathed, unable to imagine the people who gave out the Pulitzer Prize ever giving the *Kemper Times* an award for anything. "Kate was a lot more ambitious than I realized."

"She was a greedy, selfish woman who would stop at nothing to get what she wanted. We were business partners when she gave me money to do independent research but that ended when her talons became too sharp for me to handle. I told her I needed freedom from her micro-managing ways and she threatened to tell that fathead Bernard Morton that I was doing research on the side."

It sounded to me like Fritz had more of a reason to get rid of Kate than Bernard Morton did but I wisely kept my mouth shut. "So how did you break away from her?"

"I told her we were through, that's how!" Fritz's energy was returning. "She was angry, of course, and believe me, anger did nothing to improve her looks, but she agreed that we were no longer business partners."

I was stumped. How was what Fritz was telling me supposed to help me? There was no way that I believed Bernard Morton had snuck into the newspaper, killed Kate while the rest of us were there, and then snuck out unnoticed. Fritz was simply overwhelmed with his hatred of both Kate and Bernard. But there was no need to tell him that, not in his condition. I patted his arm gently. "You need to concentrate on getting better," I suggested. "We can talk more then."

"Yes," Fritz agreed, his head dropping back on his pillow. "We'll talk more when I feel better. Next time take notes, DeeDee. I want to make sure you're getting all of this down correctly."

I smiled at Fritz and then got up to leave. I was at the door when Fritz spoke again. "I know I'm right about Bernard Morton, DeeDee. Please don't let me down. Nail his murdering, thieving hide to the wall for me."

"I'll do my best," I promised. With that, I tiptoed out of the room.

"Fritz is wrong," I told Steve about twenty minutes later. We were taking a walk around the neighborhood and I was filling him in on what Fritz had said to me. "It can't be Bernard Morton. That's too farfetched."

"It does seem a little unlikely," Steve agreed. "Besides, I thought the police had arrested Kate's husband."

"I don't think he was arrested. They were talking to him as a person of interest. He hasn't formally been charged with anything. Yet."

Steve sighed deeply. "You don't think either of them did it, do you?"

"No, I don't."

"Who do you think killed Kate Weston?"

I didn't answer my husband for a few minutes. I had my suspicions but I wasn't sure if I was ready to voice them out loud, not even to Steve. "Let me chew on it for a while," I requested. "I have an idea but it's almost as farfetched as Bernard Morton being the killer. There's something I need to find out before I know if I'm right or not."

"What's that?"

"If Fritz was really poisoned or not."

"What difference would that make?"

"I'm not sure," I said slowly, "but it might confirm that who I think is the killer really and truly is the killer or at least it will knock Bernard Morton out of the running. He's a creep but I just don't see him being a murderer and I don't see how he could have possibly gotten poison into the food Fritz ate at the Coffee Hut. I was sitting at the table the entire time unless he snuck back into the kitchen and did it there. But why would he? Fritz is paranoid when it comes to Bernard."

"If it wasn't Bernard, then who killed Kate?"

"I'm working on that one too. One thing I do know for sure: the woman had a whole lot of enemies."

Steve shook his head. "I don't know that I want you working at that newspaper anymore, DeeDee."

I hugged his arm close to me. "You know what? Neither am I. I like full-time work and everything but I think I'd like to find something a little slower paced, like being the receptionist at a senior living home. I couldn't possibly get into trouble there."

"I wouldn't bet on it," Steve replied.

"He wasn't poisoned. Well, not with poison. It was food poisoning," Tyler informed me a few hours later.

It was almost midnight when my cell phone rang. I grabbed it off my nightstand and headed downstairs before it woke Steve. "Food poisoning? From what?"

"Apparently he had fish tacos for lunch yesterday at that new Mexican restaurant at the mall and there was something wrong with the fish. A whole bunch of people got sick."

"So Bernard Morton didn't poison him."

"You didn't really think he did, did you, Mom?"

"No, I didn't."

"Fritz sounds like a disgruntled employee to me. From what I've heard about Mr. Morton he's not the greatest human being in the world but he's not a murderer either."

"I agree."

"So that isn't much help with who killed your boss, is it?"

"It narrows the field and that's a help. Thanks, honey, for letting me know so quickly. How's your night going?"

"Awesome. I can play my music as loud as I want and no one cares. I love this job."

I wished I felt that way about my job. As Caroline had predicted on my first day at the newspaper, it was game over for me. There was too much work and too few people and the pay really did stink, even at twelve dollars an hour. I was so tired when I got home that I wanted to take a nap before dinner. Maybe the time had come for me to start thinking about another profession, something that suited me a little bit better. What that might be, however, I didn't have a clue.

After ending my call with Tyler, I wandered into the living room and sat in the dark for a little while, not to ruminate on my pathetic work history but to try to think through what had happened to Kate. I really didn't think that Bernard Morton murdered her. It had to be someone at the paper which meant that the list of suspects was pretty small. There was Jeff, Caroline, Ren, Frank, Bob, and Sam. Oh, and Natalie. Lou Grant Weston was also a possibility but a long shot. He was a little too obvious. Staring out through the front window into the dark night, I tried to imagine each of my co-workers doing Kate in. Kate was a tiny thing so I was sure that any of them would have been able to strangle her. Wincing, I thought about how horrible that had to have been for Kate, having her life squeezed out of her. After a little more thought I decided that I could probably strike Natalie and Caroline from my list. It would take a fair amount of strength to keep Kate quiet while she was being choked and Natalie, in spite of her youthful appearance, was around fifty and Caroline was a string bean who probably wouldn't have been able to choke Kate and keep her from screaming.

Unless they worked together. What if whoever killed Kate had a partner in crime? One to hold her mouth shut and the other to strangle her? Oh, boy. With my co-workers, that would most likely be one time when they showed some team spirit and cooperation.

I shook my head. This was getting me nowhere. Time to go back to bed. What I needed to do next was find some clues at work that would help me figure this whole thing out. There had to be *someone* working at the newspaper who knew more than they were saying. Just like there had to be someone—or possibly two someone's—who killed Kate. I wasn't at all sure how I was going to do it but I was bound and determined to find out who that someone was and then I could quit the newspaper with a totally clear conscience.

Chapter Twenty

"You can quit the newspaper right now with a totally clear conscience," Steve told me the following morning as we were drinking our coffee before heading out the door. I have to admit that I missed the old days of a month or so ago when we had time for a more leisurely morning meal. With me working, breakfast had become coffee and toast followed by a hasty kiss and Steve driving off in one direction and me in the other. "I don't see why you're taking on figuring out who killed Kate Weston. It's not your job, DeeDee. Let the police handle it."

I ignored his suggestion. "I'm thinking it has to be Bob Meredith. He might have heard that Kate was onto a big story and killed her because he was jealous."

"Seems like a mighty big step to take for professional jealousy," Steve remarked.

"Bob is a very petty person. He doesn't want to share the limelight with anyone."

"Maybe not, but murder? What about the sports writer? You've barely mentioned him."

"Frank. I have considered him but he was covering a baseball game when it happened so he's off the hook. He was the only reporter out of the building other than me so we're the only two with iron clad alibis."

"I'm glad you have an iron clad alibi." Steve gave me a quick kiss. "See you tonight. You will be home for dinner, won't you?"

"As far as I know," I promised. "Unless something comes up."

Steve sighed rather loudly as he went out the back door. "I wish you'd find something with more regular hours," he said over his shoulder.

"I could go back to catering!" I called after him but he was already in his car with the door shut. Steve can be a bit of a baby at times but I suppose that was partially my fault. I'd spent most of our marriage taking care of him so it had to be a shock to have me gone so much. Truthfully, I wasn't that crazy about it either. I missed being at home.

With my own sigh, I threw together a lunch and followed Steve's tracks out the back door. I had four stories to cover that day plus the column I'd promised Ren. I'd written two columns already that didn't quite make it. I wanted to write something original and entertaining and shocking, just like Ren had requested. Halfway out the driveway I had an idea. What if I wrote a column about Kate's murder? What if I tried to find her killer in print?

No, bad idea. I'd get fired for sure.

But as I drove toward the newspaper, my mind wouldn't stop turning the idea over. And over. And over. What if I did write about Kate's death? I'd written about Fritz collapsing at the Coffee Hut and surely murder was more compelling than food poisoning. I could write it from the point of view of a cub reporter—an older cub reporter but still someone who was new to the staff. I could describe what happened and then, without naming names, of course, suggest who might have done it. I could end the column with a plea for the guilty person to step forward.

Chewing on my lower lip at a stop light, I tried to decide if my idea sounded like something out of a corny

1930's crime movie. It kind of did but those corny movies always ended with the killer getting caught and since that was what I wanted too, then I should go for it.

Of course, it was doubtful that Ren would run it but what if I handed it in so late that he didn't have any choice but to run it? I knew that I was risking my job but I was okay with that since I wasn't all that sure if I wanted to keep my job anymore. It would be way more satisfying to flush out Kate's killer than to continue working at the paper for peanuts and having to attend school board meetings that were so boring I was sure that my rear end felt like it had turned to stone by the end of them.

"I'll do it!" I said out loud. "Let them fire me—the truth shouldn't be silenced!"

The woman in the car next to mine gave me an odd look before driving off but I didn't care. Finally I was going to write something for the newspaper that just might make a difference...and that also might catch a killer.

"How's that column coming?" Ren asked me. It was almost five and it had been a long, hard day. Any stardust that had still been in my eyes had vanished earlier that day during my interview with the director of city services who was not only dull but incredibly full of himself.

"It's all written," I told him.

"Great! Send it to me."

"It's all written in my head," I explained. "I just have to type it up for you."

"Not too momsy or folksy?"

"I think I got it right." I wanted to point out to Ren that I was doing him a favor but he looked so grouchy that I let it drop. Maybe being a columnist wasn't the dream job I'd thought it was either. Coming up with acceptable ideas on a weekly basis would be a nightmare.

Ren looked irritated, an expression that he seemed to be wearing all the time lately. "DeeDee, you do know the deadline for Sunday's paper is six o'clock tonight, right?"

"I have an hour to write it," I said.

"But I have to read it and edit it," Ren responded. "That's why I wanted it by five. How am I going to do that before six if you haven't even written it yet? What's it about?"

"It's a tribute to Kate Weston. Sort of."

Ren frowned. "What do you mean 'sort of'?"

"Well, I'm also doing a little fishing in it."

"And you think that by writing a column about it, you'll be able to make the killer confess? Wow, you are a full-time dreamer, DeeDee. I don't think you should be in journalism. Fiction is obviously your field."

"Are you telling me you don't want me to write it?" I admit that a small part of me hoped that was true since then I could go straight home, fix Steve his dinner and collapse in my recliner. I was beat.

Ren looked at me consideringly. "No," he finally said, "go ahead and write it. It might be good to shake a few branches around this dump and see what falls out. Besides, at least it won't be overly sweet if it's about murder. That's your problem, DeeDee, you're too nice."

"Just like you used to be," I pointed out.

Slightly abashed, Ren ducked his head. "Touché. It's this place. It gets to you. I'm sorry, DeeDee, if I said anything that hurt your feelings. I just want everything that goes into my section to be perfect."

I laughed. "Then why on earth did you ask me to write Sunday's column? You have to know it's not going to be perfect. I'm too new a writer to come even close to perfect."

"Maybe but you're an honest writer and that's my second favorite trait after perfect. I'll print whatever you write and I'll only edit it for style. I'll do my best to leave it exactly how you write it. Deal?"

"Deal." I paused. "Even if it makes someone who works here look guilty?"

It was Ren's turn to laugh. "Well, I know that I didn't kill Kate Weston so I'd be happy if your column figured that out. You really think someone on the paper did it?"

"I don't know who else could have gotten in here," I replied.

"Maybe you're right. Okay, I'll leave you alone so you can get it all down. Shoot it to me as soon as you're done and have a nice weekend."

"You too, Ren. Hey, Ren," I said before he vanished on me. "This column could get us both in hot water."

Ren grinned. "Doesn't matter anymore."

"What do you mean?"

"Just what I said. It doesn't matter. I've found my happy place and it sure isn't around here."

Before I could quiz him on what he was talking about, he got up, walked through the newsroom and out the door.

"So you finished your first column," Steve asked later that night. We were in bed reading. At least I was trying to read but I was so tired that I kept reading the same sentence over and over. "I'm proud of you, honey. Even though that newspaper sounds like one screwed up place to work, I think it's great that you're having your own column in Sunday's paper. That's amazing. What's it about?"

"I'm going to let you be surprised," I said. Along with everyone else. "I will tell you this: it's not about us or the kids."

"Really? What else could you write about?"

Wow, I all but had WIFE AND MOM tattooed across my chest. "Something else," I said vaguely.

Steve grew quiet. After a couple of minutes he said, "DeeDee…"

"What?"

"You didn't write about anything controversial, did you?"

"Such as what?"

"You know what. Did you write about Kate Weston's murder?"

Sometimes it's a drag being married to someone who knows you so well. "What if I did? I didn't use anyone's name."

Steve sat up in bed and peered down at me. He was wearing his reading glasses and wearing an old Bozo the Clown t-shirt so he didn't look too threatening. "Couldn't you get sued?"

"I don't think so. Fired, maybe, but sued—I doubt it."

"What did you write exactly?"

"You'll have to wait until Sunday to read it," I said drowsily. "Along with everyone else in town. Now can we turn out the lights? I'm too tired to read."

Steve snapped off his light and I switched mine off too. We laid next to each other in the dark and I was almost asleep when Steve added, "I just hope that whoever killed that poor woman gets caught soon. I don't know how much more of this I can take."

I didn't answer because I was already half asleep.

Chapter Twenty-one

Today's column is a little different from what you're used to. As the guest columnist, I've chosen to tackle a topic that has been uncomfortable for everyone at the Kemper Times, *although calling murder 'uncomfortable' is a little bit like calling a tsunami a little wave. I'm talking about the murder of assistant editor, Kate Weston. Kate was strangled in the* Kemper Times *building, and as I write these words, the police have yet to arrest her killer.*

I would be lying if I wrote that I liked Kate. She was a difficult person to work for and could be demanding, picky and quite often rude. Kate was a perfectionist but after much thought I've come to realize that a perfectionist is exactly what a newspaper needs. When I first started at the newspaper, Kate had me re-write everything I turned in to her. While I didn't appreciate how Kate showed me what to do, the end result was that I learned from her and I learned how to get better. I know that I have a long way to go, but Kate helped me by taking the time to show me what I was doing wrong. For that, I will always be grateful.

Kate set high goals for the staff at the paper and she set high goals for herself as well. Although her official title was editor, Kate was still an active journalist. Since her death, I have learned that Kate was doing some undercover investigating on her own and that she stumbled upon what might turn out to be not only highly unethical business practices in a well-known local company but also potential damage to the environment that she was determined to stop. The story Kate was working on was big—far bigger than any other story this newspaper has covered in a very long time. Unfortunately, Kate was silenced before she could put her plan into action and before she could expose the people who might be setting our town up for what could be potentially disastrous environmental impacts.

When Kate Weston was murdered, almost half a dozen people were within shouting distance but Kate didn't call out for help. Or if she did, apparently no one heard her. Since her death, her name has seldom been mentioned and her memory has apparently been snuffed out at the newspaper.

As the newest employee on the Kemper Times *I undoubtedly have the least right to voice my concerns over how the newspaper is run. It isn't up to me to point fingers at anyone. However, as the newest employee I also have the freshest eyes and as I look around the newsroom at my colleagues I see tired, jaded journalists who are underpaid, overworked and burned out. Although I've worked at the newspaper for only a few weeks, I understand where they're coming from. This is an exhausting job, one that is next to impossible to do on a regular basis.*

That said, I don't think we can in good conscience ignore what happened to our late editor. We must start asking each other, and ourselves, the hard questions. Who knows more about Kate's murder? Who has seen something that could help the police? Who has information that he or she isn't sharing?

Someone must know more that he or she has made public. Our building is small as is our staff. Please step forward and share what you know so that we can move on as a staff and so that Kate Weston can rest in peace.

Journalism is about telling the truth. The time has come for the truth about Kate Weston's death to be known by everyone.

"What do you think?" I asked Steve Sunday morning when he set the newspaper down.

His face was pale. "I think you're going to get canned," he said. Almost as if on cue, my cell phone began to ring and the caller I.D. told me that it was Jeff Hamilton.

"You may be right," I said as I picked my phone up. "Hello?"

"You're fired," Jeff said in a tone that was awfully close to hysteria. "Who do you think you are, writing that drivel? You have no right to come out and say that one of us knows more than we've told the police. Do you think you're some kind of middle-aged Nancy Drew? Come in tomorrow and clean out your cubicle and then I never want to see you again!"

"But Jeff," I began before he cut me off.

"And don't expect a reference from me!" He severed the connection.

I set my phone on the kitchen table. "I wonder if I worked at the paper long enough to get unemployment."

"He fired you?"

I nodded as I tried to decide how I felt. Relieved but also hurt and more than a little angry. "He said to come in and clean out my cubicle tomorrow."

Getting up, Steve took me into his arms. "I won't lie and say I'm not happy. That job was thankless, DeeDee. You deserve better than that and they don't deserve anyone as wonderful as you."

A few tears ran down my cheeks. "He didn't even give me a chance to defend myself!"

"From what you've told me about management at that place, are you really surprised?"

"Well, no."

"Then forget about it. You got some valuable experience that you can take to your next job and whoever hires you will be lucky to have you."

Reaching into my bathrobe pocket, I pulled out a crumpled tissue. "Thanks, Steve. I guess I didn't think that one through all the way. I knew Jeff might be upset but I never dreamed he'd actually fire me."

"Maybe you hit a little too close to home."

"Maybe I did." I wiped my eyes. "One thing is for sure. It's going to be interesting to see who talks to me and who doesn't when I go in to clean out my cubicle."

Steve hugged me even tighter. "The thing I love best about you, DeeDee, is that you always see the bright side."

Like I had any choice, I thought the following morning as I lugged a cardboard box to my cubicle and slowly began filling it up. Another job bites the dust and while I'd been able to stick a few hundred dollars in our retirement account, it felt like I'd added two tablespoons of water to an empty swimming pool. Practically pointless.

"I'm sorry, DeeDee," Ren told me when he entered the newsroom. "I was just talking to Jeff and I tried to talk him out of letting you go but his mind is made up."

I shrugged. Truthfully, I wasn't all that sad about leaving the newspaper. I didn't like the fact that I'd been fired but I knew that I wasn't a journalist. I didn't have the stamina for it and I really didn't have the disposition for it. Even if I'd been twenty years younger I doubted that I'd ever have the nerve that Caroline or Bob or Ren had. I wasn't even sure if I wanted to have that kind of nerve, that detachment that made each of them so good at what they did. *Let's face facts: you're a wife and a mom, not Maria Shriver.* "Don't worry about it. I'll be fine. How did everyone else react?"

"You mean did Caroline jump up and confess to killing Kate?" Ren grinned. "Sorry to disappoint you but no one has mentioned your column. I don't think most of the reporters read the Sunday paper."

"You're kidding me!"

"Nope, I'm not. No one cares about anything around here which is one of the reasons why I'm getting out of here."

"You're leaving too? You didn't get fired for letting me write that column, did you?"

"No, my leaving has nothing to do with that. Remember when I told you that the newspaper is no longer my happy place? I think I've found my new happy place. I got hired as a copywriter at an ad agency in Chicago. It's the bottom rung of jobs there but I'll still be making double of what I make here."

"Good for you. Won't you miss having your own section? You did such a great job with it."

"Are you kidding me? I can't wait to get out of here! I feel about ten years younger than I did on Friday. I want to see my wife and my kids and have a normal life for once. Two weeks and I'm through."

"About ten minutes and I'm through," I said. "I want to say good-bye to everyone before I take off."

Ren held out his hand for me to shake. "Good luck, DeeDee. If you ever need a reference, I'd be glad to help you out."

"Thanks. I may take you up on that." I smiled, suddenly remembering something Ren had told me. "You know, I never did get to see my job description. I wonder what my housekeeping duties were supposed to be?"

"Probably changing the toner in all of the printers and making sure the floors got waxed once a year. Be glad you never found out. I'm never going to unplug another toilet as long as I live."

The smile faded from my face as I thought about the plumber's helper that had been duct taped over Kate's mouth and I wondered if anyone had ever replaced it. Who could have known where to find the plumber's helper after Kate was murdered? And who would have known where the duct tape was? And who would have known that Ren was going to be under suspicion since he was in charge of all the plumbing problems in the building? "Ren, who writes the job descriptions?"

"Jeff and Kate."

"Are they the only ones who saw them?"

"I don't know. Probably. Why?"

"Just a thought." A blip of a thought that refused to gel properly. Something was nagging at the back of my brain, something someone at the newspaper had said about job descriptions and duties but for the life of me I couldn't recall who or what. "Well, good luck to you, Ren. I hope you love your new job and that you and your family are very happy living in Chicago."

"Thanks, DeeDee."

Picking up my cardboard box of belongings, I started on my round of good-byes. First up was Caroline Osborn. "I came to say good-bye," I told her, pausing next to her cubicle.

Caroline looked up from her computer, her eyes troubled. "I heard Jeff canned you. I'm sorry, DeeDee. You really tried and I admire that."

"Thanks. I suppose with both Ren and me leaving you'll be busier than ever."

"Don't count on it," Caroline said. "I'm quitting too. I just nailed a job at that restaurant where we had lunch on your first day. I'm going to make more money as a waitress than I do here."

"Are you serious?"

"As a heart attack. I start next week. I'm going to go tell that cheap bastard we call our boss that he can take my two week notice and stick it. Virgil makes five grand more a year than I do and he only works part-time and he's not completely exhausted like I am most of the time. This job is crap."

Wow, the paper was going to be down three reporters. Maybe Jeff would take back my firing. "Did you read my column in yesterday's paper?"

Caroline blushed. "No…I rarely read this rag but I heard about it. That's why you got fired, right? Listen, DeeDee, don't worry about who killed Kate. They'll be caught sooner or later."

"How do you know that?"

"Because I'm dating a police officer who told me that the police are very close to arresting someone and it isn't Kate's goofy husband."

"Who is it?" I asked.

Caroline lowered her voice. "This is between you and me and no one else, all right?"

I nodded, my heart thumping in anticipation. "Of course."

Caroline hesitated before leaning forward. "The police think it's—"

"Are you still here?" Bob Meredith did his usual barging in act, rudely interrupting Caroline. "I thought you were fired. What are you hanging around for?"

"I'm saying good-bye to the people I like," I said.

"You haven't said good-bye to me yet," Bob responded.

"I'm sure an award-winning journalist like you can figure that one out," Caroline said. "Look, DeeDee, I've got to get back to work. I really shouldn't say anything anyway."

"About what?" Bob asked.

"None of your business," Caroline replied before pressing her lips firmly together. I knew I wasn't going to get anything else out of her. Darn Bob Meredith anyway! I picked up my box one more time.

"Good-bye," I said to Caroline. "Maybe we can have lunch together sometime."

"I'd like that. Come to the restaurant and I'll get you a discount."

"I'm usually free for lunch too," Bob chimed in but we both ignored him. I left the newsroom for my last time. I'd say good-bye to the one other person I liked and then my foray into journalism would be over.

Walking down the hallway, I lingered outside the room where Kate had been killed. I hadn't been in there since it had happened. Taking a deep breath, I turned the knob and stepped inside.

The room was used mainly for storage and it didn't look like anyone other than the police had been in there since Kate's murder. I stared at the floor, trying to picture Kate's body there. For some reason I couldn't get that plumber's helper out of my head. It was such a macabre twist. What was the point of it? I simply didn't get it and standing in the creepy, dark room was doing absolutely nothing to illuminate me. Caroline was right; better leave it to the police.

My cardboard box and I left the room.

"Where are you going?" Natalie asked me when she spotted me carrying the box, the classic sign of an employee on the way out. "Did you quit or did you get fired? I read your column, DeeDee. Did Jeff let you go?"

"He sure did." I set the box down on Natalie's desk and sighed. "I guess I can't blame him although his response was a little extreme to me."

"Like maybe he had something to hide," Natalie suggested.

"Aren't you worried about him listening in on us?" I asked. "You never used to want to talk at your desk."

Natalie waved a hand nonchalantly. "No, Jeff's too busy to spend time watching me like Kate used to do. He has a full plate that's going to get even fuller if you're leaving."

"It was his choice," I replied.

"Hey, I just heard that the police questioned Kate's husband but they didn't charge him with anything. Looks like they don't have a person of interest anymore."

"Natalie, I wrote that column because it's making me nuts that Kate's killer hasn't been found yet and no one around here seems to really care. Why are the people who work at this newspaper so unfeeling? So cold?"

"Good question," Natalie said. "I suppose it's because they ran out of energy a long time ago. Don't get me wrong—I still love working for a newspaper but I've got to admit that the atmosphere at this place is a major downer. Especially with all that added junk they stick on our job descriptions. Like Ren doing the plumbing. If he hadn't hired someone else to do it for him, I'm sure he would have had a nervous breakdown by now."

"What are you talking about? I thought Ren did the plumbing himself."

"Sometimes when he gets swamped he has a friend of his come in and do it for him. Nice looking guy too. Looks a little bit like that old school actor—what was his name? Gregory Peck."

"What?" The only person I knew who looked like Gregory Peck was Fritz Scheider. Good heavens, could *he* be the one Ren had do the plumbing? "When was he here last?"

"I don't know. A few months ago. I think it was around the fourth of July when some wise guy flushed a cherry bomb down the toilet. I always suspected Kate of doing that just to get Ren's goat."

My mind was racing. If Fritz had been to the newspaper then he knew where the plumbing supplies were kept and he also knew his way around. Plus if he came in to murder Kate, since they knew each other she wouldn't have been alarmed. Oh, my gosh, and my daughter was interested in Fritz and might be visiting him at the hospital at that very moment! "I forgot something upstairs. I'll see you later."

"Sure," Natalie said but I was gone before she had the word completely out of her mouth.

Upstairs I found Ren in the break room. "Ren, Natalie just told me that you outsourced your plumbing work. Is that true?"

Ren blushed. "Yeah, I did do that on occasion. A friend of mine is great at plumbing so when I couldn't stand it I asked him to help me out."

"What's your friend's name?"

"You know him, DeeDee. It's Fritz Scheider. He's great at everything—plumbing, brilliant chemist, knows everything about computers. I don't think the guy has ever failed at anything."

"Why didn't you tell me this before?" I demanded. "You knew I was with Fritz when he collapsed."

"Yeah, I knew that but I didn't exactly want to tell everyone that I was getting a ringer in here to do my job. Besides, what's the big deal?"

I stared at Ren, my mouth unable to form a coherent sentence. I had to get to Jane and tell her to stay away from Fritz because if what I was thinking was true, I knew who had murdered Kate Weston. Without another word, I ran out of the newsroom, out of the building and dashed to my car moving faster than I had in years. I had to find Jane and make sure she was safe.

Chapter Twenty-two

"Pick up, pick up, pick up!" I kept chanting as I sped toward Kutrate Kemicals with my cell phone pressed to one ear. Normally I never attempt to talk on my phone while I'm driving but this was a definite emergency. I kept getting Jane's voice mail and after my third attempt I tossed the phone on my seat in a panic. Common sense had reminded me that Jane wouldn't be visiting Fritz on a Monday morning. She would be at work but just to play it safe I drove past her apartment building on my way to the plant. My motherly sixth sense paid off; Jane's Avalon was parked in its usual spot. She wasn't at work and that in itself was a major red flag. Standing on the brakes, I made a sharp left into her building's parking lot.

If Jane was at home and not answering my phone calls, something was seriously wrong. I parked my car and then called 911. "Hurry!" I shouted. "Send someone to 1924 Southbridge Road, apartment 706! My daughter's in trouble!" I ended the call and then ran to the building. Jane had reluctantly given me a key a year earlier and as I rode up in the elevator I searched for it on my key ring. I knew I should call Steve or Tyler but there wasn't time. I had to get to Jane before Fritz did.

Outside her apartment door I could hear muffled voices coming from the inside. Jane was in there and she was talking to someone. The thought occurred to me that I might be about to burst in on an intimate moment—that would explain why she hadn't answered my calls—but I didn't care. I'd much rather be embarrassed by catching my daughter in a romantic interlude than devastated if a deranged killer murdered her. But I needed to calm down. If Fritz was holding her hostage I needed to keep my wits about me.

Slipping the key into the lock I slowly opened the door. The voices were coming from the small den at the back of the apartment. I recognized Jane's voice. Straining my ears, I recognized the other voice. It was Fritz. My heart thundered in my chest as I tiptoed down the hallway.

"...we are so close to winning, my little pet! Bernard Morton is going to have to admit that he poisoned me and then I'll be in the position to get my formula back and I won't have to share it with anyone—except you, of course, my darling."

"That's wonderful, Fritz, but I really do need to get to work." Jane sounded calm but I could hear the faintest strain of tension in her voice. "We can celebrate tonight, all right?"

"You aren't going into work," Fritz announced. "We are going to go to the airport and fly somewhere where no one can find us, not anyone from work or any of your friends or that nosy mother of yours. It will be just the two of us. I have to say that your mother has been a great disappointment to me, my little cupcake. I thought she'd help me nail Bernard Morton but instead she was a waste of my time."

"I'm sorry about that and what you're describing sounds lovely, darling, but you know me. I can't stand to leave any loose ends. I want to go into work and clear off my desk."

"That's one of the things I love most about you—we have so much in common. I, too, can't abide loose ends." Fritz chuckled. "Especially ones that have big mouths which is why I had to take care of that horrible woman, Kate Weston. She was about to ruin everything. That was one loose string I enjoyed tying up."

"You…you killed Kate Weston? Why?"

"Because she betrayed me. Betrayal is something else I can't abide. She said she would help me with money to do extra research and then she changed her mind. She said she'd help me break my contract with Kutrate but she didn't. She said she'd never tell anyone about my brilliant secret diet aid but she lied. She lied about everything." Fritz's voice had become as cold as ice. "You'll never betray me, will you? You'll never, ever lie to me, will you, Jane?"

"But I don't see how you could have killed her. Everyone thinks it was an inside job, that someone on the newspaper killed her."

Fritz chuckled again. "Like your idiot mother wrote in her column yesterday? Truly, Kate, she should stick to tweaking Toll House cookie recipes and putting them on her Facebook page. I thought she was a true journalist but she's just a mommy. No, I did it. I snuck in, hid in a closet, killed her and then left via the back steps. I even thought to tape the plumber's helper over her mouth so that it would look like my so-called friend at the paper did it. Easiest thing in the world."

"Why would you want to do that?"

"Because Ren never thought twice about asking me to come in and unplug toilets for him but he also never thought twice about forgetting to thank me adequately. A free subscription to that rag of a newspaper is not my idea of true gratitude."

"I thought there were cameras everywhere. That's what my mom said."

"Cameras can be disabled if one knows what one is doing. I, my love, always know what I'm doing."

I heard Jane gulp. "Fritz…I don't know…murder…that's too much for me."

"Are you judging me, Jane?" Fritz asked harshly.

"No! It's just that—"

I heard him take a step toward her and I couldn't stay in the hallway a second longer. The police would be there at any moment but I couldn't wait. "Stop it!" I yelled. "Get away from her!" Grabbing the object closest to me, I jumped into the den and brandished a rolled up umbrella at Fritz. To both of our amazement, it popped open and one of the spikes poked him in his right eye.

"Ow!" Fritz screamed while Jane cried, "Mom! Mom! He's crazy! Get out of here!"

Footsteps came from the hallway and within seconds, two burly police officers entered the room. "She blinded me! Arrest her!" Fritz shouted, pointing at me.

"What's going on here?" one of the officers asked.

"Arrest him! He killed Kate Weston! I heard him confess!"

"Arrest *her*! She's a menopausal crazy woman who tried to poke my eye out!" Fritz screamed.

The next few minutes were pandemonium as everyone shouted at each other. After several fruitless minutes filled with accusations, the police put the three of us in separate cars and drove us down to the station. Jane and I rode in the back seat of one police car while Fritz rode in the other. Jane was crying quietly the entire way and I patted her hand, feeling about as useful as a turnip. "When will I ever meet a nice, not crazy, not married man, Mom?" she asked when we arrived at the police station.

"It will happen," I predicted. "One of these days you'll meet someone wonderful, just like I did."

Jane sniffed. "I don't think that's ever going to happen."

I wasn't so sure it was ever going to happen either but I didn't say so out loud. "We're here," I said. "Let's get this over with."

"DeeDee, you either have the worst luck or the best luck in the world," Steve told me a few hours later. "You both could have been killed, you know. One of the policemen told me that Fritz is having a complete break from reality. He's still convinced that Bernard Morton poisoned him and refuses to accept that what he had was food poisoning. I'm wondering if all of this isn't related to that cockamamie drug of his. Maybe homicidal tendencies are a side effect of long term exposure to 'Fat Off.'"

"Maybe Kate figured that out," I said. "What I can't figure out is why he volunteered to be my Deep Throat when he was the killer."

"He must have thought he could outfox you," Steve suggested.

"Maybe. I suppose we'll never know. I'm just glad I only got a couple of whiffs of that spray. Being skinny isn't worth any side effects." I snuggled up next to Steve. He had come home early once he heard what was going on. Jane was upstairs taking a bath and Tyler was asleep, blissfully unaware how close Jane and I had gotten to, well, I'm not sure what but something mighty scary. My whole family was under the same roof and all was right in the world. Even better, Kate's killer had been caught and our daughter had been rescued before she got really involved with a homicidal maniac. "I even got my job on the paper offered to me again. Jeff Hamilton called and apologized."

"Are you going to take it back?"

"Maybe for a while but I think I've had enough of newspapers. I think I'd like to try something new."

Steve groaned. "Why don't you take some time off and just hang around here for a while?"

"What about our retirement account? I didn't have the chance to add much to it, you know."

"So we'll be old and poor. So what as long as we're together?" Steve kissed me.

I returned his kiss. He was right; as long as we were together we could handle anything.

The End

ABOUT THE AUTHOR

Marlo Hollinger is a Midwestern author who enjoys reading, cooking, walking her dog and watching old mystery movies. For as long as she can remember, Marlo has wanted to write books that solved mysteries. Like her protagonist, DeeDee, Marlo has been married to the love of her life for almost 40 years. The cat in the photograph is Boo.

The first book in her Midlife Crisis mystery series was *Catered to Death. Black and White and Dead All Over* is the second in this series.

Proof

Made in the USA
Charleston, SC
13 August 2016